IMPORTUNITY

JON LUNN

First published in Great Britain in 2023 by:

Carnelian Heart Publishing Ltd
Suite A
82 James Carter Road
Mildenhall
Suffolk
IP28 7DE
UK

www.carnelianheartpublishing.co.uk

Paperback ISBN   978-1-914287-19-0

eBook ISBN   978-1-914287-20-6

Editors: Lazarus Panashe Nyagwambo and Samantha Rumbidzai Vazhure
Cover art: Emma Minkley
Cover layout: Rebeca Covers
Typeset by Carnelian Heart Publishing Ltd
Layout and formatting by DanTs Media

For Suzan and Nancy

L'idée, la mouche importune.

- Aimé Césaire, *Discours sur le colonialisme* (1955)

Contents

Part 1   Testimonies and origins

Chapter One

Evidence given in the High Court of Southern Rhodesia, Bulawayo Criminal Sessions, by Iolo James, 7th March 1923

I live with my wife Doris James in Lobengula Street. On 19th January, at about 10 pm, I was in my house. I had my coat off and boots unlaced. I saw two people come to my front gate. One of them was Violet Harper. I went to the front gate. Harper asked, "Are you Mr James?"

I said "yes". She then told me she wanted to see me about business. I opened the gate and went out. Immediately, two or three men caught hold of me; I think they had been hiding along the fence. I struggled with them for some time and one of my boots came off.

I was dragged along the street through bushes and stones. I called for help. Some distance from my house, I was placed in a motor car. As I was being put in the car, my son, aged thirteen, came to my assistance. He was shouting for help and caught hold of me. I saw someone pull him away from me. When the car moved on, I saw my son jump onto *the footboard before someone kicked him off. My wife was near the hind wheel of the car and called my son to come away.*

***

"Origins" – unpublished manuscript found in the house of Iolo James after his death in 1958

I sometimes wonder what possessed me to migrate to South Africa in 1906 at twenty-nine years of age. But then I remember what I was leaving behind.

I was born in 1877 in Corris, a slate mining village in the Dulas Valley, Merionethshire, in mid-Wales. The village was surrounded by mountains that rose to more than fifteen hundred feet. My father, Owen James, worked in numerous quarries – I remember Abercorris, Braichgoch and Abercwmeiddaw – in the surrounding area over the years, mainly as a slate getter but sometimes as a supervisor.

The quarries around Corris were small and rarely profitable. For big profits, you looked to much larger quarries like the Penrhyn and Dinorwic. As a child I visited a lot of them, sometimes with my father, but more often while roaming around with my friends. Even at a young age I could see that the work was brutal and hard. Death as a result of accident or injury was not uncommon. Wages were low and could not be relied on.

Many men drowned their sorrows in the local pubs. The Slaters Arms in Bridge Street was a favourite. Wives (and widows) often held households together on a pittance. My mother, Bronwyn, had worked as a slate enameller in a nearby town until she married my father in 1870.

I was the third child of six. My two elder brothers both went to work in the quarries at fourteen and I was expected to do the same.

14

But I was a good student. I was quick to pick up reading and writing at school – in the Welsh language, of course.

The class teacher, Mr Williams, told my mother that I had the ability to aim higher than the quarries. Although my parents were suspicious of the English as a people, they agreed that he should teach me English outside of class.

In contrast to my elder brothers, my health was not robust. My parents sometimes struggled to make sense of me. Father often said that I appeared lost in my own world and worried that I spent more time than was good for me looking at books. We didn't have many in our small cottage but there was a small library in the Rehoboth Chapel, where we worshipped. I'd devoured everything in it by the time I was eleven and was hungry for more.

***

The car then moved off. I recognised the driver, Mr Lawson, who used to be a friend of mine. I had been wounded in the face during the struggle and was blinded by blood, so I could not recognise the man beside me in the car. Including myself, there were six persons inside the car. There was a seventh on the footboard. Among the six persons was Violet Harper.

The car went up Main Street. Another car followed us. I was taken down 8th Avenue into the Market Square. As the car was proceeding, Violet Harper thrust a tar brush at my face which I caught and warded off and threw out of the car. She said she was prepared to do time for me. The man who sat on my knee asked if I was not ashamed of myself. I replied that he did not know all the facts.

***

15

The time came when my schooling was due to end. Neither I nor my parents could imagine me thriving as a rubble man in the bottom-rungs of the quarry industry. When I reached eleven, Mr Williams told my parents that he might be able to secure me an apprenticeship with a local butcher, Richard Pugh. Ignorant of what this would involve, I was keen.

In September 1888, I walked the short distance from the family cottage to Mr Pugh's shop. Within minutes, he was asking me to cut the throat of a lamb in the backyard. I was terrified and could barely hold the knife he gave me. I just about managed to nick an artery before I fainted. When I came to, Mr Pugh was laughing. He said that having failed this rite of passage, I might be more useful in the office, running errands or serving customers.

This was how things turned out. Although there were always carcasses and joints for company, mercifully I never had to kill a living creature myself. I stayed in the job for six years. I mainly made deliveries but, as I got older, I helped out with the books too. It was hard work but I enjoyed it and made myself indispensable to the family business. I earned a tiny wage, most of which I handed over to my mother to help meet bills. But I had a little for myself, and from the age of fourteen onwards, I began to spend some of it exploring the world beyond the Dulas Valley.

I would hop onto the rickety Corris Railway and go to Machynlleth where I remember standing outside what was said to be Owain Glyndwr's Parliament House. What a great Welshman he was! Sometimes, I would travel on from there, on the Cambrian Railway, to the slate, lead and agricultural wharves at the port of Aberdyfi. I would spend many happy hours watching the dockers at work, wondering where the boats being loaded were destined for.

But I was no roustabout. Apart from regular peregrinations on the Corris Railway, I was a member of one of several male choirs to be found in the village. With the help of Mr Williams, I also continued with my English studies.

Unusually for boys of that age, I didn't give much thought to girls. I think I was considered odd but inoffensive by them. My father and my brothers were bemused by me. I was closer to my mother and my three younger sisters. Our family life was often penurious but still harmonious, for which I remain grateful to this day. The desperate poverty that was everywhere was much more destructive to the lives of many others who lived in the village.

My father did bequeath one gift to me, if that is the right word: an abiding interest in politics. He brought leaflets or pamphlets home which I read avidly. He was a strong supporter of William Gladstone and the South Wales Miners' leader William Abraham, known as Mabon. Mabon advocated cooperation between employers and workers to build a better society in Wales.

My father was a lay preacher, a fluent Welsh speaker and had a superb tenor voice. His views shaped my own thinking, although I was eventually to disavow his radical liberalism in favour of socialism. Mr Pugh was a Tory, so I kept my thoughts to myself at work.

***

I was taken to the southern side of Market Square. Both cars stopped there. I was taken out of the car and all my clothes were taken off, with the exception of my shirt and socks. One of the men had a drum of tar. I shouted "police" but to no avail. The men made a ring around me; there were about eight or nine of them. Several persons then put tar all over my body, leaving only my face. One person held his hand over my mouth and I held my own hands over my eyes.

After I had been tarred, someone produced a bag and threw some woolly material over me. Someone then shouted to the others to hurry

17

away as quickly as possible. They all went away in the two cars and left me there. I went to the Police Station and reported to Sergeant Sheppey. I made a statement to him. In the struggle in Market Square, my top artificial teeth had been broken. I still have wounds and scratches all over my body and my skin has been burnt by the tar. My nerves are also upset. I was put in fear and terror by my assailants, as I thought I was going to be killed.

I know of no provocation for the assault; Violet Harper told me it was because I sided with a black boy against a white woman. I gave evidence in this Court in a case on 17ᵗʰ January 1923. I appeared in defence of one of my African servants charged with indecent assault of my wife. My wife made no protest when I was forced into the car.

***

By 1895, aged eighteen, I was beginning to feel restricted by life in Corris. I wanted to find a bigger stage. I made my first ever visit to South Wales in July of that year, staying for two days in Cardiff. I was overwhelmed by the architecture and energy. On my second day there, I saw a job advert in the window of a well-kept butcher's shop in Butetown, near the docks. On impulse, I went in and expressed an interest.

I was interviewed on the spot by the owner, Mr Morgan, and offered a job, starting straight away. Clearly, I'd made a good impression. When I said that I'd need a couple of weeks to make arrangements, I was told I could have a week or forget it.

A week later, I was back. My father did not object when I told him about my new plans, saying that it was now my life to lead. My mother and sisters were more upset, but nothing was going to stop me from taking the job. Once back in Cardiff, I found basic lodgings in a shabby house in Butetown, sharing with five men and one family. A meagre breakfast and dinner were provided by the taciturn landlady. But I was happy enough.

For the next two years, my life revolved around work. Mr Morgan was a hard taskmaster. Armed with good writing and numeracy skills, I became more and more involved in the administration side of the business.

There were many temptations in Cardiff but I resisted them. I dedicated myself to further study, signing up for evening classes in all sorts of subjects; religion, history and politics were my passion.

This was a time of growing industrial strife in Wales and gradually I found myself getting caught up in public campaigns to support workers fighting unreasonable employers. I became involved in raising funds for the Quarrymen's Union in North Wales which, at the time, was perpetually in dispute with the most powerful slate quarry owner, Lord Penrhyn, and his notorious agent E.A. Young.

The union was on strike between 1900 and 1903 – the longest strike ever in British history. But it was an unequal contest. Lord Penrhyn, who also owned sugar plantations in the Caribbean worked by a slave workforce, was implacable and not bothered by the fact that he never won in the court of public opinion. I remember putting up a poster in our window in Butetown in support of the strikers. It declared: "*Nid oes bradwr yn y ty hwn*" (There is no traitor in this house).

I was also involved in raising money for soup kitchens and emergency feeding schemes during the 1898 coal stoppage when tens of thousands of miners were locked out by the coal owners. I became radicalised, and in 1899 joined the Independent Labour Party.

***

Evidence given in the High Court of Southern Rhodesia, Bulawayo Sessions, by Sergeant Frank Sheppey, 7th March 1923

On the night of 19th January 1923, I was on duty in the Charge Office. About 10:30 pm, the last witness came into the Charge Office alone. His whole body, except his neck, face and hair, was covered with tar. There were spots of tar and a lot of blood on his face. There was a lot of white wool fluff on his body sticking to the tar and in his hair. In his left hand, he had some false teeth and a broken plate. He appeared very distressed and agitated and was suffering from shock.

He made a report to me. He asked for paraffin, but I could not give him any. He left the office after a minute or two as he stated that the tar was burning and he wanted to get it off.

I do not think the complainant is of an excitable nature. His speech was hurried when I saw him in the Charge Office and the insult to his modesty obviously affected him. I think he was genuinely distressed.

***

My father died in November 1900 and Mr Morgan allowed me to return home to Corris for three months to support my mother and sisters. My elder brothers by now had their own wives and families and showed little interest in meeting their responsibilities. I believe that my father died of sheer exhaustion in the end. It redoubled my determination to avoid the same fate.

I returned to Cardiff, but within three months, I was back in Corris. In June 1901, my beloved mother, Bronwyn, followed my father into the next world. We had been very close, so her death was a grievous blow. I took a long time to recover.

I was fortunate to have good friends to support me back in Cardiff. By this time, I was living in better quality lodgings on the edge of Butetown. I shared them with three other single men. We spent many happy evenings there, discussing public affairs or literature. On the weekends, we often went out together although we were certainly not wild types. Our landlady called us the "monks of Butetown".

***

Evidence given in the High Court of Southern Rhodesia, Bulawayo Sessions, by Henry Livermore, 7th March 1923

I know Mr James, who lives close by, at the back of my house. On Friday evening, I was in my house and received a call at about 10 pm. Mr James's little girl called me saying someone was hurting her father. I went down the sanitary lane to get to the front of James's house. When I came to the front of the house, I saw a number of men pulling James along the ground. James was calling my name all the time. I asked the men what they were doing and told them to leave James alone.

One man had hold of each leg and another was holding him by the body. They took him towards 1st Avenue and I followed. A car appeared into which James was taken. I saw Violet Harper standing near the car before it moved off. Violet Harper said to me, "Don't worry, Mr Livermore, I am Mrs Harper of the Empire. We are going to tar and feather this man."

I ran after the car for a short distance. It went up 2nd Avenue and I did not see it again. I returned to my house and found James's children there, very alarmed. His son asked me to go with him to find his father. I went with him to the Police Station. There, I saw the complainant, all black except his face, with a few white spots about him. He appeared distressed.

I am not a friend of the complainant. The complainant had spoken to me about the case of the assault by an African on his wife. I did not say that I approved of the complainant's conduct in that case. I did not intend to go down to the Police Station and lodge a charge against the assailants.

***

In 1904, Mr Morgan offered me the Number 2 position in the butcher's shop. Being without sons of his own and in his late sixties, he indicated that he might be willing to hand over the shop to me when he retired. At first, I was delighted at this prospect, but soon I was having doubts. Did I want to be a butcher in Cardiff for the rest of my life? I wasn't sure I did.

A young woman from a good family had begun to take an interest in me but I could not reciprocate her feelings. We'd met at an Independent Labour Party meeting but, while we shared much in common, I never thought of her as anything more than a friend. It reached the point where I began to feel haunted by her.

In a somewhat restless mood, fate intervened once again. Walking past Cardiff Railway Station in February 1906, I saw a poster advertising jobs on the Cape Government Railways. I knew little about Southern Africa but, no great supporter of the Empire, I had been appalled by the cruelties inflicted on the Boers in the course of the war of 1899-1902. I had also been interested to read in the newspapers about the campaigns being led in Natal by Indian lawyer Mohandas K. Gandhi.

I knew even less about railway work; however, I remembered happy days on the Corris Railway as a boy. Feeling that I had nothing to lose and much to gain by throwing everything up in the air, I went to the address given on the poster and arranged an interview the next day.

The gentleman who interviewed me was encouraging, assuring me that my skills would be much in demand on the railway. Two days later, I returned to see him and he made me a job offer as a goods checker.

Suddenly it was real. While not reckless, I did sometimes act on impulse as a young man. I accepted the offer and signed up on the spot. Mr Morgan was astonished and disappointed, but he had no hold over me and could do nothing more than wish me well.

It was with excitement and some relief that I took the train to Southampton, boarding RMS Walmer Castle for the two-week journey to Cape Town the next day. The Cape Railways paid for my third-class passage. At the time of departure, I had no thoughts of spending the rest of my life in Southern Africa. Yet, for better for worse, that is how it has turned out.

***

Evidence given in the High Court of Southern Rhodesia, Bulawayo Sessions, Iolo James (recalled), 7th March 1923
I did not say in the car that I would sooner take the word of my domestic servant than that of my wife or any other white woman. I did not shake hands with the African in question after he had been convicted of indecently assaulting my wife.

I was stationed at Belmont some years ago in the employ of the South African Railways. I did not assault my wife then. I was dismissed from the railways on misrepresentations. I was later reinstated. I did not know that it was through my wife's intercession.

I know nothing of any women chasing me with a chopper and a broomstick owing to my behaviour towards my wife when we were living in Belmont. I did not take refuge at the top of a water tank. I remember a rooster of mine disappearing; this happened at Belmont. There was trouble between myself and my wife at Hartley; my wife may have gone to the magistrate about it. I was not chased by anyone there. I did not take refuge down a well.

I have never assaulted my wife at any time. I do not keep my wife short of food. She has money of her own in the bank.

23

When I was taken from my house, I fully believed I was going to be murdered.

Part 2 Belmont and Kimberley, South Africa, 1906-11

Chapter Two

Belmont, March 1906

Iolo James reached for his suitcase from the luggage rack as the train juddered to a halt. At five foot eight, it was a bit of a stretch. The stop was Belmont Station, eighty miles or so south of Kimberley. He had arrived at his first posting with the Cape Government Railways.

He had landed in Cape Town a week earlier after an uneventful passage. Apart from one casual encounter, he had kept to himself on the voyage, sticking to superficial conversation when forced to engage with other passengers.

The encounter had been unplanned, as they often were. A tall man of Eastern European extraction had caught his eye as they both gazed at a faraway ship headed towards Madeira from which they had just departed. They'd found an empty cabin. It was all over in ten minutes.

Familiar emotions surged through him afterwards – shame, guilt, self-loathing – but they did not last long. These feelings had been overwhelming when his teacher, Mr Williams, first propositioned him at thirteen years old. But over time he had become expert at suppressing them.

Once in Cape Town, he had spent three days being trained for his new job. The recruiter in Cardiff had recommended that he work as a goods clerk to make use of his education. It turned out that he was just one of ten men on the boat who were coming out to work on the railways. They were a diverse lot, with a range of backgrounds and nations represented. Some were rough-and-ready. They tried to rope him into their social plans, which involved much rowdiness and heavy drinking, but he turned their invitations down.

He preferred to read on his bunk rather than explore the city. His passion was the lyric poet John Ceiriog Hughes, once a railwayman in the county of Merionethshire, albeit a less than dedicated one by all accounts. The national mourning when Hughes died in 1887 was one of Iolo's earliest memories.

Some called Hughes the Robert Burns of Wales, which Iolo thought sold him short. Like many Welsh people, he could recite numerous poems and folk songs from the Hughes canon. His favourite poem, for its melancholic simplicity, was *Nant y Mynydd* (The Mountain Stream). Hughes had written it as a young man after moving to Manchester to find work. Although the poem evoked sadness in many, it comforted Iolo. It carried him home again.

His nose deep in a book, a couple of the trainees tried to turn the rest of the group against him, charging him with aloofness. "You're always reading, James," said one, accusingly. "It's just not healthy."

"Each to their own," Iolo replied, keen to bring the exchange to a close. Everybody was aware that soon they would be heading off in many different directions, so nobody pressed things too far.

Iolo looked on as the others became instant experts on 'the African and his ways'. He had not given such matters much thought ahead of his arrival, but he was instinctively disinclined to join in triumphal celebrations of white superiority. He remembered something one of his comrades in the Independent Labour Party had said before he left Cardiff, "Too many British workers lose their humanity when they sign up for the Empire."

On his final day of training, Iolo was told that he would be going to Belmont, a small settlement on the line of rail not far south of Kimberley, known worldwide as the city of diamonds. Another member of the group, a young Scotsman called McCartney, was heading to the same *dorp*, with a job as a ganger waiting for him.

Iolo and McCartney were met on the platform by the Station Master, a middle-aged Englishman called Walter Snow. "Gentlemen, welcome to paradise," said Snow without much trace of humour. Snow ushered McCartney into a room to meet the ganger's foreman for that section of the line. Iolo hoped this would be the last time he saw the tiresome man. Mr Snow then took Iolo into his cramped office by the station entrance, gesturing at a chair.

"Right, Mr James," Snow said, "We've been short of a goods clerk for some time now, so you are eagerly anticipated. We don't actually have a separate shed for items being sent off from here or received. Everything is crammed into a couple of small rooms at the end of the platform. I suspect there are some items that should have been sent off long ago. And we have several irate Boer farmers and businesses locally that are sure we should have received something for them by now. So, there is a big job of work for you to do and no time to delay, I'm afraid."

"I'm keen to get started, Mr Snow," Iolo replied. "Just show me where the goods rooms are."

"I'm pleased to hear that. But it's only fair to give you the rest of the afternoon to sort out your accommodation and take a look around the place. Let me show you to your quarters. They are next door to those of my wife and I, as it happens. They are modest, but you are a single man and therefore have minimal needs, I assume."

"You are right," said Iolo, smiling.

"Let's go. I need to be quick, the twelve thirty from Kimberley is coming through shortly."

Twenty feet later, they were outside Iolo's living quarters. Mr Snow ushered him in, gave him his key, saying as he left, "There are now three European workers permanently based here in Belmont. I propose that we meet for dinner on Saturday evening if that is acceptable? I can then introduce you to Mr Carmichael, the ganger's foreman, who is also coming. You have one African working under you, by the way. I will bring him along tomorrow morning. Until then, I'm sure you can fend for yourself."

"Thank you for the kind invitation, Mr Snow. I'll be fine until tomorrow."

Snow disappeared around the corner. Within a minute, Iolo heard the twelve thirty train pull into the platform.

Mr Snow had not misled him. His quarters were extremely basic. They had mud walls and a corrugated iron roof. There was a single bed in the corner, draped with a mosquito net. A paraffin lamp stood beside it, along with some matches. This would be his first night ever under a net. He worried that he might get claustrophobic.

There was a narrow chest of drawers for his clothes. A small desk and chair stood in front of the sole window. In a tiny side-room was a sink without taps and a bar of soap on it. A bucket of water stood under the sink. That was it. He spied an outside toilet nearby. Iolo was not disconcerted. He had not expected much.

He unpacked his suitcase in five minutes. His belongings were minimal. There were more books than clothes. He stood a small, framed photograph of his mother on the desk. Then he headed out to familiarise himself with the rest of Belmont.

That, too, did not take long. The railway station apart, the town comprised two small, run down stores, several homesteads and a small location where Africans and other non-whites lived. The first was a grocery, doubling up as a post office. The second was an agricultural equipment store. He could hear the sound of Afrikaans from inside the grocery.

He went in to get something for dinner. There was little to buy and when he took his paltry purchases – a tin of corned beef and a couple of tomatoes – to the counter, the middle-aged woman behind it looked at him distrustfully. He was sure he'd been due more change than she gave him.

As he walked out of the shop, he spied a row of rocky hills nearby. In due course he would learn their names. Some joker had dubbed two of them Mont Blanc and Table Mountain.

After twenty minutes, he was back in his quarters, in part because there was nothing else to see, but also because he was still struggling to adjust to the unfamiliar climate. Wales, let alone the lush green landscapes of the Cape winelands, this was not. He was slowly becoming accustomed to the dry heat, but he was unsure that he would ever get used to the fierce light. Squinting through his shabby glasses had given him a headache.

Having retired to his rooms, he did not leave again until the sun rose the next day except to ease himself. He had a disturbed night's sleep under the mosquito net.

The next morning, Mr Snow showed Iolo the locked brick storeroom on the northbound platform where basic provisions for railway staff were kept and gave him his own key. Access to the storeroom reduced the need for awkward encounters of the sort he'd had at the grocers on his first day in Belmont.

At dinner that first Saturday evening, Mr and Mrs Snow gave him a potted history of Belmont and its environs. Mr Carmichael had been called away to Kimberley at short notice. Mr Snow said that this was not much of a surprise. There were rumours that he spent a lot of time in drinking dens there rather than checking up on the gangers along the line of rail under his authority.

This, Mr Snow told him, was border country – an area where the Orange Free State and Cape Colony met. Nor was the Transvaal far away. Most of the whites in the area were Afrikaner farmers. Belmont had seen serious fighting during the war. In 1899 there had been an important battle there between British troops under Lord Methuen and Afrikaner forces under the command of Jacobus Prinsloo, in which the British prevailed.

Mrs Snow added that the woman running the grocery store, Mrs du Toit, had lost her husband and son during the war. Both had been members of a local Boer militia. She and her younger children ended up in a concentration camp. Iolo remembered reading about the terrible conditions in the camps. Thousands of Afrikaner women and children had died in them. The woman's expression whenever he visited the shop made more sense to him now.

The Snows had arrived soon after the war ended in 1902. The Cape Railways decided to post British employees along the line of rail between Beaufort West and Kimberley in the immediate aftermath – Afrikaners could not be trusted, at least not for a while, it reasoned. The upshot was that railway staff in Belmont were an island of Britishness in an ocean of Boers. The station began to feel more like a fort to Iolo than a public building.

Evidence of the war was still easy to find in the town and nearby hills. Bullet casings lay everywhere. Abandoned, rusty rifles turned up from time to time. There had been some reconstruction; the telegraph line and the sole road had been repaired. The station had been given a lick of paint. Nonetheless, Belmont had an air of abandonment and neglect. Several nearby farms lay unoccupied.

At first, the two goods rooms that were Iolo's main responsibility were in a disorganised state. There were several bags of putrefying produce to dispose of. Within a week, some order had been created. Word soon got around the area that the railway was once again sending and receiving goods.

The local farmers had no choice but to bring their produce to the railway side if they wished to get it to big markets like Kimberley. Conversations were brief and to the point. None had so far picked a fight with Iolo. Although they noticed his Welsh accent, he decided not to mention that he was not really British. After all, he was working for them. And word might have got back to Mr Snow, who was highly patriotic. A framed image of the King adorned the Snows' living room wall.

Iolo had not got the goods rooms functioning properly by himself. He'd had Samuel to help. This was the name of the African Snow had mentioned on the day he arrived. Samuel was probably in his thirties. He walked with a limp, but he was strong, hard-working and reliable. When Iolo arrived for work, Samuel was always already there.

Iolo tried to engage Samuel in conversation, but he was not keen to say much about himself, or indeed anything else. Snow had assured him that this was for the best; too much familiarity could lead to laziness and insubordination, he said. Iolo was not convinced but did not challenge him.

Iolo was not sure where Samuel lived and had not asked. He presumed it was the town's location. Apparently, he had arrived in town in 1903, approached Snow for work and been taken on.

Snow said that, when questioned, Samuel had assured him that he was loyal to the British. He'd worked under Iolo's predecessor, a Mr Stewart, who had been employed by the railways in Belmont until the end of 1905 but who had now got a more attractive job in Cape Town's goods sheds. Iolo was pleased that he and Samuel had a harmonious relationship but regretted there was so much social distance between them.

Iolo's days had a steady rhythm. He was on duty from 6 am to 6 pm, the hours during which trains came through Belmont, six days a week. He had half an hour for a lunch break every day. Work was not always intense. The busiest times were the first and last three hours of the day when he and Samuel checked in and checked out the goods they handled.

When he had time, which was mainly on Sundays, he liked to take short walks. At first sight, there appeared to be little vegetation, but as his eye grew more accustomed, he was able to identify the numerous bushes and plants that survived in the semi-arid environment. His favourites were the yellow, flowering *granaat* and the dark blue 'Karoo violet'.

Most evenings, he'd eat his main meal and then spend time gazing at the heavens. The night sky was astonishing. Borrowing a book about astronomy from Mr Snow, he'd quickly identified the five stars of the Southern Cross.

Newspapers were the highlight of his day. The railways were the main artery for delivering them around the country, so there was a regular supply. Iolo read every paper he could get his hands on, but his favourite was *Indian Opinion*, edited by Mohandas K. Gandhi, in whose exploits Iolo became keenly interested.

Iolo had plenty of time to reflect on his own life and what he wanted from it. He was now approaching thirty years of age. The Christian faith which had been so central to his family and community life in Corris – they were Calvinist Methodists, a Welsh strand of Presbyterianism – remained strong. His political convictions ran alongside that faith. The Independent Labour Party's socialism often had a decidedly evangelical tone.

He was quiet and solitary in temperament. He often felt that he was more an observer than a participant in life. While he sometimes felt this was a weakness, usually he was comfortable with it.

He loved ideas more than people. He felt ambivalent about physical intimacy. Mr Williams had taken advantage of him when he was a boy, causing him considerable distress. His teacher had tried to persuade him not to feel guilty, telling him that God was forgiving when it came to the weaknesses of the flesh. Iolo had always struggled to accept this injunction.

Until now, all but one of his physical encounters had been with the male sex. His years in Butetown had provided many opportunities. His one assignation with a young woman had been successful enough, at least from his point of view, but it had not ended his episodic encounters with men.

Three encounters in Butetown had been with African sailors. For a while, one of them looked like it might develop into a passionate relationship. Mohamed was an older Somali man with over a decade at sea who was thinking about putting down roots in Cardiff. They had met when Iolo was proselytising for the Independent Labour Party with a group of comrades by the dockside one weekend. Most people had simply walked straight by,

35

but Mohamed had come up and asked him several probing questions.

The question which Iolo remembered most vividly was about the British Empire. Mohamed said that he had heard many avowed socialists defend what surely was indefensible. Iolo thought he had a point. He'd heard several compatriots go so far as to argue that Wales was an oppressed colony of the English. This was the first of many important conversations between them. Their friendship crossed into the realm of the physical, but it was never primarily about sex.

Butetown was a rough-and-tumble area. Most people were relaxed about relationships between races. Nor was there necessarily great censoriousness about men being intimate with each other, as long as it was not spelt out. But there was a minority who objected, so it was important to take care. From time to time, church groups and the municipal authorities became agitated about the lax morals of the area. This would lead to campaigns to 'save Butetown'.

One day in late 1905 an acquaintance warned Iolo that somebody had reported him and Mohamed to the police and that they should take action to protect themselves from arrest. A panicky Iolo warned Mohamed, who decided to return to the sea for a while. He signed up with a merchant shipping line which operated in East Africa and the Indian Ocean. Within two days, he was gone. Iolo was sad but hoped that things would now return to normal.

Unfortunately, his troubles were not over. Not long after Mohamed left, a policeman came to Iolo's home when he was out, saying that he wanted to interview him about something. Although he was reluctant to admit as much, this unwanted visit played a big part in Iolo's own decision to leave Cardiff. The railway recruiter for the Cape Government Railways was knocking at a half-open door.

Mohamed had visited South Africa on two occasions during his sailing days and educated Iolo about the country. It was he who first awakened Iolo's interest in Mohandas K. Gandhi's peaceful campaign against the colour bar dividing white people and Indians there. But Mohamed was critical of Gandhi's failure to make connections between the injustices suffered by Indians there and the even deeper discrimination experienced by the African majority.

Iolo had acknowledged the force of Mohamed's opinions, but they did not put him off. Since arriving in Belmont, Iolo had read about how Gandhi had established a commune near Durban called the Phoenix Settlement. He was experimenting with living on the land, without personal possessions, on the basis of interfaith harmony. Europeans and Indians lived alongside each other at Phoenix. *Indian Opinion* was published there.

With little else to do in Belmont, he decided to undertake a sustained study of Gandhi's philosophy. Maybe one day, he thought to himself, he might visit the Phoenix Settlement.

Chapter Three

Kimberley, April 1908

Iolo disliked Kimberley. Everything revolved around the diamond mines. It was a company town. De Beers controlled everything. The city was dirty, noisy and dangerous. Coal, most of it from Wales, echoing Iolo's own migratory journey, cast a permanent smog over it. Tremors rippled through Iolo's body, generated by the rumble of machinery and underground dynamite blasts, as he moved around the centre of the city.

He had twice been the victim of theft. Illicit diamonds could be purchased on street corners and down narrow alleyways. Once, near the Malay Camp, he had been offered diamonds for sale by Black Abrahams, one of the best-known illicit traders. But he was never tempted. He knew that the mining companies had established a department to catch those involved in the illicit trade.

Europeans spoke of nothing but the 1900 siege and its heroic relief by British forces. He had little time for such talk. However, the city had clothes and shoe shops which he needed to visit, despite his natural frugality. It also had two good bookshops.

Kimberley was also a marketplace for sex. At first, he'd hoped that he might find some of the freedom there that he had enjoyed back in Butetown, but he was quickly disabused of this notion. There was a tavern down an alleyway off Long Street where likeminded men congregated. He went several times in his first year but then lost courage. He'd realised that the difficulties which he'd faced in Cardiff could be multiplied many times over in Kimberley, where the moral climate was less relaxed. This created an undertow of frustration in Iolo. He had an itch which, from time to time, he needed to scratch.

In November 1906, on his fourth visit to the city, Iolo discovered a small, informal, club of free-thinkers which held occasional talks about social and political matters. They were held in the backroom of a Europeans-only bar, near the Public Library.

The club kept a low-profile to avoid the disapproval of the so-called right-thinking majority. Its meetings became the main reason why he came to Kimberley. Mr Snow was happy to let him go, provided he was back on the first train the next morning.

In April 1908, the club held a talk that really excited Iolo. The speaker was Mr Albert West, a resident of the Phoenix Settlement. He talked about Gandhi's life and campaigns.

Expecting a large audience, the venue was changed to a meeting room in the Grand Hotel on Market Square. As Iolo entered, he looked around. About sixty people were there. There were more women than usual. He thought he might have seen some of them at other meetings, but he could not be sure.

Mr West's talk was absorbing. He spoke at some length about the *Satyagraha* campaign currently being led by Gandhi. There were murmurs of agreement from several members of the audience when he spoke about the injustice of official efforts to disenfranchise Indians. He described Gandhi's experience of prison.

West argued that the Indians had proven their loyalty to the Empire during the recently concluded war with the Boers and were in no way uncivilised like the Africans. This elicited widespread 'hear hears'.

It was when Mr West went on to talk about Gandhi's personal beliefs that Iolo became most intently engaged. Gandhi's struggle to master his mortal passions intrigued him. His quest for mastery included a long-standing commitment to vegetarianism, as well as a more recent decision to embrace poverty and celibacy. Iolo agreed that man's unruly physical desires often got in the way of what mattered most in life, which was to be faithful to your principles.

The talk concluded after about an hour. Applause rang out. Mr West bowed in acknowledgement. When questions were invited, Iolo raised his hand.

"Mr Gandhi advocates celibacy but he is a father of four children. Is that not inconsistent? And he is married. Has he got the agreement of his wife to this change?"

Mr West replied, his hands plunged deep in his pockets, "Mr Gandhi believes that there is a time and place for everything. His natural desire to have a family is satisfied, hence he can now focus on purifying himself and freeing his wife from the disrespect he feels he showed her in the past through his lustful desire. She supports him wholeheartedly in this decision."

He went on, his face blushing a little, "It is also interesting to note that, notwithstanding his own decision, Mr Gandhi has been encouraging me to get married for some time – something I intend to do in June! My wife-to-be has already joined me at the Phoenix Settlement." Mr West's expression turned serious again, "This shows that he does not want to deny others the right to a family.

Maybe in time I will follow his course of action and embrace celibacy, but for now it is certainly not on my mind."

Iolo nodded in response. It was gone nine o'clock when the meeting finally ended. As the audience was filing out, a woman approached him. "Your question was a good one, sir. But I am not convinced that Mr Gandhi's wife has been afforded a genuine opportunity to have a view when it comes to his decision on celibacy!"

Iolo's first instinct was to avoid the woman, but she had blocked his path. He felt he had no choice but to respond. "Perhaps you are right. We only have Mr West's word for it."

The woman was a bit shorter than him but, at first sight, of similar age. She was slender in build but with piercing eyes and bright auburn hair in a bun. Her female companion was taller with similar reddish hair. His interlocutor said, "My sister Hannah and I came on a whim, to be honest, but we are glad we did. Mr Gandhi is an interesting man, and his cause appears just. But he has some strange foibles, would you not agree?"

Iolo replied cautiously, "Well, I am not sure. I am still formulating my opinion."

"Ah, it is good to meet somebody who considers, rather than rushes to judgement. My name is Doris, by the way, Doris Maxwell. I live here in Kimberley, for better or worse, along with my sister and mother. I wonder whether you might be kind enough to accompany us both home? It is not far and my mother was worried about us getting back safely."

Iolo was taken aback by the woman's forwardness. But he could hardly refuse; it would have been unchivalrous and he had nothing else to do. He had a room for the night in a hotel just round the corner, much humbler than the Grand. He'd planned to go back there and read.

41

"It is unusual for two young women to be out on their own, unchaperoned. You are clearly independent of spirit as well as mind! I'm very happy to accompany you home," he replied.

"Sorry, I should have introduced myself. I am Iolo James, a railway worker living down the line of rail. Do you have a carriage waiting?"

They did. It was right outside the hotel. The carriage set off for Beaconsfield, a suburb not far from the city centre. Within twenty minutes they had arrived at a small brick house with a thatched roof. Even though it was dark, Iolo could see from the front garden that the residents loved roses.

During the journey Doris talked non-stop, telling Iolo much more about her life story than was customary on a first meeting. Their father, an engineer of Scottish origin working for De Beers, had died during the Siege of Kimberley, leaving the family in straitened circumstances. Doris informed him that both she and Hannah were unattached and that their prospects had been harmed by the loss of their father. Her mother, also Scottish, prized respectability, but achieving this through a good match for her daughters was no longer straightforward.

Iolo felt obliged to reciprocate Doris's openness by revealing more about himself than he would have done otherwise. She smiled when she learnt that Iolo was stationed at Belmont. "There is nothing for a man of culture there, Mr James," she said. "No wonder you rush to Kimberley at the first opportunity."

"No, I assure you, I am perfectly content in Belmont. I prefer the peace and quiet. It is easier to think there."

"It is late and my mother will have already retired for the night, so it would not be appropriate for you to come in at this hour. But perhaps you could come back tomorrow morning? I feel that we have more to discuss about Mr Gandhi. And my mother would be very happy to meet the kind gentleman who chaperoned her daughters home."

"I would like to, but sadly I am expected back in Belmont tomorrow and have a return railway ticket for the morning."

"Then let us say you will visit next time you come up to Kimberley? Write me a letter ahead of your visit and we can send a carriage for you." Hannah, who had barely spoken, nodded in assent.

"I would be delighted," said Iolo. He took details of their address and bowed. "I wish you good night."

"Thank you, Mr James. It has been a pleasure meeting you." And with that he left.

Once he was in his hotel room, rather than get ready for bed immediately, he sat down in the rickety chair by the window and thought back over the events of the evening. He couldn't put his finger on it, but he sensed that something significant had happened.

At the same time, not far away, twenty-six-year-old Doris Maxwell was wondering whether she had met the knight in shining armour who might help her escape her intolerable confinement.

***

Kimberley, May 1909

Iolo and Doris walked out of the church into the blinding light. They had been married by an elderly presbyterian minister who'd struggled to remember their names during the service, calling Iolo 'Ivor' and Doris 'Doreen' on several occasions. It hadn't mattered. The titter of laughter from the small congregation behind them had helped to relieve the tension.

As people threw confetti in their direction on the steps, Doris looked at Iolo. She laughed and he smiled back. His smile seemed genuine, but Doris was still sometimes uncertain about what was real and what was not about Iolo.

The basic facts about his past and present life she was confident about: his childhood in Wales, his butchering days and his current employment with the railways. But he was somebody who held things back, residing behind a façade.

The wedding party moved on to the Grand Hotel, where the reception was being held. It was, of course, where the newly married couple had met. Doris had started going to the club six months before Mr West's talk. While some of the talks had appealed to her, in truth her main reason for going had been to find a husband.

The death of her father during the siege had not just deprived her of a father. Eighteen at the time, she had been engaged to a promising young man who cruelly cooled towards her when faced with responsibility for the whole family rather than her alone.

As the years passed, Doris had begun to fear that the life of a spinster would be her fate. Her sister Hannah appeared unbothered by the prospect, but she was not. Doris felt like it would be the end of the world. She wanted her life to grow and change. For that to happen, she needed a husband. Children would inevitably follow. She had long wanted to be a mother and envied the women in her small social circle who had bred successfully.

Iolo James was the third potential candidate she had identified while attending the talks. The other two had not reciprocated her interest. The speaker at the meeting, Mr West, attracted her more but, sadly, he was taken.

She had watched Iolo intently when he was asking his question. He was presentable enough, if on the short side. There was an air of tentativeness and circumspection about him which encouraged her. He might be amenable to direction by a more forceful personality.

44

Her approach that evening had born fruit. Iolo did visit the family home on his next visit, which was pleasingly soon after the talk, suggesting keenness. Her mother, who had never recovered from the loss of her husband, said that she had formed a favourable impression, notwithstanding the fact that she did not usually like the Welsh.

Hannah expressed indifference. She was worried that Iolo might prove a disappointingly dull husband in the long run. She thought there was something missing. Doris soon began to worry that she might be right, but she felt that it was now or never. She decided to accentuate the positive.

Iolo started coming to Kimberley for an overnight stay every month. With Hannah always in tow, they would meet at the house or take late-afternoon walks, usually in the vicinity of the Honoured Dead Memorial, which commemorated those who had died defending the city during the siege.

In front of the Memorial was Long Cecil, the enormous, custom-made gun named after mining magnate and politician Cecil Rhodes, which was used to repel the Boers during the 1900 siege. The Memorial had become something of a tourist attraction. Doris had been disconcerted by Iolo's dismissive sneer at the sight of it but had let it go.

Mr Snow was unhappy about how much time Iolo was spending in Kimberley, but his wife had impressed on him that good Christian people should be facilitating rather than obstructing those contemplating the marital state. Her argument was immensely strengthened when, in January 1909, Iolo proposed to Doris and was accepted.

Although Iolo had offered to help with the arrangements for the wedding, Doris and Hannah took most of the organisational strain. Their mother was a spectator. Doris set Iolo the task of trying to secure a transfer to a railway job in Kimberley. To her frustration, Iolo was slow to submit his request and had to be repeatedly chivvied about it.

By the time of the wedding, no transfer had been secured. But Iolo assured her that his request was under active consideration and that it was only a matter of time. In the meantime, she could stay in Kimberley with her mother if she wanted. She said no to that. A married woman should live with her husband. Living apart would be unnatural and unconducive to intimacy. If this meant living with Iolo in a backwater like Belmont for a short while, so be it.

Neither Iolo nor Doris had much money for a honeymoon, so after the reception had ended, it was simply a matter of Iolo returning with her to the house in Beaconsfield. They spent their first three nights together there. Doris found it hard going back to the house where, as she put it, "nothing ever happened". She had counted down every day since her engagement.

Iolo seemed not to mind. He was waiting to receive a telegram from Mr Snow confirming that his new accommodation was ready. When Doris said she was coming to Belmont come hell or high water, he'd realised that his current spartan quarters would not be acceptable. And as it became clear that a transfer to Kimberley was not going to happen before the wedding day, he had begun to look around for something bigger.

It turned out that Mrs du Toit, the Boer widow running and living in the grocery store, owned a small three-room house on the edge of Belmont. It had a bedroom, bathroom, living room and, like most houses in South Africa, a *stoep* – Afrikaans for veranda – at the front. It had no electricity or running water, but Iolo felt it would do.

Mrs du Toit, who only began to give Iolo the time of day a year or so after his arrival in Belmont, viewed him as a friend by now. Her attitude changed after Iolo told her that he was Welsh, rather than British, and condemned the behaviour of British forces during the war. "Back in the fifteenth century, Wales was England's first colony," he had told her. Iolo asked her not to let the Snows know that he'd said this.

Mrs du Toit congratulated him warmly when he told her that he was getting married. The property had been unoccupied for nearly a year and she welcomed the idea of receiving some income from it. Having lost her husband in the battle of Belmont, she and her children were living hand-to-mouth in a tiny place beyond the grocery store.

Iolo said nothing to Doris about the lack of electricity or water. He was a little worried that she would find it wanting on those grounds, accustomed as she was to both in Kimberley. It had not occurred to her to ask. Hopefully, she would not be too disappointed.

Privately, though, he hoped that Doris would warm to Belmont and perhaps Kimberley could be avoided. He had indeed been rather dilatory in putting in his transfer request. Unbeknown to her, he only submitted it the week before the wedding.

He was pleased to become a married man. Until he met Doris, it had not been in his plans at all. But Mr and Mrs Snow had often told him this was a country where Europeans put a premium on fitting in. It was vital to demonstrate civilised standards of morality. Unless Europeans did so, their authority over the Africans would be undermined. Single white men above a certain age could be viewed with mistrust. Iolo was now over thirty. Mrs Snow warned him that he might begin to stand out if he remained a bachelor.

While he had never felt strongly drawn towards women and had little experience with them, Iolo did not recoil at the prospect of conventional married life and all it involved. Nor was he repelled by the idea of fatherhood. So, as he sat on the train home following their first encounter, he had resolved to take up Doris's offer of another meeting. And as he got to know her better, Iolo came to like Doris's energy and apparent sense of direction. He got caught up in the excitement of the unfamiliar and began to imagine a future with her by his side.

The marriage was furtively consummated in the Maxwell family home that first night after the wedding. He knew his duty. With her encouragement, Iolo crept into Doris's adjoining bedroom – sleeping together had been deemed too much for her mother to accept – and into her bed. The electric light was off, but the light of a full moon shone through the closed curtains sufficiently for them inexpertly to conjoin.

Although there were stifled giggles and gasps, neither sought nor expected great pleasure. For both, the main point of this first time was to satisfy expectations. After twenty minutes, Iolo was back in his own room, content that these had successfully been met. He slept well that night.

On the third day after the wedding, Mr Snow sent a telegram confirming that the new house was ready. Within hours, he and Doris were at the station, boarding the train south. Doris had promised her mother and sister that she would soon be living in Kimberley again and in the meantime, would visit every few weeks. Iolo was not sure that their funds would stretch to that but said nothing.

They sat close together on the train to Belmont, holding hands and staring out of the window at the vast expanse of open country which would be their new home. Iolo and Doris James. It sounded good. It sounded right. Both were thinking the same thing, although neither said it – this will be a happy marriage.

Chapter Four

Belmont, May 1910

Doris reached into the Moses basket on the *stoep* floor and picked up three-month-old baby Mervyn. Michael, their new domestic servant, looked on through the kitchen door. Mervyn had begun to cry, something he did a great deal. Doris put the baby to her breast. She was exhausted by early motherhood. She had desperately wanted to be a mother, but it had happened far faster than she'd anticipated. By her calculation, she may well have become pregnant at the first attempt, on the night of their wedding.

The pregnancy was hard. Morning sickness took hold several weeks after their arrival in Belmont. She was quick to retreat back to Kimberley, where her mother, miraculously reanimated, could take care of her better than Iolo would. Iolo had tried but he was nonplussed by pregnancy and struggled to engage with it. Mrs

Snow did her best to help, but she and Doris barely knew each other, so that could not work for long.

Doris had also been dismayed by the house which Iolo had rented for them. It was all so rudimentary. She was used to much more comfort. It was another reason for her to return to Beaconsfield despite having only just escaped. Iolo visited for a night every month, as he had prior to their marriage. Time passed but there was still no news of his transfer to Kimberley.

Mervyn's birth in Kimberley hospital in February 1910 went smoothly, although she had been shocked by the pain involved. There were tears in Iolo's eyes when he was shown his first-born later that day, but thereafter he had done little for the baby – or her. Once again, he became strangely distant. When she mentioned it to Hannah, she nodded as if it came as no surprise. Doris couldn't muster the energy to object.

Doris returned to Belmont once Mervyn reached three months. She wanted to try living there as a family. Iolo said that she was under no obligation but seemed happy enough when she insisted. Mr and Mrs Snow made a fuss of her when she returned, although Mrs Snow hinted that she should have stayed in Kimberley for longer.

One day, Iolo brought home an African, Michael, announcing that they should employ him as the family's domestic servant. Doris had been thinking that she needed help around the house, so she agreed readily. Samuel knew Michael and had recommended him to Iolo.

Until recently, Michael had worked for a nearby Afrikaner farming family. He was probably in his mid-twenties. Tall and well-built, he spoke Afrikaans well and English serviceably. His cooking skills were limited, but he cleaned the house and did the laundry competently. Mrs Snow brought food up to the house most days.

Occasionally Mrs du Toit brought up a meal too – invariably *Frikaddel*, an Afrikaner meatball dish.

Could Doris get used to living in Belmont? She was willing to try. But in the end, she could only stick it out for another two months. She became more and more exasperated with Iolo. Not only was he normally at work at the station, he was semi-absent even when he was present. He was quick to retreat into his books and newspapers. He hardly touched his son.

Doris joked, not without bitterness, that he seemed to be "married to Gandhi rather than her." Missing the underlying reproach entirely, Iolo replied that Gandhi had been their matchmaker – both of them, he asserted, were in his debt.

Iolo's detachment deepened further after something happened to Samuel, the African who worked under him in the goods rooms. When Doris asked what was going on, he was unforthcoming, saying only that Samuel had got into trouble and needed help.

Her patience stretched to breaking point, she announced that she could bear the isolation no longer and would return to her mother and sister. She'd hoped for a reaction from Iolo. But instead of remonstrating with her, he simply said that it might be for the best, adding that he would accompany her to Kimberley, where he had business to attend to.

So, in July 1910, Doris and Iolo returned to Kimberley by train, now with baby Mervyn in tow. The atmosphere this time was flat. There was no hand holding. As the train entered Kimberley, Doris found herself asking, *Have I made a terrible mistake?* She dared not answer.

***

The same thought was crossing Iolo's mind. While he could still see the intellectual and social arguments for marriage, soon he was

51

doubting whether he could perform the role of husband and father with sufficient conviction. Doris's energy and enthusiasm had palled on him. She made demands on him that he resented. Although he knew it was not her fault, he was angry with her for falling pregnant so fast.

He felt ambushed. Doris wasn't really interested in ideas and philosophy. He suspected that she had been looking for a husband when she went to Mr West's talk and almost anybody would have done. He was bemused by Mervyn. Babies were a puzzle he had no wish to solve. He had been happy enough with his life beforehand but now it was all just so complicated. He barely had any time to read his books and newspapers. There were piles of unread copies of the *Indian Opinion* by the bed.

When Samuel was arrested, he was shocked. While they had not become friends, over time they had begun to speak more openly. He discovered that Samuel was a highly intelligent man, with many interesting ideas about the world. There was much they agreed upon.

Samuel spoke critically about Afrikaners. He knew from personal experience, having grown up on an Afrikaner-owned farm in the Pilansberg region of the Transvaal, that they mercilessly exploited their African tenants, compelling them to undertake back-breaking labour without pay in return for staying on the land.

Samuel had strongly supported the British side in the war because he'd believed their promises that things would be better after the Boers had been defeated. Those promises, he claimed, had not been kept. But he would never work voluntarily for an Afrikaner again. For this reason, he had left the farm in 1903 and made his way to Belmont.

Samuel told Iolo that he was a Kgatla, one of the Tswana peoples. Iolo was fascinated by Samuel's descriptions of the history, life and culture of his people. They were an independent people, with a homeland that extended from the Bechuanaland Protectorate into Western Transvaal, all ruled over by King Linchwe. But the Europeans had split the Kgatla living in the Protectorate, in what was today called the Kgatla Reserve, from those settled around Pilansberg. During the 1899-1902 war, the two areas had been reunited. Samuel felt Linchwe could have done more to resist the restoration of partition once the war was over.

These conversations, conducted as they worked together in the goods rooms at the station, opened Iolo's eyes to something that had been staring him in the face but which until then he had barely noticed: This was an African country. Whatever the Europeans might claim, Africans had been here for centuries before their arrival and would still be here long after the Europeans had gone.

One Thursday morning in July 1910 Iolo and Samuel were packing up goods for the next train south which was due in an hour. Both were absorbed in their task and did not see two policemen armed with pistols appear in the doorway with Mr Snow next to them. Snow coughed to alert them to the arrival of visitors.

As Iolo and Samuel turned to look at him, he announced, "I am afraid that these gentlemen have come to arrest Samuel and take him to Kimberley. He is accused of a crime."

Iolo, incredulous, replied, "Crime? What crime?"

"This man is accused of being a ringleader in the illegal occupation of a farm during the war and violently resisting the return of that farm to its rightful owner once the war was over. He is also accused of stealing livestock. He has been on the run for seven years. Samuel is not his real name," said one of the policemen.

Mr Snow added, "These are serious charges. I have the authority to dismiss this man from his job here and now and must do so."

"But no man should be judged guilty based solely on an accusation. Only a judge is qualified to do that," Iolo retorted angrily. "Surely, we owe him something for the service he has given us?"

"We owe him nothing, Mr James. There is no smoke without fire and we have the railway's reputation to consider."

"Samuel, I will see what I can do to help," said Iolo. Turning to the policemen, he asked, "Where will he be kept in Kimberley?"

"The prison, of course, pending trial," said the other policeman with a look of contempt on his face as he tied Samuel's wrists with a piece of rope.

Samuel said nothing as he was taken into custody. When Iolo looked at him, he saw little emotion. Samuel looked like a man who had half-expected this to happen one day. He sat with the two policemen on the platform for two hours while they waited for the next northbound train to arrive, then stepped on board and was gone.

Iolo struggled to concentrate on his work for the rest of the day. In the late afternoon, Mr Snow called Iolo into his office. Looking stern, he told him bluntly, "Do not think of pursuing this matter further, Mr James. I have often felt that you hold some naïve and misguided views about this country and your reaction to today's events confirms my fears."

The Station Master became increasingly agitated as he continued his peroration. "There can be no equality or friendship between Europeans and Africans in South Africa. The African is inferior in civilisation and prone to criminality. Samuel, or whoever he really is, took advantage of the war to violate the laws of property. He must be punished. You are a married man with responsibilities now, so any poorly judged actions you take will affect your family too. Do not bring shame upon them by your conduct."

Iolo left Snow's office without replying, but he was hot with emotion and adrenalin. That evening at home, he hardly spoke to Doris and ignored Mervyn entirely. He had no idea what to do, but he knew that he could not let this matter lie. As he lay sleepless in bed, he determined to go to Kimberley at the first opportunity, visit Samuel in prison and make representations to the railway management.

***

The next day, still fuelled by a sense of injustice on Samuel's behalf, Iolo wrote a short letter to Mr Cooper, the most senior railway manager in Kimberley, asking him to allow Samuel to return to his job if he was found innocent. He told neither Doris nor Mr Snow about this.

When a week or so later, Doris said she wanted to return to Kimberley with Mervyn, Iolo was relieved. It gave him an acceptable reason to go too. If she and the baby were being looked after by her mother and Hannah, he would be free to do what he could for Samuel. He asked Mr Snow for a few days' leave. Reassured that Iolo's priorities were as they should be, Snow granted it.

They drew into Kimberley in the afternoon and went straight to Beaconsfield. To Doris's pleasure, Iolo put Mervyn to bed and joined everybody for dinner. She wondered whether it was perhaps his job that made him so unapproachable in Belmont.

However, the next morning at breakfast, Iolo told her that he would be out for the whole day. Her heart sank. By this time, he had told her that Samuel was under arrest and being held in Kimberley. She suspected that his business had something to do with Samuel but decided not to pry in order to avoid an argument.

Iolo was at the entrance to Kimberley prison by eleven o'clock. It was a forbidding building at the edge of the town. He approached the prison officer at the front gate and asked when the visiting hours for African prisoners were. The officer, an elderly Afrikaner man in an ill-fitting uniform, pointed him to a notice board on which a piece of paper said: *Visiting hours for European prisoners: 1-5 pm Tuesdays and Thursdays.*

"No, sorry, you misunderstand me," said Iolo, "I want to know the visiting hours for African prisoners."

"Why are you visiting an African?" asked the officer, looking at him with suspicion. "No white man visits an African here."

"I wish to do so," said Iolo plainly, unwilling to elaborate.

At first Iolo thought he was going to be turned away. But then the officer said, "Wait here a moment."

When he came back, he was accompanied by another man who announced himself as the deputy governor of the prison. An Englishman, he repeated what his officer had said and told him that his visit was impossible. Iolo could see his efforts coming to nothing. As a last resort, he tried deception.

"The African I want to see used to be in my employ. His mother has died and his elderly father lives too far away to come in person to tell him, so he has asked me to communicate this sad news on his behalf."

"People die all the time, but white men do not visit African prisoners here. If you want us to pass the prisoner a note or tell him on your behalf, we can do so as a favour to you. But a visit – no."

Iolo was not going to get anywhere. He thanked the two men through gritted teeth and made his way back to town with a view to visiting head office and following up his letter to Mr Cooper.

Near the Public Library his gaze was caught by a headline of that day's issue of the *Diamond Fields Advertiser*. It ran: *African convicted for wartime crimes – refuses to recognise court.* He bought a copy from the street vendor and began reading it on the spot. Within a few lines, it was obvious that the story was about Samuel. Iolo was too late.

> *Thirty-year-old native Gopane Mpisidi caused a sensation in Kimberley High Court yesterday when, after being found guilty of theft and injury to property, he shouted at the judge that he did not recognise the court.*
>
> *On handing down sentence, Judge Stewart condemned the African Mpisidi for contempt of court and said that he would add a year to the six-year sentence he had originally intended to mete out.*
>
> *The African made to shout back at the judge but was bundled out of court before he could say anything.*
>
> *The African was accused of being at the head of a mob of squatters which drove Mr Marius Botha and his family off their farm in the Pilansberg region, Transvaal, in January 1900 during the war. The squatters expropriated Mr Botha's cattle and then proceeded to live off the land as if they were the rightful owners.*
>
> *Giving evidence in court, Mr Botha said that when he and his sons returned in February 1903 to reclaim the family property, Mpisidi and his retinue told them that they no longer had any right to the land. They said that it belonged once again to the Kgatla people, as it had done before the Boers arrived.*
>
> *Mr Botha was obliged to call in the constabulary to re-establish his ownership. However, when he arrived with a party of four policemen, the Africans fired warning shots over their heads.*
>
> *The party was forced to retreat. Only after it was reinforced by another ten policemen was the farm recaptured,*

following a two-hour pitched battle. Mr Botha was shot in the leg during the exchange and still suffers from his injuries. Three Africans were shot dead.

Believing him to be the ringleader, as soon as the gun battle ended, the constabulary searched for Mpisidi in order to arraign him, but he had escaped. It was only a week ago that his whereabouts was accidentally re-established.

One of Mr Botha's sons was travelling from Kimberley to Cape Town on the train when he saw Mpisidi loading goods onto the train at Belmont Station, working alongside a European railway employee. On arrival in Kimberley, the son alerted his father on the farm back in the Transvaal, who in turn told the authorities. The African, who had adopted the false name of Samuel Opusu, was taken by surprise and duly arrested in Belmont.

In order to expedite justice, Mr Botha agreed that the African should be tried immediately in Kimberley rather than sent on to Johannesburg. For the same reason, he also agreed that the African should be tried on the charges described rather than even more serious ones, under which the African might have faced a death sentence.

The article ended with a commentary:

Mpisidi was far from the only African to feel that the conflict between the Boers and the British gave them licence to break the law. Such cases emphasise the need to ensure that our new Union of South Africa brings to an end such disunity forever. If it does not, European dominion in this country could be gravely imperilled.

Iolo stared ahead, motionless, for a good few minutes. Given the outcome of the trial, it dawned on him that he might have been a little precipitous, indeed naïve, to write to Mr Cooper on Samuel's behalf. But no, there was no cause for regret. Iolo was sure that there was more to all of this than the official version. Hopefully, reasonable people would understand.

There was no more he could do for Samuel – that is, Gopane. He abandoned any idea of going in person to the railway head office. After wandering the streets for another hour, lost in thought, he returned to Beaconsfield.

***

Gopane Mpisidi dragged his bruised and battered body off the floor of the cell. Following his outburst in court, he had received a brutal beating at the hands of court officials and prison warders. The beating was accompanied by curses and insults. His wounds would take a while to heal.

He would do it again, he told himself. Botha and his sons were notorious for their brutality. The civil war between the white men had unexpectedly offered him and his fellow Kgatla tenants an opportunity to seize back what was theirs.

But he had always suspected that the whites would close ranks eventually. He had tried to persuade his Kgatla brothers to form an armed militia with other ethnic groups living in the area, but few could see the point. He recalled one foolhardy man proclaiming, "We don't need them. Our regiments are strong enough on their own to defend what is ours."

Gopane Mpisidi pledged to bide his time. When he was released, he would try to find his wife and three children. After Botha returned with the police in tow to take back the farm, he'd told his family to go to Kruidfontein 649, one of the few Kgatla-owned farms in the area, if anything happened to him. Hopefully, they would still be there.

In the meantime, he had to survive. *One day, the tide will turn again*, he promised himself. He looked around the cell at the dozen or so other inmates, none of whom had spoken a word since he had been thrown in through the door. He could sense their sympathy, but there was nothing to say.

His thoughts turned to Michael. He hoped he would take care. He was not safe either.

At that moment, a harsh English voice rang out, "Alright you kaffirs, outside now – exercise time." Gopane Mpisidi and the other men filed out into the baking hot yard.

Chapter Five

Iolo was exhausted by the time he reached the house back in Belmont. It was early evening. He asked Michael, who was sitting in the kitchen, to get him a glass of water. Iolo slumped into an old chair he had inherited from Mr and Mrs Snow a few months earlier.

Normally, by this time Michael would have gone to his quarters at the back of the house, but on this occasion he had stayed. After five minutes of silence, he asked Iolo, "How is the Madam and your son? Will they come back soon?"

Iolo, too tired to say much, said brusquely, "They are well. I don't know."

"And Samuel, did you manage to help him?"

Iolo was startled. "What are you talking about? How do you know about that?"

"I saw the letter you were writing on the desk. I can read a little English."

Iolo was aware that Samuel and Michael knew each other, but perhaps they were closer than he'd realised? "Yes, I did send that letter. I tried to visit him in prison but could not. He has already been found guilty and sent to jail. There is nothing I can do."

"Ah, poor Samuel!" exclaimed Michael, a tinge of anger in his voice.

"Yes, he seems to have been involved in a battle with British forces at the end of the war back home. He has been on the run."

"I am also unable to return home, although not for the same reasons," said Michael. Iolo looked at him. Michael as well? It was another reminder that he understood little about this country.

"Were you alongside him in Pilansberg?"

"No. I was part of a regiment sent by King Linchwe from the Kgatla Reserve into Western Transvaal. We took back land from the Boers and stopped their commandos from operating in the area. Sometimes we worked with British intelligence, but we were never under their command. When the war ended, the regiment returned home to Mochudi. But I had some problems and left six years ago. King Linchwe wants me arrested and returned to Mochudi for trial. I have moved from place to place, taking whatever work I can. Samuel and I met last year. He told me you were looking for a new domestic servant."

Michael stopped speaking and looked at Iolo, waiting to see what his response would be. Iolo could see from his expression that he did not want to say any more about what his problems had been and so did not press the point. "Will you move on again now?"

"I don't know. After what has happened to Samuel, it does make me think that perhaps I need to get further away from home. Will you tell the police about me?"

"Why would I do that?" exclaimed Iolo. "But now I know all this, something occurs to me. I could not visit Samuel in prison, but you can. Perhaps you might take him a parcel of food and clothing and make sure he is alright?"

Michael's face lit up. "I would like to. Gopane Mpisidi is Samuel's Kgatla name. He has supported me. Yes, I would be willing, but once only; it could be dangerous."

"I understand. Thank you, Michael. I will put the parcel together and pay for your journey. You should go the day after tomorrow. Now, good night." Michael made to withdraw, but before he could do so Iolo asked, "Is Michael your real name? I would like to know what it is."

Michael smiled. "Ah, yes. It is also Gopane. It is a common name amongst the Kgatla. Gopane Matala. So easy to remember. But please do not use it in public."

"I promise," said Iolo. Patting him on the shoulder, he added, "See you in the morning, Michael. And, once again, thanks."

Iolo spent most of the following day collecting items for Samuel's parcel. The goods rooms were emptier than usual, so there was little work to do. He bought some food from Mrs du Toit's store and helped himself to a few things from the railway storeroom too. He identified items of clothing from his wardrobe which he thought would fit Samuel. Iolo could buy replacements the next time he was in Kimberley.

Around lunchtime, Mr Snow came up to him and handed him a letter from the head office in Kimberley. He felt a surge of panic but, when he opened it, he found that it was about his transfer. It had finally been approved.

When he told Mr Snow, his superior expressed pleasure, saying that Kimberley would be far more conducive to family life than Belmont. Doris would be overjoyed. Iolo still preferred his Belmont bolthole but realised that the move could not be put off forever.

That evening, once home, Iolo gestured to Michael. He handed him an amateurishly wrapped parcel, along with money for the train journey. Michael nodded as he received his instructions and undertook to return within three days with news of Samuel.

As he settled down on his bed that night, he began to reconsider. Could he really trust Mr James to keep his mouth shut? He decided it was best to leave Belmont as soon as possible.

The following morning, Michael took the train north. As the train chugged and swayed its way through the outskirts of Kimberley, he was overwhelmed with sadness. If he just stayed on it instead of getting off, it would soon reach the Kgatla Reserve.

He missed his son, Molemane, so much. The boy would now be talking. Tears flowed as he tried to imagine the conversations they would have, if only he could see him again. Hard as he tried, he couldn't remember what Molemane looked like.

Gopane Matala had come to adulthood as a member of the Makuka Regiment in 1901, the last cohort of Kgatla boys to undergo *Bogwera*, the traditional initiation ceremony.

After embracing Christianity, King Linchwe had abandoned many Kgatla traditions. Michael's family had moved to Morwa, eight miles west of Mochudi, from Western Transvaal in the mid-1890s as life became more difficult for Kgatla tenants. The family was part of the minority which had enthusiastically followed the King's lead. He had undergone *Bogwera* only because his grandfather had insisted.

Soon after coming back from serving with his regiment in Western Transvaal during the white man's war, Michael married Keletso – or Grace, as she preferred to be called – from a neighbouring family of the same rank. It was a love-match. A year or so later, Molemane was born. *Bogadi,* a bride price of cattle or other property, would normally have been paid to Grace's family at this stage, rendering the betrothal final, but under missionary influence, Linchwe had suspended the practice.

Nonetheless, Michael and Grace had their own cattle and a home near that of his parents. Their future looked settled. But within a few months of Molemane's birth, Linchwe ordered members of Michael's regiment to leave the Kgatla Reserve and work on the Rand gold mines for the Europeans. In return, the King would receive five pounds for each labourer from the employer, with which he planned to build a large new church in Mochudi.

Michael objected. He argued that if Linchwe claimed to be a modern ruler, why did he continue to treat his people as if they were property? Despite the pleas of his wife and both their families, he refused to comply. His mother was inconsolable. She understood all too well the risk her son was taking. His father complained that he had always been too stubborn for his own good. The senior headman tried to persuade him to change his mind but without success.

Because he was disobeying a royal edict, his case went straight to the *Lekgotla*, the King's Court. Michael had little confidence that he would receive a fair hearing there and decided to abscond beforehand. So it was that in early 1904, he fled to Kimberley, where he found work with De Beers.

It was not long before Michael started to regret what he'd done. Word reached him that the *Lekgotla* had, in his absence, banished him from all the Kgatla lands. And within a year of his departure, with the blessing of a local court, Grace's family had the marriage annulled, finding her a new husband. Molemane became that man's son.

Michael had been sentenced to social death. Too late, he now realised that he had been blind to the consequences of his actions,

65

even if his anger had been righteous. He had ended up working for the white man for a pittance anyway. But he could see no way of repairing things. All he could do now was get on with his life.

Over the next three years, he'd moved between Kimberley and Johannesburg for work. He encountered lots of other Kgatla men and never felt entirely safe from the reach of King Linchwe. In 1909, he decided to seek out somewhere more remote. He took the train south from Kimberley to Graspan, where he'd found employment on a European farm. Then he'd met Samuel in Belmont. They soon found that they had much in common. In due course, with Samuel's encouragement, Michael had moved to Belmont and started domestic service in the James household.

**

Michael had brought a bicycle with him on the train; he'd helped himself to it on the way to the station. He planned to sell it when he got to Kimberley. The extra money would come in useful. On arrival, he took the bicycle to a man he knew in one of the many private locations dotted around the city. Within ten minutes, another man came by, paying Michael a tidy sum for it. Michael then made his way to the prison.

Visiting hours for African prisoners began in an hour's time, at three o'clock. He took his place in the queue and waited. By three thirty he had been admitted and his parcel searched. He was shown to a crowded meeting room. There were no seats and all business was to be conducted standing up. An African warder asked him for the name of the person he wished to see and, ten minutes later, Gopane Mpisidi was led in, looking surprised.

"You have twenty minutes," said the warder. "If you want to hand over that parcel to this prisoner, give it to me and I will search

66

it again." The two Gopanes nodded in his direction. The warder took the parcel away.

The two men spoke to each other in Setswana. "I did not expect you. You shouldn't have come," said Samuel.

"I know, but Mr James asked me to," Michael replied.

"What is he hoping to achieve? He understands little about this country!"

"I agree. But he has a good heart. He is not like most white men."

"Maybe. When the day of reckoning comes, we shall let him live. He can work as a domestic servant in the King's household."

"Hopefully there will be a new King by then," cried Michael, suppressing a laugh. "How is it here? Will you get out alive?"

"I think so. There are a lot of Kgatla in this prison and some, like us, took part in the fighting during the white man's war. We take care of each other."

"That is good. You must survive."

"Yes. You too. So, what are your plans?"

"James expects to see me in two days. But I am not going back. It is time to move on again. Staying anywhere for too long is not safe."

Samuel grimaced. "Yes, as I have found. You are right. So, where will you go?"

"I am not sure, but maybe Southern Rhodesia. I hear there is plenty of work and nobody will know me there. I have the money for a ticket from a bicycle I stole at Belmont Station."

The warder came over, handed Samuel the parcel, and told them their time was nearly up.

"Ah, what Mr James calls redistribution of wealth! Well, my friend, it was good to see you. Thank you for coming. Hopefully, we'll see each other again one day," exclaimed Samuel, embracing Michael.

"You never know. Stay well, Gopane Mpisidi. When you open this parcel, try and do so where you cannot be seen. Look carefully in the bread. There is something special for you inside."

"I will. Thank you, Gopane Matala!" said Samuel, laughing. "A present and it is not even my birthday! Now, goodbye."

As Michael walked away, Samuel started singing the Kgatla anthem, *Tlotlang Kgosi e kgolo banna*.

Tlotlang Kgosi e kgolo banna. Chaba di maketse. Diabo di maketse. Tlotlang Kgosi e kgolo banna.

Revere the King. Nations are astounded. How astounded they are. Revere the King.

Every Kgatla man and woman knew the words by heart. Michael turned, grinning, and began singing too, forgetting for a moment his antipathy towards the current monarch. Then several other men in the room joined in. As they sang, some of the men took three steps to the right and then three steps to the left, a dancing style common in *Dikopelo*, Kgatla folk music.

The warders started shouting at the prisoners, demanding quiet, but elated, they refused to stop. Michael was pushed out of the room and escorted at speed out of the prison. He was still humming the Kgatla anthem as he walked towards where he would be staying overnight. First thing the next day, he was back at the railway station, boarding a train to Bulawayo.

It was not easy, but that evening Samuel found a quiet spot in the latrines to check out the bread. In case he was observed, he made as if to eat some of it. Something glinted in the half-light. As he extracted the object, he saw it was a knife – a long, sharp one. Michael had done well, he thought. His survival chances had improved. Now to find somewhere to hide it.

***

Iolo did not make too much of Michael's failure to return on the appointed day. Something had obviously cropped up. As long as he had avoided trouble. But as the days passed, Iolo realised that he might not be coming back. He had no idea if he had visited Samuel as agreed. He was angry, but there was nothing to be done.

Mr Snow was also in a bad mood. His bicycle had gone missing. He rarely rode it these days – he was not fit enough – but that was not the point. Iolo could not help him. He turned his thoughts to his transfer to Kimberley which, now it was imminent, he was quite looking forward to. For a start, it would be easier to attend the public talks he so enjoyed.

A week after Michael's disappearance, Iolo went to Mr Snow's office to discuss the date of his transfer. He took with him the day's post which had just arrived. One letter was from Doris; he could recognise the handwriting. Another was for Mr Snow from Mr Cooper.

Snow took the letter, muttering his thanks as he gestured to Iolo to sit down. As he read, his complexion turned puce. When he'd finished, he put the letter on the table and stared intently at Iolo.

"This letter is about you, Mr James. Its contents are hard to credit. I am instructed to dismiss you immediately. It says a separate letter to the same effect will be sent to you. It is probably on the next train."

Iolo's throat tightened. He struggled to breathe but managed to say in reply, "For the love of God, why am I being dismissed?"

"Here, see for yourself." Mr Snow handed Iolo the letter.

As Iolo scanned its contents, Mr Snow continued, "Mr Cooper writes that you have interceded inappropriately in the dismissal of an African employee and brought the railway into disrepute by doing so. He says you wrote a letter to him on Samuel's behalf. Is that true?"

Iolo swallowed. "I simply wrote to Mr Cooper saying that a person is innocent until proven guilty and that Samuel should be reinstated if found not guilty of the charges against him."

"What nonsense!" shouted Mr Snow. "If we all took that view, there would be chaos. The African has no understanding of law or justice. It is up to the European to educate him about it. It requires the firmest of hands. What is worse, you have challenged my authority and gone behind my back."

Mr Snow calmed himself. His voice deepened. If he'd had a black cap, he would have put it on. "You are a strange man, Mr James. Mrs Snow and I have done our best to welcome you. We have shown kindness to you and your wife. You have been a good employee in many ways, but by these actions you have placed yourself beyond the pale. The letter gives you one week's notice, so we will carry on as we are until then. I will also begin the process of finding your replacement. It goes without saying that there will be no transfer to Kimberley now. You may return to your work, Mr James."

Iolo left the room in a state of shock, nearly tripping over a chair leg. He walked in a trance back to the goods rooms. He faced disgrace. How was he going to tell Doris?

***

Iolo did not sleep that night. Doris's letter to him had been full of happy chit-chat about their future life together in Kimberley. They would have their own house in Beaconsfield and take part in polite society. If Michael didn't want to come with them, they would hire a new servant and a wet nurse, freeing her from the everyday burdens of motherhood. Mother and Hannah could also help with Mervyn.

Iolo was paralysed. He knew he had to tell Doris straight away but could not bear the thought. As his remaining days as a railway employee passed by, he kept finding reasons not to contact his wife. Finally, his last day came and went. Mr Snow approached him to say goodbye.

"I can't pretend to understand you, Mr James, but I want us to part on good terms. Let this be a lesson to you. If you can't play your part here as an upstanding member of the white race, you should consider returning to Britain. I wish you well. Mrs Snow asks me to say that you should pass on her best wishes to your wife. And may your son grow and thrive."

"Thank you, Mr Snow. My rental of Mrs du Toit's house has a month to run, so I shall return to pack up after I have visited Kimberley to see Doris and Mervyn. I intend to leave for Kimberley tomorrow."

"As you see fit," said Snow. He turned to leave.

That evening Iolo drank too much; a bottle of whisky which he had hardly touched for months disappeared in under an hour. The next day, battling a foul hangover, he packed a case and caught the train to Kimberley.

He arrived at the house mid-afternoon. Doris, Mervyn and her mother were in the front room. When he walked in, Doris leapt up and greeted him with pleasure.

"Ah, Iolo, what a wonderful surprise. Have you come to Kimberley to finalise arrangements for your transfer?"

"Yes, the transfer..." he said, his voice trailing off. "There is something urgent we need to discuss on that matter. Would you mind if we did so in private, mother? Perhaps you could take Mervyn with you?"

Doris's mother picked Mervyn up and walked out. "Now, what is it, husband?" There was nothing for it. Iolo told her everything that had happened, with the exception of his attempts to see Samuel in prison. Doris sat silently, her eyes betraying her shock.

"So, there will be no transfer and we must start again," Iolo said in conclusion. Doris still said nothing. "Say something, Doris," he begged. When she did speak, her tone was almost monotonal, but the anger beneath was palpable.

"You have been a fool, Iolo James. You have acted like somebody who just got off the boat. Nobody who has lived here for any length of time would have behaved as you did. We must try to reverse the railway's decision. Nobody else will employ you with this stain against your name. My parents knew Mr Cooper and his wife. Since my father died, our families have lost touch. Indeed, my mother has hardly socialised with anybody. But I will ask her to approach Mr Cooper's wife about the matter. There is still some hope."

Iolo was embarrassed by the thought of his wife and mother-in-law taking charge, but it was evident that Doris would brook no contradiction. There was a chance of salvation and he had no choice but to take it.

Over the next few days, none of the Maxwells spoke to him. He had no idea what was going on. He was left to watch Mervyn. To his relief, his son was quiet and cooperative. On the second day, his mother-in-law forsook her usual black widow's dress and put on something more colourful. She and Doris left by carriage and were gone for several hours.

When they returned, Doris told him, "We paid a visit to Mrs Cooper. She was sympathetic and promised to have a word with her husband. Now we must wait."

Doris kept her own counsel as they waited for news. She could not imagine ever respecting Iolo again, let alone loving him. And yet they were tethered together. If she left him, she would be shunned and trapped in perpetuity with her mother. Her best hope was to get his dismissal reversed and his transfer reinstated.

Time crawled by. August became September and still there was no news. Doris began to doubt whether their intercessions had done any good. Then, after three long weeks, a letter arrived from Mr Cooper asking Iolo to come to his office the next day. He put on his best outfit and went to see him.

Mr Cooper kept Iolo waiting in the corridor for over an hour. When eventually he was called in, the meeting ended almost as soon as it had started. Mr Cooper said simply, "I have reviewed your case and decided to give you a second chance. You were misguided rather than malicious in your actions, and I have been assured that there will be no repeat of such behaviour. But your transfer to Kimberley will not be going ahead. Do not challenge our decision. You are lucky we are being so understanding. You must return to Belmont. A telegram will be sent to Mr Snow. I am informed that he has been unable to fill your post and is willing to accept you back."

Iolo expressed his gratitude and reversed out of Mr Cooper's office. He was relieved to have his job back but feared Doris's reaction when he told her that the transfer to Kimberley was still off.

He was right to be afraid. With a look of cold fury, she slapped him on the cheek. "What have you done? You are killing me," she hissed. "Get out of my sight." Iolo judged it prudent to obey.

He spent the rest of the day in the bar of the Grand Hotel, drowning his sorrows. When he sneaked back to the bungalow, his possessions had been moved into the bedroom next door, out of which he had crept on their wedding night.

The next day, after breakfast, Doris spoke to him in the drawing room. "Word has got out about what has happened. Mr Cooper's wife has been helpful, but indiscreet. Your behaviour is now well known. There are rumours all round town that you are a Kaffir lover and that our marriage is in trouble. God knows, both are true enough. But I have no choice but to follow you back to Belmont to show that we are still happy together. You probably do not care much about being treated like an outcast, but I do. We must renew our efforts to make our marriage work. I have no love for Belmont, but I can pretend to like it. You seem indifferent to me and Mervyn, but you must act as if you are not. After a decent interval, you can try and find another posting, although obviously it cannot be Kimberley now. That is probably for the best. I would be a laughingstock here."

It was decided. That afternoon, Iolo caught the train back to Belmont. Doris and Mervyn would follow the day after.

Chapter Six

Belmont, September 1910

Mr Snow was in his office when Iolo stepped off the train, the only person who did. He came out to speak with Iolo. "Well, you've pulled a rabbit out of the hat, Mr James. Reinstated. I'm surprised, but there you go. I am willing to let bygones be bygones. Let us resume as if nothing has happened."

"I thank you for your understanding, Mr Snow. My wife and child are returning tomorrow and we will be based permanently here from now on."

"We have found a new assistant for you, Mr James," added Mr Snow. "His name is George. A coloured mission boy, he has the levels of literacy and numeracy required for the job. I have been supervising him in the absence of a goods clerk. You'll meet him at work tomorrow. Mrs Snow has kept an eye on your house in your absence. You are fortunate that Mrs du Toit was unable to find a new tenant."

Pleasantries over, Iolo walked up to the house. Nothing had changed beyond an accretion of dust. He set about cleaning the house and otherwise preparing it for Doris. He tossed and turned all night and ended up going into work early. There was a lot to sort out.

In the early afternoon, the southbound train to Cape Town arrived, Doris and Mervyn on it. As he accompanied them to the house, there was an awkward silence between man and wife.

Doris was the one to break it. "Do we have some food for supper?"

"I bought some vegetables from Mrs du Toit. Mrs Snow has given us some fish. I will cook once I return from work. In the coming days I will find us a new servant," replied a relieved Iolo.

"Michael has gone?" Doris had not known about his disappearance until then. She sighed but said nothing further on the subject. "Tomorrow I shall try to make this place more homely. You live like a monk, Iolo."

Iolo returned to work for the rest of the day. As promised, he cooked that evening. It was barely edible. Doris put Mervyn to bed and then sat mutely on the *stoep* for two hours before announcing that she was turning in for the night.

Iolo slipped in beside her once she had fallen asleep. He wondered if her anger at him would ever relent. Yet it caused him remarkably little anguish.

Maybe Doris is right and there is something wrong with me. How can I care so little for her feelings? She only wants what most people want. I thought I wanted it too. For all our sakes, I must make more of an effort from now on.

***

Doris returned to Belmont in a state of despair. But as the days, weeks and then months passed, communication improved between her and Iolo. Both of them tried hard to be a real family.

Mervyn grew into a burbly, chatty toddler and Iolo seemed to enjoy spending time with him more. His nose was less often in his books. They found a new domestic servant, an elderly Xhosa woman called Gertrude.

She had always felt somewhat uneasy about being alone in the house with a male servant, but it was the norm in European society. It was a relief to have Gertrude. People in Belmont did not seem to be bothered by this break with custom. Gertrude quickly became devoted to the baby.

Doris set about making the house a nicer place to live. They began to keep chickens. She found them dirty and noisy and left their care to Iolo. Like most children, Mervyn loved them. His favourite was the rooster, whom Iolo christened Mabon.

Doris was still bored rigid in Belmont. She and Mrs Snow met for tea two mornings a week and played bridge from time to time. Mrs Snow was sweet and kind, but she was dull, so dull. To avoid going mad, Doris started to knit and sew. By the time winter came, the whole family was wearing the fruits of her labours, Gertrude too.

Conjugal relations resumed. Iolo was a proficient but unengaged lover. It was over fast, but Doris was desperate for intimacy and lapped it up. She hoped that they were through the worst. Provided she could keep Iolo away from flights of fancy of the sort that had possessed him over Samuel, all would be fine. Later in the year, Doris thought to herself, perhaps it would be possible for Iolo to request another transfer to somewhere less misbegotten than Belmont.

Then, one day in April 1911, Iolo came back from the station with a smile on his face. "Mr Snow has just informed me that I am entitled to some extended leave, having served for five years. Four weeks! We could have a holiday!"

The idea excited Doris. "Yes, perhaps a trip to Cape Town or even Durban? Mervyn would love the seaside!"

Iolo frowned. "I have a better idea. You and I were brought together by a common interest in Mohandas K. Gandhi. I've always wanted to visit the Phoenix Settlement in Natal, but it is just too far away. He and his followers set up a new community called Tolstoy Farm, twenty miles south of Johannesburg, last year. He has written about it a great deal in the *Opinion*. He recently wrote that visitors are always welcome, children included. How do you fancy that?"

Doris had never been interested in Mr Gandhi, but it was embarrassing to admit as much, given that it left her looking like somebody trivial and lacking in substance. She felt a sense of foreboding but decided to ignore it. Perhaps while passing through Johannesburg, Iolo could also make approaches to the railway management there to see if there might be a job for him. So, the trip could serve her purposes too.

"Let's think about it. I am willing to consider the idea," Doris replied.

***

Tolstoy Farm, May 1911

A tired and bedraggled European family by the name of James arrived unannounced one afternoon at Tolstoy Farm.

They had spent an enjoyable week in Johannesburg, staying with the Mackenzies, well-to-do friends of Doris's family, in the suburb of Kensington. Iolo, looking forward to the coming pilgrimage, was in fine fettle. He had been happy to attend social engagements with Doris and her mother who had joined them for this leg of the holiday. Doris was in her element. Mervyn, now in his second year, charmed everybody, enjoying the company of other children. Doris wanted to extend their stay in Johannesburg for as long as possible. But in the end, she had to be satisfied with a promise to spend another few days there on the way home.

The final mile of the journey from Lawley railway station to Tolstoy Farm was on foot and seemed to go on forever. Mervyn could walk, but only a few steps, so he had to be carried most of the way.

Tolstoy Farm had been established after the focus of Gandhi's *Satyagraha* campaign shifted from Natal to the Transvaal. It stood on land donated by a Mr Kallenbach, a sympathetic German architect. Although he was there only intermittently himself, Gandhi had instructed his family to move up from the Phoenix Settlement. While not all had obeyed this injunction, his wife, Kasturbai, had complied.

As Iolo and Doris reached the gate, an Indian man walked towards them. "Greetings, friends. Have you come to stay with us a while?" The unannounced arrival of visitors was a common event.

"Do you have room? We would very much like to," replied Iolo in high spirits.

"Of course! Our accommodation is simple but acceptable to most. We share everything. You are no doubt familiar with how we live here. My name is Krishnan, but you may call me Krish. You're lucky. The great man is here at the moment. You're sure to meet him at supper."

Iolo's heart pumped with excitement. "How wonderful," he sang. He turned to his wife, "Isn't it, Doris?"

"Wonderful," she muttered. They followed Krish. Their room was indeed basic, with only two single mattresses on the floor and a table in the corner.

"Do you need another mattress for the child?" asked Krish.

Doris indicated yes with a nod of her head. Krish smiled, "Fine, I'll see if I can find a small one for your little boy. I'll be back soon. Supper is in an hour, at 5:30 pm. Follow everybody else and you'll find where we eat."

Doris saw there was a communal bathroom and, suppressing her unease at the lack of privacy, went off for a much-needed wash. Iolo kept Mervyn occupied while she did so. Then it was his turn. When he got back, feeling refreshed, he found Doris half-asleep on the mattress with Mervyn sitting next to her, looking confused. He picked up Mervyn's teddy and calmed him with an adventure story about his precious toy.

At dusk, a bell rang out; it was the call to supper. *I can't believe it*, thought Iolo. *I am going to meet Gandhi.*

Doris stirred and, picking up Mervyn, they walked to supper together.

***

There were about fifty people sitting on both sides of a long table – significantly more men than women and a few children, several of them around Mervyn's age. Most were Indians. The rest were Europeans. As they ate in silence, Iolo glimpsed Gandhi to his right, but it was difficult to get a good view. There was no meat served, which he had expected, but Doris had not. The meal was soon over and everybody dispersed.

Iolo was disappointed. He turned to the European man next to him, briefly introduced himself, and then asked whether there would be an opportunity to hear from Gandhi that evening.

The man replied in friendly tones, "We have not met. I am Hermann, the owner of the farm. Don't worry, we hold a meeting every night at 7 pm at which Gandhi speaks and we discuss matters of the day. Come back here then."

When he told Doris about this, she only said, "You go. Mervyn will need to be put to bed. I'll see to him." She'd felt somewhat uncomfortable in the presence of so many non-Europeans at supper.

"Thank you, Doris. Perhaps you can go another night."

When Iolo returned at seven, he found a smaller group of around twenty people on the *stoep*. Krish introduced some of them, but the introductions were curtailed by the sudden emergence through an open door of the small, slim figure of Mohandas K. Gandhi, accompanied by his wife, Kasturbai. All eyes turned in their direction.

Gandhi, shaven-headed and in labourer's clothes, began to speak, talking with a measured, surprisingly deep voice about the challenges of the *Satyagraha* campaign in the Transvaal. He said that establishing the farm had helped to revive what had previously been a flagging campaign. It had proved an ideal place for training *Satyagrahis* in the spiritual and mental discipline required for successful, non-violent resistance. But there was more, much more, to do.

Looking around the group, he said, "I see many who have subjected themselves to arrest for our cause over the years, some here in the Transvaal, others when we were living at Phoenix. Men, women, Hindus, Muslims, Christians, Europeans. Our campaign is powerful only because we have prepared ourselves through a life of simplicity and arduous labour. We have abandoned all hostility to other religions. We have disavowed meat. Some of you have, as I did in 1906, taken the vow of *brahmacharya* – celibacy. But this is a long struggle. The Black Act extending the pass laws to Indians here in the Transvaal will be difficult to defeat. In the meantime, we are very short of money. We must economise further, I am afraid. No railway journeys to Johannesburg, please, we must walk from now on. We also have to wean ourselves off goods purchased in the city which we can produce ourselves here. We are now making our own sandals. This is the way forward. We need to think about what else we can make for ourselves."

Gandhi went on to talk about the school for children recently established on the farm. As he spoke, his disciples listened, occasionally responding or asking questions. But overall, it was more of a sermon than a discussion. Kasturbai seemed lost in her own thoughts.

Iolo found the whole thing fascinating but did not feel qualified to contribute. After an hour, Gandhi smiled at the gathered throng and concluded, "Well, tomorrow is another long day. Let us sleep well and see each other at 6 am for breakfast."

As Gandhi got up to leave, Hermann spoke softly in his ear and pointed in Iolo's direction. Gandhi glanced at him. Hermann came over and told Iolo, "Gandhi would be happy to have a one-to-one meeting with you tomorrow afternoon should you wish?"

"That would be much appreciated," beamed Iolo. "What should my wife and I do tomorrow?"

"You can join in the farming work in the morning. Your wife could move into the women's quarters and perhaps assist with the tailoring."

"She is a good seamstress, as it happens."

"Excellent!" said Hermann, walking away.

Iolo returned to their room in a happy mood, although he was worried about Doris's reaction to the news that the family was to be separated. Fortunately, she was already asleep, exhausted by the day's exertions. The conversation could wait.

***

They had been at Tolstoy Farm for a week now – a very long week for Doris. Although the other women were friendly and supportive, she had been caring for Mervyn virtually single-handed. She enjoyed sewing but had never done all-day sessions like these. Her fingers were sore. Worse, she found the food revolting and the meetings bored her to tears.

She had seen little of Iolo since, under duress, she had moved into the women's quarters. When she did, he appeared invigorated. He looked healthier and fitter following days of tilling the fields.

The day after he met Gandhi, Doris and Iolo had talked ahead of supper. "He has such a force of personality," Iolo had said. "I now have a keener appreciation of why a pure spirit needs a pure body, how gross appetites demean the soul. He encouraged me to start my own personal journey by becoming a vegetarian. So far, so good! Celibacy, well, that is a bigger step. I just wish I had remembered to challenge him on why he doesn't have more sympathy for the plight of the Africans in this country, but I plain forgot in all the excitement."

Doris ignored his last sentence, seizing instead on Iolo's remarks about celibacy. "Don't even think of it! You are a married man. Celibacy would be a betrayal of the vows you made to me."

"Thinking is not a crime, Doris," Iolo had replied, annoyed now. "But don't worry, I have no immediate plans. I must go, I am helping in the school for the rest of the day."

The days passed slowly for Doris. After a while, she could hold back no longer. She sought out Iolo again and told him, "I know you are happy here, but I am not. I've had enough. Can we bring our stay to an early conclusion? We can have some extra days in Johannesburg before going home."

A look of distress crossed Iolo's face. "But there is so much more to do, so much more to learn. If you must leave, I understand, but I want to stay. Perhaps if you try harder, you will get more from it."

"How dare you? Most women of my background would never have agreed to come in the first place!" Fury was written all over Doris's face.

Her misery was obvious to the other women with whom she was living. The following day, one of her fellow seamstresses, Indira, approached her. "Doris, I am worried about you. Your smile has disappeared. Is life on the farm disagreeable to you?"

Doris burst into tears at the show of concern. Indira listened to Doris spilling out her woes, all the while gently stroking her hair. After Doris had finished speaking, she said, "Many of us have felt this way at times. Our men get carried away and forget their obligations, leaving us, their wives, to pick up the pieces. But we at least share a commitment to the cause. You do not have that to draw upon."

"I have sympathy for the cause," said Doris. "But try as I might, I cannot make it my own."

"Don't feel guilty. Perhaps it might help to talk with Kastur? She wrestles with many doubts about which her husband, for all his brilliant qualities, sometimes seems wilfully indifferent. If you want, I could arrange a meeting."

Why not, thought Doris. *If Iolo can talk with Gandhi, I can talk with Kasturbai.* "Yes, I would like very much to talk with her. Thank you, Indira."

The meeting was swiftly arranged. Only an hour later, she and Kasturbai were sitting together in the main building. Until that moment, Doris had paid her little attention. She was just the plump, middle-aged Hindu wife sitting next to Gandhi at supper or in those interminable meetings. The two women talked for a long time.

Kasturbai proved to be empathetic and kind. Her words had a big impact on Doris; one comment really hit home. "Let me speak to you strictly in confidence, woman to woman, mother to mother," said Kasturbai. "Wives have a duty of loyalty to their husbands. Mine has imposed on me ideas and ways of living, many of which were initially repugnant to me. Only the fact that he is a great man has made my great sacrifice worthwhile. Is your husband a great man?"

As Doris walked back to the tailoring workshop, she answered Kasturbai's question. *No, Iolo is not a great man*, she thought.

The next time she saw Iolo, she again suggested that they leave early. When he said no, she replied, "Well then, Mervyn and I will leave alone. You can accompany us to the station tomorrow morning and then join us in Johannesburg in time for the journey back to Belmont."

This time, Iolo put up no resistance. Doris's early departure was good for all concerned, Iolo told himself. He spent a further ten days at Tolstoy Farm, plunging ever deeper into life there, before returning to the city. If he could have, he would have stayed longer.

***

Doris enjoyed her bonus time in Johannesburg, staying with her friends in Kensington once more, throwing herself back into the hectic social whirl.

When Iolo appeared, it was evident that he was there more in body than in spirit. Doris warned their bemused hosts about his vegetarian turn. In order to avoid awkward exchanges about his new dietary habits, he did not go with her to dinner appointments, instead staying behind to look after Mervyn and read. Tolstoy and the *Bhagavad Gita* lay on his bedside table.

Things did not improve when they returned to Belmont. Sexual intimacy ceased again. Doris and Gertrude worked hard to cook food that met Iolo's exacting new requirements, but it was a struggle. Mrs Snow shook her head at news of his vegetarianism.

Their execution cancelled, Iolo spent more and more time tending his chickens.

Another month passed. Iolo was still wholly absorbed by his life changing experience at Tolstoy Farm. Unbeknown to Doris, he was mulling over what he saw as the final step on his spiritual journey: celibacy. He was increasingly convinced it was the right thing to do.

While at the farm, Krish had become a good friend. His wife, he said, had been inspired by Kasturbai's example and was happy when he'd taken the *brahmacharya* vow the previous year. Mastery over the sexual organs, Krish asserted, was the ultimate act of self-restraint and raised marriage to a higher spiritual plane.

Iolo just couldn't get what Krish had said out of his mind. He resolved to take the plunge. It would be an understatement to say that winning over Doris was not going to be easy. He would speak with her about it soon, he assured himself, when the time was right.

Chapter Seven

Kimberley, September 1911

Officially, Iolo was attending a talk about Theosophy at the free-thinkers club. It was a plausible claim, given that Gandhi had often written about the impact of Madame Blavatsky and her followers on his thinking when he lived in Britain, before coming to South Africa. When he'd read up about Theosophy himself, Iolo had found much to recommend it.

Instead of making his way from the station to the Grand Hotel, where the talk was being held, he stopped for some food at a cheap restaurant and then walked towards Long Street. There was a chill in the evening air. Winter was giving way, but summer had not yet arrived. Despite having lived in South Africa for over five years now, Iolo could still not get used to the way that the seasons had swapped places in the calendar.

Down the alleyway, there was a Europeans-only club known locally as Eliza's Molly House. Of course, this was not the name over the entrance; that was Maguire's Tavern. But Eliza's was an open secret.

There were occasional police visits, but they were token in nature. When they came, the Constables appeared to be there more for their own titillation than to enforce the law. Eliza, a middle-aged Irishman who dressed in matronly women's clothes, was skilled at handling the police. She would offer them a drink on the house and entertain them with racy stories. She had spent time in the cells but, so far, her lawyer had been expert in extracting her without things coming to trial. It helped that one of the most senior judges in Kimberley was a regular.

While some of the men who visited Eliza's knew each other, nobody harped on about it. Privacy and discretion were highly valued. Encounters could be with somebody whose name you never discovered. This was Iolo's preference. He felt nervous but excited as he walked in. It was some time since he had last been. One last scratch, he said to himself.

Iolo headed straight for the bar and ordered a beer. The barman obliged silently. The beer was cheap, but an additional hospitality fee was added to the bill.

Iolo knew from his previous visits that all you had to do was wait to be approached. He took a seat and sipped his beer, his anticipation growing. After five minutes or so, a man came up to the bar, a beer in his hand, and stood next to him. They exchanged glances. The man had a long, lugubrious face with a deep scar running from his left eye down to his jawbone. He was well-built.

Iolo liked men who had the muscles he so conspicuously lacked. Lack of good looks was not a problem for him.

This man would do nicely. Iolo ventured a smile and got one back. The man then nodded in the direction of one of the small cubicles at the back of the bar and asked, "Shall we go and sit down?" Iolo replied in the affirmative. These were the only words the two men would say to each other.

To keep up appearances, the cubicle had two chairs and a table in it. More importantly, there was a long curtain that could be drawn across the front. Iolo was the one to draw the curtain.

An hour later, Iolo and the man came out and went their separate ways. Iolo thought about leaving but then reconsidered. *If this is my last time, let's make the most of it,* he said to himself. He bought another beer and settled back on the same stool he'd been on before.

Eliza's was busier now. The hostess herself had appeared, dressed but not yet performing. She was talking to several people near the entrance. Iolo barely had time to take things in before another man, younger this time, approached him. They soon retired to the same cubicle Iolo had used before. It had been cleaned, albeit rather perfunctorily.

When they came out it was ten o'clock and the evening was in full swing. Tired by his exertions, Iolo decided he had had enough and made to leave. As he turned out of the front door, sliding around two men who were just arriving, he all but collided with the ganger McCartney, the unpleasant young man who had travelled on the same train as Iolo from Cape Town to Belmont. He was in the company of an older woman. Both were drunk and laughing. Iolo and McCartney exchanged glances but neither said anything before rushing away from the scene in opposite directions.

Back on Long Street, Iolo felt sick to the stomach, overtaken with panic. His worst fear had been realised. He could only pray that McCartney would be too inebriated to remember their near-collision or decide not to make anything of it. Perhaps he too was engaging in illicit pleasures and would not want to advertise the fact.

Iolo and McCartney had not seen much of each other since their arrival in Belmont. For several years, McCartney was based along the line of rail in various gangers' cottages. Then, when Carmichael had moved on, he had become the gangers' foreman for the stretch of line between Beaufort West and Kimberley.

McCartney visited Belmont from time to time in his new capacity. They had eaten together at the Snows on a couple of occasions, although there continued to be no great rapport. McCartney had confirmed himself to be a man of conventional views on race and morality.

Iolo was now at McCartney's mercy. In a daze, he made his way to the house in Beaconsfield where he always stayed the night before catching the first train home. Doris's mother had retired upstairs. Hannah greeted him without warmth before going to bed herself, saying only, "You are later than we expected. We will see you at breakfast."

***

Sunk in deep depression, he returned to Belmont the next day. Life resumed. Iolo did his best to keep up appearances, but he felt like a man upon whom sentence had already been pronounced.

Doris tried to engage him about the Theosophy talk but found him even less forthcoming than usual. Over the following days, he soothed his nerves by tending to his chickens.

"They seem to have more to offer you than your wife and child do, Iolo!" Doris chided him one evening as he got up from the dinner table and went to check on them again.

A week after Iolo's return, Doris went down to the Station Master's house for her customary morning tea appointment with Mrs Snow. Needing somebody to unburden to, Doris had started to confide in her.

Mrs Snow had been incredulous when regaled with stories about the so-called family holiday at Tolstoy farm the year before. She promised Doris she would say nothing to Mr Snow about it but had been unable to resist. He had been outraged, exploding, "Will that man never learn?"

The front door of the Snows' house was ajar. Doris walked straight into the sitting room, issuing a greeting as she entered. She was surprised to see not just Mrs Snow but her husband as well. Both were grim-faced.

"You look like you have seen a ghost!"

"If only that were the cause of our distress," Mr Snow replied. "I hardly know how to say what I have to tell you." Greatly alarmed, Doris looked at Mrs Snow who was staring at the floor, unwilling to meet her gaze.

"I have had a visit from Mr McCartney." Doris heard everything and nothing that Mr Snow said after that. As he spoke, she felt a powerful, tingling pressure grow in her forehead, a stiffening of her neck muscles and a tightening of her abdomen. Only a few – utterly shameful – words lodged in her mind as Mr Snow continued speaking. "I have no choice but to report this disgusting behaviour. Your husband cannot remain in his post now. No further allowances will be possible."

Tears streamed down Doris's cheeks, but no sound emanated. Mr Snow looked at her, adamantine. Mrs Snow overcame her paralysis and placed an arm on Doris's left shoulder. "You do not deserve this. I am so sorry." Then she withdrew it and turned away, an involuntary expression of disgust crossing her face, "Goodbye Doris."

Mrs Snow's combination of sympathy and distaste was humiliating. Doris had to escape. She half-ran back to their home, her grief and confusion turning to burning rage. She was overwhelmed with a desire to hurt Iolo as he had hurt her, not just this time, but many other times too. In a little over two years of marriage she had been repeatedly wounded by him. He had to be wounded back.

She strode into the house, past Gertrude and Mervyn on the *stoep*. They were absorbed in a game with Mervyn's teddy. Gertrude looked up to speak but Doris was gone before she could say anything. Doris walked into the kitchen and picked up a knife. It didn't look sharp enough, so she found another.

***

Iolo and George were locking up the goods rooms for lunchtime. George had done a good job of distracting Iolo from the existential dread that was hanging over him. George had his own family dramas. His two older brothers could not stand each other and had come to blows the night before over something trivial. Iolo was not required to say much, merely to listen.

As Iolo walked past Mr Snow's office, through the almost closed door he glimpsed McCartney gesticulating in front of the seated Station Master. Neither man saw him. Iolo speeded up. This could only mean one thing. He broke into a sweat. What could he do now? Where could he go? He was cornered.

All he wanted to do was flee before he was confronted by anybody. He'd dodged Snow and McCartney, perhaps he could get home before Doris found out, invent another talk in Kimberley, pack a few things and then just disappear. Doris and Mervyn were better off without him now anyway.

As he walked furtively past Mrs du Toit's store, he heard a cry and the bustle of feet. There, at the front door, was Mrs du Toit, along with a couple of other women he had seen in the back of the store once or twice in the past, seated and chatting.

Mrs du Toit showed no sign of being well-disposed towards him anymore. She was brandishing a broom and shouting at him, "You monster! You disgusting man! You are an abomination in the eyes of God-fearing people. You and your family must leave my house now! Just go away from Belmont!"

McCartney had enjoyed telling anybody he met about where he had seen Iolo in Kimberley that night. Iolo kept on walking, not looking back, but the women nonetheless rushed after him, shouting insults. He broke into a run. So did they.

"Turn round and face us!" Mrs du Toit cried, waving her weapon with menace. Another woman shook a knife at him.

Fortunately, the women were slowed down by their skirts and he was able to pull away from them. He reached a neighbour's house and ran through its front garden into the back yard, where he sheltered behind a water tank. He climbed several rungs up the ladder to the top. The women saw him but felt constrained from chasing him beyond the front gate. While he tried to make himself as small as possible, he could hear them negotiating with Mrs Maasdorp, the elderly widow who lived there. She had come out of her house to find out what was going on. Voices were raised, protestations uttered.

The exchanges went on for what felt like an eternity to Iolo. For a moment, he felt an urge to jump and put an end to it all. *Then at least this nightmare would be over*, he thought. But he probably wasn't high enough up to guarantee death. The impulse faded.

Then, all of a sudden, it was quiet. Mrs Maasdorp came to her kitchen door and looked up in Iolo's direction. Iolo was easily visible. In a calm voice, she said to him, "Please leave, Mr James. I have forbidden your pursuers to enter my property and they have agreed, although not without protest. But they asked me to warn you that they will be coming to your house tonight with their men

93

to chase you and your family away. I think you should heed their warning."

"I am sorry to have troubled you, Madam," whispered a still-breathless Iolo as he climbed down from his hiding place.

Mrs Maasdorp looked at him coolly. "I was due to go to Graspan later this afternoon to visit my brother. If you can be ready within two hours, I will let you have my cart and driver instead. You can catch a train there. I am doing this for your wife and child, not you."

"I am very grateful for your kind offer," Iolo said. "We'll be ready." He looked anxiously towards the town as he exited through the open garden gate. He could see the women looking in his direction two hundred yards away, still shouting. He could not hear what they were saying. There was no time to lose. They must pack and leave that afternoon.

***

Doris had watched Iolo's pathetic flight from Mrs du Toit and her entourage. She had watched him disappear into Mrs Maasdorp's garden and climb up the water tank. Now she watched him make his way home.

When Iolo reached the *stoep*, he talked to her in stuttering, staccato sentences. "It was a misunderstanding... grave danger... we must go straightaway." This was as much as Doris could make out. But it didn't matter. She knew everything she needed to know.

She interrupted him. "Shut up, Iolo. Yes, we'll leave, thank God." Then she said, to his astonishment, "But first we must have lunch. Food is ready. Come and sit down." He looked inside the house. There was a fully laid table in the front room.

Gertrude brought the food through. It smelt unfamiliar, but its odour was good, rich. Iolo could not help asking, as if it was just a normal family mealtime, "What are we having?"

94

"Chicken," replied Doris, adding, "and I shall carve."

***

The cart bounced and rattled along the rough stone road. As they rolled north, the country became flatter. In the distance, Doris could see smoke rising from two homesteads on the edge of Graspan.

As a settlement, it was even smaller than Belmont. There were no facilities here, only a platform at which trains would stop by prior request. Iolo was not sure that a train driver would respond to being hailed impromptu, but he would try. If unsuccessful, they would have no choice but to find a way of getting to the station at Modder River further to the north.

After that strangest of lunches was over, they had hurriedly packed three suitcases of possessions, one for each of them. Iolo found room for a few favourite books but accepted that most of them would have to be abandoned. Doris asked Gertrude to do the washing up and then said she could have the afternoon off. She was surprised but asked no questions and withdrew to her quarters.

While they waited, Iolo went into the yard to feed the chickens one last time. He hoped that Gertrude would take them with her once they had gone. He looked around for Mabon, the rooster, but he was nowhere to be seen.

Mrs Maasdorp kept her word. The cart, pulled by a tired-looking horse, drew up outside the house at four o'clock in the afternoon. They piled their luggage and themselves into the back of the cart and urged the driver to move off.

They did not want to be caught in the act by Mrs du Toit and her fellow vigilantes; thankfully, there was no sign of them. Iolo felt overwhelming relief as they left Belmont, but he was dreading the painful and humiliating conversation with Doris that was coming.

For the first two hours of the journey, Doris spoke only to Mervyn, who refused to sit still in the back of the cart, careering between his parents. They repeatedly set him right, taking care to stop the boy from plunging over one of its sides. When she did look in Iolo's direction, her gaze was full of scorn.

Eventually, Mervyn tired himself out and fell asleep in his mother's lap, his arms around her waist. The day faded as the cart rolled on. A full moon and a clear starlit sky meant that the night was far from dark. The land had an almost lunar hue.

Iolo could bear it no more. He broke the silence between them, "Doris, I will understand if you have had enough of me. I can –"

"No," she spat back at him, "no more speeches, no more expressions of contrition. You listen to me." Iolo was overpowered. He looked down at his feet. "You have betrayed me. You have lied to me. You have humiliated me. Not once, but several times. I am sure that you'd like me to say that this marriage is over and I never want to see you again. God knows, it is tempting. The episode over Samuel last year was embarrassing but it was nothing compared to this. But you are not getting off so lightly. You have no idea. To be a lone mother without a husband in our society is to be cast out. I refuse to be forced back to Beaconsfield, condemned to live the rest of my days there with my mother and sister, raising Mervyn on my own, an object of pity."

Doris jabbed a finger in his face. "You will discharge your responsibilities, which are mine to define from now on. I want another baby, which you will provide. After that is done, we will have no further physical contact. You have toyed with the idea of celibacy, so take the vow for all I care. But you will play the role of loving husband. As for me, I will do as I wish."

Suddenly aware that she was shouting, she quietened her voice so as not to wake Mervyn. "We will not stay in Kimberley. We will catch a train north, away from South Africa. Where to, I care little, as long as we can begin afresh. You will find work somewhere. I will control the money. I'll give you a stipend. These are my terms. If you don't like them, you can get out of the cart now. But be in no doubt that if you do, I will reveal your perversion to the world. Then your life will also be over."

Iolo stared at her, cowed. She was right. At one level, he'd been hoping to be dismissed, with both of them agreeing to bury what had happened. He was confident that the railway management would not pursue him if he got far enough away. McCartney lacked the power or connections to keep the affair alive, although Iolo would always be looking over his shoulder.

A lifetime of being tethered to Doris, jumping to attention, kept like a pet, was a heavy price to pay. But he didn't feel he had much choice. It was in his interests to concede with as much grace as he could muster in the circumstances.

"It seems that you have decided," Iolo replied, his hands held out in supplication. "As for where we should go, I suggest Southern or Northern Rhodesia."

"Very well," replied Doris. "As soon as we get to Kimberley, we will buy onward tickets to Bulawayo, where you will look for another railway job."

Iolo nodded in agreement, at which point Doris looked away. The conversation was over. The future had been decreed.

The cart dropped them off at Graspan around midnight. The driver, who had neither looked at them nor spoken with them all journey, departed. There was no shelter, no seat to sit on. Exhausted, the James family slept on the ground until dawn.

Mervyn was the first to wake and soon was demanding the attention of his parents. Iolo blearily kept him occupied while Doris got out the chicken legs she had packed for the journey. All three of them were starving.

At nine o'clock, the first train north arrived in Graspan. Iolo waved his hands and jumped up and down to attract the attention of the driver, who at first seemed disinclined to stop. The driver had not been told about a request for a stop here, but when he saw the man was accompanied by a woman and a child, he relented. Iolo threw their bags onto the train, pushed Doris, Mervyn in her arms, up the steps and then clambered aboard.

As they settled into their seats, Iolo looked around. There was nobody there that they knew. The conductor approached him. "Two adult tickets to Kimberley. One-way, please."

***

In the house, all was quiet. Mrs du Toit was doing an inventory. They had left almost everything behind. She would sell some of the furniture to compensate for lost rent. There were some nice shawls and dresses that might fit her or some of her friends. Some of it, though, would have no resale value and would have to be thrown away – all those books and newspapers, for example. Nobody would want them.

She'd been a little disappointed that they had disappeared so promptly. Mr McCartney, who had told her about the man's disgusting proclivities, had been keen to take part in the commando operation. The young farming lads she recruited had been looking forward to some argy-bargy. Nothing this thrilling had happened in Belmont since the end of the war.

The party had dispersed reluctantly. One or two helped themselves to a few chickens in the yard as booty, but most had been taken by the domestic servant, who now was nowhere to be seen.

While Mrs du Toit and her allies surveyed the house and yard for spoils, Mr Snow sat in his office, pondering what to do. Iolo

James had not shown up for work, which meant that he was not going to have to sack him in person. Word had got out that the family was gone. Mr Snow had a decision to make. Should he report everything that had happened to the railway management or simply tell them that James had resigned?

McCartney wanted the world to know all the sordid details, but Mr Snow, who saw himself as a man of the world, had no appetite for that. It would only create embarrassment for the railways and even more trouble and strife for him.

Despite James's faults, Mr Snow had liked him. And Mrs Snow kept saying, "Think of his wife and child." She had a point. In the end, he ruminated, which of us is perfect? No, he would keep it simple. Best to draw a veil over the sorry episode.

And he would warn McCartney to keep it to himself as well. Mr Snow had heard about some of his escapades. McCartney might not want those aired in public. He would include in his letter to the management an urgent request for a replacement. George could not manage on his own for long. Mr Snow reached for pen and paper.

Part 3   Hartley and Bulawayo, Southern Rhodesia, 1919-23

Chapter Eight

Bulawayo, July 1920

Mervyn stamped his foot with frustration. He was starving, he said, and could not wait any longer. His younger sister, Gwerfyl, stared at him, impressed by this outburst. It was supposed to be her who threw the tantrums. An exhausted Doris sat in the lounge in the only comfortable chair in the house, unmoved. Eventually, she forced herself up and entered the kitchen.

"There is some bread and butter on the side, Mervyn. Help yourself and give some to Gwerfyl while you are about it."

Mervyn was tempted to respond that he'd been hoping for something warm, but seeing the expression on his mother's face, thought better of it.

With the children becalmed, Doris returned to her chair. She should be happy about being back in Bulawayo after another five years of boredom and misery in the bush, but she just could not shake off the blues which had dogged her for what felt like ages.

Since arriving in Southern Rhodesia in September 1911, her mood swings had got worse and worse. No doctor had been able to make much of a difference. They used terms like 'nerves', suggesting that it was part and parcel of the female state.

She suspected that her problems were rooted in her life, in particular, a marriage that was beyond salvation, but somehow this could never be admitted as a valid cause in respectable society.

She longed to be free from Iolo, who had heaped endless indignities upon her. Belmont had only been the beginning, it turned out. She had had no friends she could confide in for nearly a decade now. What did she have to share with other people beyond feelings of shame and humiliation about how things had turned out?

She missed her sister Hannah, still in Kimberley and by all accounts enjoying life since their mother passed away in 1918, leaving each of her daughters a small bequest. Doris and Hannah were no longer in touch much. Although Doris had written often, she had heard just once from Hannah since then. Hannah had written that she was living contentedly in "no man's land." A longstanding friend, Olivia Hastings, of whom she was fond, had moved into the house. Doris chose to ignore Hannah's not so coded message.

Life had been just about alright for the first few years after they got to Southern Rhodesia. Iolo had got a job in the goods sheds in Bulawayo as soon as they arrived. They had lived in a decent enough house in Raylton. In 1914, Gwerfyl was born.

Her name was Iolo's idea. Where he'd got it from, she had no clue. As part of the bargain reached on their flight from Belmont, sexual relations were terminated once and for all thereafter. The relief was mutual.

Then the war broke out and Iolo dusted down his principles again. This was an imperialist war, he'd announced. He started to sound off about it, annoying a lot of people. As ever, he took things too far and started to proselytise among his fellow railway workers, and not just the white ones.

By mid-1915 they had been transferred up the line of rail to Insiza as punishment. They spent a dreadful year living in a *pondokkie* on the edge of town, a shack with two rooms, mud walls and a corrugated iron roof. Iolo seemed not to care much. He said he had done the right thing and that was what mattered. He continued with his campaigns in Insiza.

Another transfer, this time to Gatooma further north up the railway line, followed in 1916. Still, Iolo would not desist. But life had been a little better there. There were even a couple of decent stores. Their house, made of brick, was a marked improvement, although it was some way out of town.

Gatooma was not spared by the Spanish influenza which swept through the colony like wildfire in October and November of 1918, claiming thousands of lives. Africans in crowded and unsanitary compounds and locations were particularly affected, but nobody was entirely untouched.

Doris was terrified that the children would catch the flu and die. Although Iolo had to go to work, she kept herself, Mervyn and Gwerfyl at home. Miraculously, none of them caught it.

In December 1918, Iolo was transferred again, this time to Hartley, twenty-five miles north of Gatooma. Hartley's goods clerk had succumbed to the influenza. By then the war was over, so Iolo's pacifistic agitation came to an end.

Iolo had been told that this would be a longer-term posting. Doris hoped that the family could at last put down some roots and have some stability. She was determined to create a civilised domestic environment suitable for a European family, something which, to her chagrin, had been conspicuously absent until now.

Yes, Hartley was yet another *dorp*, but it was less dusty and ugly than most. The capital, Salisbury, was within relatively easy reach by train. Like most towns along the line of rail, the area was a mix of European-owned farms and mines, but the tone of the place was better. Recently, the roads had been improved and electric street lighting had been installed.

The family's new house was made of brick and had a thatched roof, which Doris felt was a big step up. It was the largest place they had rented since their arrival in Southern Rhodesia, with a good-sized garden at the front. She would make it a Victorian garden, she told Iolo.

Iolo was unenthusiastic. "What's wrong with the indigenous flora? We are in Africa, Doris, not Kent." But he did not press the point. He mooted getting some more chickens, but she vetoed it.

"We are not peasants," she countered.

They found a good African servant from Nyasaland called Ignatius, who doubled as a gardener. A shy, elderly man who never looked her in the eye, he seemed to understand her kitchen kaffir well.

Doris was gratified that Ignatius was not like those mission boys who thought they knew everything because they'd had a bit of education. She didn't tell Iolo, but she'd set Ignatius's monthly pay at twenty-two Shillings, two Shillings below the going rate. He lived in the town location, rather than in a *kia* behind the house. This meant he was not around all the time. She preferred it that way. It got stressful having Africans around all the time.

Ignatius looked smart in the white uniform she bought for him to wear when he waited at table. She liked how assiduous he was when boiling water for the family to drink, something that she was anxious about. Enteric diseases were everywhere. Doris instructed him to add Jeyes fluid to the water after boiling it, just to make sure.

Soon she was drawn into fund-raising activities for soldiers injured in East Africa. She attended several local meetings of the Women's Christian Temperance Union at which she heard dreadful stories about British men who had succumbed to the demon drink.

All present agreed that this damaged European prestige in the eyes of the Africans. At least Iolo was not prone to that vice, she thought. As she got to know other European women, she also started to receive invitations to morning tea.

Hartley suited Doris. Her moods improved. But then all hell broke out again. Iolo, as ever, was the cause. Doris shuddered at the thought of it. She reached for the Luminal pills in her dress pocket. The doctor had prescribed them soon after their return to Bulawayo.

They were helpful in calming her down. She swallowed down two as prescribed and then added one more for luck. In the kitchen, Mervyn and Gwerfyl were bickering loudly about something. She took no notice.

***

Bulawayo, July 1920

Iolo had finished work an hour earlier but he was in no hurry to get home. He headed instead to the Waverley Hotel and read the newspapers for an hour until hunger got the better of him. But instead of returning to the family's rented property on Lobengula Street to eat, he stopped off for a pie at a canteen on 1st Avenue.

It was gone nine when he walked into the house. He found Mervyn and Gwerfyl still awake, reading and doing colouring quietly in their joint bedroom. Doris was asleep in the front room but stirred when she heard him. She went to put the kids to bed without acknowledging his presence.

The tension between him and Doris had become unbearable. If he let it, it would ruin his life. But he wasn't going to allow that to happen. In the scheme of things, he thought, what does a failed marriage matter? This was a historic moment in human affairs, holding out the prospect of making many things anew. Where he could make a difference, he believed he should give it a go.

He had delivered on his promise to Doris with the birth of Gwerfyl. He had chosen that name as a private joke but felt bad about it now. The poor child did not deserve it. He would provide for his family and be a good father to the children. Beyond that, Doris could expect nothing from him.

For a while, fears that she might reveal to the world what had happened in Kimberley in September 1911 had held him back from following his conscience. But with time, he became sure that she was bluffing. She would probably pay for any such revelation more than he would. All too often, that was how white society in a colony like Southern Rhodesia worked.

As for that itch, he was careful not to provoke Doris by getting caught in the act again. He was committed to honouring his vow of celibacy and had only succumbed once since the Kimberley incident. That was during a short posting in 1915 to cover a vacant post in Broken Hill in Northern Rhodesia, when his family had not accompanied him. He was full of self-reproach afterwards.

His growing confidence that Doris would not expose him had shaped his calculations when he got involved in pacifist campaigning after the outbreak of the First World War. Iolo became the local representative of the No-Conscription Fellowship, which was established In Britain in 1914. The Southern Rhodesian chapter had a grand total of three members, including him. Conscription was never introduced in Southern Rhodesia, but it was actively considered for a while. Iolo wrote letters and handed out leaflets against it at every opportunity.

Of course, he was a true believer in the cause. It was consistent with his Christian and Socialist beliefs, not to mention Gandhi's pacifism, although he felt that the great man could be too equivocal on the subject. But he was not sure he would have had the courage to raise the banner aloft if Doris had threatened to unmask him.

She never did. Doris told him he was a traitor. But she did not present him with a white feather, or anything like that. His stance attracted the ire of the railway management; however, with so many men away fighting and skilled white labour in short supply, it decided against sacking him. Instead, his punishment was internal exile in Insiza, followed by stints in Gatooma and Hartley.

He hadn't minded greatly. He could see that Doris hated these small-town postings as much as she had hated Belmont, but he and the kids were happy enough. He was aware of her escalating reliance on medication to maintain her equilibrium but did not get involved. It was a shame that she seemed to be shrinking away from life, rather than moving towards it.

In 1917, while they were living in Gatooma, Iolo came across a book which piqued his interest: *Bay Tree Country* by Arthur Shearly Cripps. Cripps was an Anglican missionary living alongside the Africans outside another small town 250 miles to the southeast called Enkeldoorn.

The novel told the story of a European grain trader, Lyndhurst, isolated from other whites, who came to love and understand the Africans he lived amongst. He saw his African flock as closer to God than his fellow whites, becoming obsessed with the idea of the Black Christ.

So deep was Lyndhurst's identification with Africans, he darkened his skin and joined the labour force on a white farm in Makoni District, where he discovered that the life of an African farm worker was one of coercion, violence and exploitation.

Lyndhurst tried to save a governess from marrying the farmer but was shot dead by a supervisor. The supervisor thought that an African was harassing the woman and that this was a case of the Black Peril, the shorthand phrase used by whites to describe the supposedly existential sexual threat posed to white womanhood by African men. Lyndhurst was posthumously vindicated.

Iolo could not get Cripps's story out of his mind. He asked around about the priest. Several people had heard of Cripps but were unanimous in dismissing him. He was a queer cove, apparently, a kaffir lover. Iolo discovered Cripps was also celibate and a vegetarian, heightening his interest. He resolved to go and meet Cripps but discovered he was away, serving as a chaplain with British forces in East Africa. Iolo decided he would visit Enkeldoorn once Cripps had returned from the war.

He also became preoccupied with the dramatic events unfolding in Europe. Change was in the air, not before time. He read everything he could find about the unfolding Russian revolution. But he recoiled from the Bolsheviks, who were too violent for his taste. By the end of 1918, now living in Hartley, he had come to sympathise more with the Socialist Revolutionaries, for whom the peasantry was a class to be mobilised, rather than extinguished.

Good things were happening closer to home too. Iolo was encouraged by the growing militancy of the Rhodesia Railway Workers' Union. He'd been quick to join. But once again, he couldn't help having some reservations. It was avowedly socialist yet fatally blind, in Iolo's opinion, to the fundamental unity of interest between workers of different races in Britain's colonies.

The family was now back in Bulawayo. But after what had happened in Hartley the previous year, they had returned under a cloud. Iolo decided it would be best to keep a low profile for a while.

***

Rewind: Hartley, Christmas 1918

Arthur Shearly Cripps was back from East Africa. The idea of visiting Enkeldoorn resurfaced in Iolo's mind.

He had come across a new pamphlet by Cripps called *A Million Acres*, in which he decried a decision by the British South Africa Company, which governed Southern Rhodesia under a charter granted by the British Government, to take land from the Native Reserves and hand it over for white settlement.

Iolo was fired up afresh by this pamphlet, yet he could see no sign of African agitation against the plans. He became convinced they must be unaware of what was happening. He had to do something about it. But what? He hoped that Cripps could give him guidance.

In January 1919 Iolo took two weeks off work and set off for Enkeldoorn. When he told Doris about his plan, she said contemptuously, "Well, at least this time I don't have to trail after you to sit at the feet of some crank. Do what you will."

The journey was slow and arduous. There was no direct route by rail or road and much of it had to be done on foot. He began by walking through rural areas which had played a major part in the African revolt against colonial rule in 1896-7.

On his journey, he met Africans who were willing to talk to him, particularly when he mentioned the name of Cripps. Some of them appeared to view Cripps as an ally of sorts. He heard from them about the role of Chief Mashayamombe and other local leaders such as the spirit medium Sekuru Kaguvi in the *Chimurenga*, as the Shona called the 1896-7 revolt. The Chief had been killed in the fighting. Kaguvi was tried and hanged after the rebellion was defeated, along with his sister medium Mbuya Nehanda.

Finally, he reached Beatrice. From there, the journey went faster. Several ox-wagons gave him lifts south. When he finally arrived in Enkeldoorn, Iolo asked after Cripps in town but discovered, to his consternation, that he was actually living at a mission called Maronda Mashanu, ten miles away. Fortunately, an elderly Afrikaner farmer was heading back to his farm near the mission and offered to take him there.

The farmer was less negative about Cripps than other whites. "You know, nobody can accuse Father Cripps of being a hypocrite. He lives like an African. I once heard that a fellow priest said about the man, 'I know in my heart he is right, but I still can't agree with any of his conclusions.'"

The old man eventually dropped him off at a junction and pointed into the distance, "About half a mile up there is the mission. I hope you find him. He is always on the move."

Cripps was not there. When Iolo got to the mission, he was met by a Shona man called Pfumojena. He was the head of one of several families that had moved with Cripps, just before war broke out, to Maronda Mashanu.

Pfumojena spoke no English. Nor did anybody else there. But the man appeared unsurprised to see him, showing him to a room with a bed in the corner in the main building.

Nobody could tell him when, if at all, Cripps might arrive. Iolo was disappointed but his exhaustion meant that leaving straightaway was out of the question. As he lay on the bed, he felt his eyes close. Soon he was deeply asleep.

There was no sign of Cripps the next day. He was given food but otherwise left to his own devices. Nobody objected to him wandering around. Wherever he went, he encountered Africans of all ages and sexes engaged in activity on the land, with not a

European in sight. Yet Iolo knew that officially this land was intended for white use only.

At sunset, he returned to the main mission building. More food – thick porridge again, this time with chicken and vegetables – was provided. Iolo felt rested. He decided to leave the following day unless Baba Cripps, as everybody called him here, appeared by then. He comforted himself with the thought that, even if he did not manage to meet with the man himself, the trip had been worthwhile; his horizons had been expanded.

Then, just as he was preparing to turn in for the night, voices were raised and exclamations uttered. A tall, thin man in a bush hat marched out of the gloom towards the mission, exchanging words in Shona with people as he walked. Pfumojena appeared, spoke with Cripps and pointed in Iolo's direction.

The missionary looked puzzled at first but then approached him. "Good day to you," he greeted Iolo wearily. "I am Arthur Cripps. I understand you have been waiting for me? I'm very tired after a long walk. If you'll forgive me, can we speak tomorrow after breakfast?"

Iolo smiled and said, "It is an honour to meet you. I am Iolo James, a railwayman currently living with his family in Hartley. Tomorrow morning is more than fine. Sleep well."

***

Cripps was as good as his word. "I hope you had a good night, Mr James," he said. "Now, let us talk. I'm afraid that I only have half an hour before I take the morning service, so please get straight to the point."

Iolo suddenly felt unsure exactly why he'd come, but he marshalled his thoughts as he spoke. "In a nutshell, Father Cripps, I have been greatly impressed by your writings, including the most recent pamphlet. I have heard European farmers in the town discussing how to take advantage of the Company's decision to take land from the reserves. I'd like to do something to protect the interests of the Africans but am not sure what."

Cripps looked at Iolo and sighed. "I am afraid we have missed the boat, Mr James. It is too late to reverse the decision. I and other people have written, lobbied and campaigned about this in London and in Salisbury. We have tried our best, but we have failed." Seeing the pained look on Iolo's face, Cripps went on, "The main thing we can do in future, I suggest, is try to raise African awareness about these growing efforts to make Southern Rhodesia a white man's country forever. With awareness, hopefully will come action."

"But African action seems so far off," replied Iolo. "Will it not be too late if we take a slowly-slowly approach?"

"It may seem that way. I am more optimistic. This is an African country, Mr James. In the end, the power of numbers will count. But not just that. If you are familiar with my work, you will know that I am sure God is on their side. There may be suffering along the way, in fact, I am certain of it, but Africa will again be for the Africans one day."

"Yes," said Iolo, "The Black Christ. Your idea had a powerful effect on me. Perhaps I should look for those who embody that idea."

"I cannot tell you who or what to look for. But keep looking," Cripps replied. He stood up. Their exchanges were over. "I must go now and take a service. Mr James, you are welcome to stay for as long as you like. But there are many demands on me, so I cannot promise you another chance to talk."

"One last thing, Father Cripps," interjected Iolo, "You have taken a vow of celibacy, I understand. I have too, under the influence of Mr Gandhi. Yet I am married, somewhat unhappily. How do I square this circle?"

Cripps raised an eyebrow and looked at Iolo penetratingly. "You don't. The two are not compatible. You and your wife are in an impossible situation. I once contemplated marriage but didn't go through with it. That episode, brief and cut short as it was, has had lifelong consequences for me. I am sorry to speak so harshly, but I fear that your current arrangements can lead only to bitterness and tragedy."

Over the next few days, as he travelled back to Hartley, Iolo reflected on what lessons to take from the trip. Cripps was an impressive man. *"I cannot tell you who or what to look for. But keep looking,"* he had said. Cripps was right. That's what Iolo would do – keep looking.

But what of Cripps's warning about his marriage? Iolo really wished he hadn't asked that question.

Chapter Nine

Hartley, April 1919

The preacher paused for breath before continuing with his sermon, "The days of the white man are coming to an end," he said, speaking in English. In the background there was a quiet murmur as what he said was translated for those in the congregation who did not speak the language of the colonisers. "God wills it and nothing can stop it." There were shouts of assent from the worshippers.

"They have taken our land and enslaved us in order to enrich themselves," the preacher declared. "This is true whether you are Shona, Ndebele, Nyasa or Lozi. None of us have been spared. If we unite under *Mwari*, we will be redeemed. And when the kingdom of God is established, blacks will become white and whites will become black!"

This statement elicited another roar of enthusiasm from the congregation. The preacher drew his sermon to a rousing close.

"Many here come from Nyasaland, where only a few years ago we rose up under the blessed John Chilembwe. Yes, we were defeated in that battle, just as our Shona brothers and sisters lost their *Chimurenga*, but there are more battles to come. Let us pray to our Lord for his guidance in our coming struggle!"

The congregation knelt in the dust. The service was being held outdoors in the veld under a collection of Msasa trees, about ten minutes' walk from Hartley's location. Dry and drooping after a fierce summer, the trees nonetheless offered essential shade from the daytime heat.

The organisers, members of an independent African-run church called Watchtower, sought out places of worship which were less likely to be spied on by the police. The mere idea of an African-run church was a threat to public order as far as the colonial authorities were concerned. Apparently, only Europeans were civilised enough to be priests or bishops. Watchtower had originated among labour migrants from Nyasaland, but increasing numbers of Africans in Southern Rhodesia were flocking to its cause.

Prayers were followed by a final hymn, after which the preacher dismissed his flock. It dispersed in multiple directions. The preacher's name was Paul Kamwana. Kamwana walked in the direction of Simpson's maize and cattle farm where he worked as a plow driver. He was accompanied by a member of the congregation, Joseph Mashingaidze, a worker in Hartley's goods shed.

As they walked, Joseph handed Kamwana an envelope. He opened it. Inside, as he had hoped, was money. He nodded to Joseph, patted him on the arm, and walked on. Joseph turned around and headed in the opposite direction towards the location.

The envelope contained a five-pound note from Iolo James.

Iolo had stumbled across Kamwana giving his Sunday service a month earlier while wandering around the African parts of Hartley.

Kamwana's first response had been hostile. As soon as he saw him, he'd waved Iolo away. Other members of the congregation shouted at him and began to scatter. Iolo withdrew a short distance but did not retreat completely.

Kamwana brought the service to an early end and marched toward him. A member of the congregation – Iolo thought he recognised him – rushed to join the preacher, speaking with him as they approached. Kamwana was gesticulating angrily.

When the two men got to Iolo, Kamwana was direct. "Are you going to report us to the authorities, sir? Are you a spy?"

Iolo, unused to being spoken to so forcefully by an African man, stammered his reply. "Neither, I assure you. I am a white man who is ashamed of how we treat Africans in this country. Like Baba Cripps I want to help change things here."

"Baba Cripps?" replied Kamwana. "Ah, I see. You want to be another white father to the Africans. We do not need any white fathers! Glancing at Joseph, he continued, "My friend tells me that he knows who you are and does not think you are a spy. But having any contact with you is dangerous. I ask you to leave and not come back."

Kamwana was right. Iolo could only say, "I understand. I am going." In turmoil, he returned home and sat down in his favourite chair on the *stoep*.

Doris could see that Iolo was in distress about something but decided she would rather not know. She left him to his own devices. The anguish stayed with him for several days. Mervyn and Gwerfyl's efforts to engage with their father in the evenings met with no success. He told them to leave him alone, protesting that he was tired.

Then, just as Iolo was beginning to feel that he could put the embarrassing episode behind him, Joseph came up to him at work and introduced himself, "You recognise me, I presume?"

"Yes, of course I do. But isn't it dangerous to talk to me?"

"I have a message from Kamwana. He wants me to tell you that there is something useful you could do. We need money for our work. Kamwana proposes that you give a monthly tithe, which the Bible says is one-tenth of your income."

Iolo was disconcerted. Ten percent was a lot. Could he afford that much? Could he prevent Doris from finding out? She'd be furious. He needed some time to think. "Come back to me tomorrow. I will have an answer for you then."

Iolo slept poorly. His mind was racing. When he dozed off, he had vivid dreams. In one of them, Samuel, who he had watched being taken away by the police in Belmont, appeared and intoned, "Stand up and be counted, Mr James."

The next morning, his mind was made up. When Joseph approached him again, Iolo had an envelope ready. "I agree with Mr Kamwana's proposal. Here is my first tithe."

Joseph looked surprised at first but then smiled, saying, "Thank you. I will give this to Kamwana when I see him next."

Iolo was euphoric. That evening, he played football with Mervyn and read Gwerfyl a bedtime story. Doris looked on, bemused, as she supervised Ignatius, who was folding the washing.

I will never understand that man, she thought to herself.

***

Hartley, July 1919
At the end of July 1919, Joseph came up to Iolo after work and thrust a piece of paper into his hand. "Your support has allowed us to pay for some leaflets, Mr James!" he exclaimed. "We have been handing them out in the location and around some of the white farms. Here is one for you to read."

Iolo stuffed it into his pocket and walked home. Once there, he got himself a glass of water and sat down on the *stoep* to read it. As he did so, he became more and more agitated.

> *Goliath was a big man. David was a small man. The white race are now powerful. But it will be the same as happened to Goliath. David, the small man, rose up and killed him. So it will be with the white and black races. The king of the white man shall cease to be king and we shall reign. When England was at war with Germany they promised the natives of this country that if we fought for England we would all be free men. Many of our people did fight and were killed and yet we are not free. If there is any more fighting, you must remain in your kraals – that is white against white. Only the fool natives will go. I warn you now that sometime between September and November of this year there will be great trouble come to Rhodesia.*

It dawned on Iolo that he was out of his depth. The leaflet was treasonable and seemed to be advocating violence. Flustered, he scrunched up the leaflet and dropped it into the nearest bin. He needed to extricate himself as quickly as possible. He would speak to Joseph tomorrow and tell him that he would no longer pay the tithe.

After an uneventful morning at work, Iolo looked around for Joseph and found him still hard at it, unloading crates from a farmer's wagon. "Joseph, we need to talk." But before he could say anything else, Joseph replied, "Mr James, I have some worrying news. Kamwana has been dismissed and deported to Nyasaland."

"What?" exclaimed Iolo. "Why?"

Joseph looked at Iolo, incredulous. "Why do you think? Our congregation has decided to stop meeting for a while. I am confident that Kamwana will not give the authorities any information, but it is a sensible precaution."

"You should stop giving your tithes," Joseph added, criss-crossing his hands to emphasise the point. "Maybe in a few months everything can start again." But he did not look convinced.

They agreed to stop associating at work – there had been some quizzical looks from white colleagues. Iolo was relieved. He hadn't had to say anything. With one bound he was free.

***

But it was not that simple. Over the coming days, things unravelled. Three days after his conversation with Joseph, he was intercepted on his way to work by the Native Commissioner, Mr Smith, and Mr Simpson, an uncouth local farmer and Kamwana's former employer.

Mr Smith asked Iolo if he might come to his office for a quick chat. His manner was pleasant enough. By contrast, Simpson looked like he might erupt. While Iolo and Smith sat down, Simpson remained standing, hovering over him.

Mr Smith spoke. "So, Mr James, let me get straight to the point. A police informer has made an extraordinary allegation against you. He says that you have been giving money to a local branch of the Watchtower movement. The informer, who I won't name, is not always reliable and we are strongly inclined not to believe him. But you have taken some unorthodox stances in the past from what I hear. So let me ask you directly: is there any truth to this claim?"

"Absolutely not," Iolo retorted. "I know nothing of this Watchtower movement. What is it about?" he added, improvising as he went along. Mr Smith, who clearly rated himself an expert on African affairs, looked pleased to be asked this and embarked on a lecture. It went on for some time. He ended with a flourish, "Religion is the vehicle of this movement, but not the end of it. This sect has no ritual or separate doctrines of its own, being, so to speak, a go-as-you-please church, *sui generis*, so loosely made that it seems unlikely to last very long. But it may yet prove itself strong and permanent because of the central, animating ideal of racial self-assertion embodied within."

Looking pleased with himself, Mr Smith glanced toward Simpson for backing. A much more direct man, Mr Simpson glared at Iolo and said, "You are far too relaxed about this, Smith. This cult seeks to foment another rebellion, like the one that nearly did for us all in 1896. If we take it too lightly, there is a real danger we'll be murdered in our beds."

"No, no, no, Simpson," retorted Mr Smith, "It is premature and alarmist to say that. For now, we are content to keep a close eye on Watchtower. If it really does turn out how you describe, be assured that we will clamp down on it vigorously."

Iolo was starting to feel that the two men had forgotten he was in the room. This feeling was curtailed when Mr Simpson turned to him, "Mr James, I have heard stories about you and am less inclined to believe you than Mr Smith here. Something smells wrong to me. If I find out you are lying, God help you."

Iolo blanched. Mr Simpson looked like a man who meant what he said. All he could do was repeat his protestations of innocence. Mr Simpson was still glaring at him as he left.

***

Meanwhile, back at home Ignatius had told Doris that he was unwell and could not work that day. She was annoyed, but he was coughing a lot, so she dismissed him and began doing some of the tasks she'd had in mind to give him.

The bins needed emptying. Her attention was caught by a piece of paper in the one on the *stoep*. It seemed to be in a mixture of African languages and English.

She sat down, unscrunched it and began to read. It seemed to be the work of a madman. *The king of the white man shall cease to be king and we shall reign...* What was that about? She was about to dismiss it, but something impelled her not to. She put it in her apron pocket instead. She would ask Iolo about it later.

Later that morning she walked to one of Hartley's stores to buy food for tea. Mr Moncrieff, the owner, saw her come in and raised his hand in greeting. As she browsed the shelves, he came over to her.

"Mrs James, I heard that your husband was interviewed by the Native Commissioner this morning. I hope it was nothing serious." Moncrieff, a notorious gossip, was shamelessly fishing for information. Alarm bells set off in Doris's head.

"I've no idea, Mr Moncrieff. I have not seen my husband since breakfast. I will no doubt hear about it from him this evening," Doris replied.

Moncrieff smirked. "I am sure you will." Doris detected a hint of malice in his voice.

Doris finished her shopping and went home. Standing in the kitchen after unpacking her purchases, she took out the piece of paper and looked at it again.

As she read the document, her expression darkened. It was threatening rebellion. Perhaps Iolo had reported its contents to the Native Commissioner? *No, he'd never do anything that sensible.*

She knew Iolo. This was just the sort of thing that would excite him. He might even be in on it. No, surely not. He wouldn't go in for violence. But he could not be trusted to report it.

It came to her. It was her duty to inform the authorities and there was no time to lose. The leaflet spoke of an uprising between

September and November. That was now! Mervyn would be home from school soon. If she hurried, she could report it and be back in time for his return.

She set off at pace for the Native Commissioner's office. However, before she got there, she changed her mind. She didn't trust Mr Smith. He had a reputation as a kaffir lover, a bit like Iolo.

She had to inform somebody who would be more likely to take stern action. Yes, the Magistrate, Mr Pinnock, would be more appropriate. She turned left instead of right at the junction between Main and Rhodes Street and headed towards Mr Pinnock's office.

She was shown in straight away by Mr Pinnock's secretary. Pinnock was in the company of another man who Doris recognised as Mr Simpson, the local farmer. His wife was a stalwart of the Temperance Union. "How can I be of assistance, Madam?" said Mr Pinnock, looking at her with curiosity.

Doris got straight to the point. "I am Doris James, the wife of the goods clerk, Iolo James. I have reason to believe that some Africans are planning an uprising imminently."

Mr Pinnock had heard many such allegations in the course of his duties. All had turned out to be false, but he could not afford to ignore them if he was to retain the confidence of the community, so he gave the lady his full attention.

After she had told him everything she knew, Doris checked her watch and said, "I must get home. My son is getting back from school any moment now. Can I leave this in your hands, Mr Pinnock?"

"Of course, Mrs James," responded Mr Pinnock. "This is indeed a serious matter. But rest assured, I will be careful to ensure that your husband doesn't get into too much trouble. After all, a wife needs her husband and her children, their father."

Doris looked at Pinnock. "Yes, of course, however you have the law to uphold. I do understand that."

Mr Pinnock was taken aback by this answer, but before he could reply, Doris was gone. "I knew that bastard James was lying!" shouted Simpson, the veins on his forehead pulsing. "This is exactly what I wanted to talk with you about. Kamwana had stacks of those seditious leaflets under his bed. They must have known each other. I hope you will be taking strong action. He deserves everything coming to him!"

"Steady on, Mr Simpson. I need to talk to him first and then confer further with Mr Smith."

Simpson looked at him with undisguised irritation. "You make the right noises, Pinnock, but when push comes to shove you are as bad as Smith. If you won't act, then some of us may have to take matters into our hands."

Mr Pinnock raised his hand in warning. "Don't even think of it, Mr Simpson."

Simpson stormed out, shouting, "You have a day to do something about James."

***

Pinnock sighed as he scribbled a short note to Iolo. The note summoned him for a meeting within the hour. An African messenger was instructed to deliver it to the goods shed. Twenty minutes later, Iolo appeared, having made his excuses at work. He was out of breath.

At Mr Smith's, Iolo had been nervous. Now he was terrified.

When he saw that Pinnock was holding the Watchtower leaflet, he knew that the situation had got much worse. If asked whether he had knowledge of the document, he could hardly deny it – it was the same leaflet he had thrown in the bin a few days back. How

had it got into Pinnock's hands? Ignatius? That seemed unlikely...
Doris? Probably.

"Yes, I have passing knowledge of this document, Mr Pinnock,"
said Iolo. "I found it on the ground on the way home after work a
few days ago and took it home to read. As soon as I saw what it
said, I threw it in the bin."

"That is all very well, Mr James," replied Pinnock. "Why did
you not report it to the authorities? A strong, if circumstantial, case
has built up against you."

"I swear on my life, Mr Pinnock, that I have never funded
Watchtower activities," exclaimed Iolo. "The fact that I know of
this leaflet is pure coincidence. I dismissed its contents as the
ramblings of deranged people. It didn't seem worth reporting."

"Maybe so, Mr James. But you should let us be the judge of
that. Your wife, I am pleased to say, took it more seriously than you
did."

Then Pinnock said, "I think we have gone as far as we can with
this now. I will be discussing your case further with Mr Smith.
Once we have settled on a course of action, you will be informed.
You can go."

It was too late to return to work, so Iolo trudged home. At first,
he was determined to have it out with Doris, to confront her for
her treachery, but as he neared the house, he was overcome by
weariness. What was there to say? This was how it was between him
and her. They were mortal enemies trapped in the same household.

Doris had reached a similar conclusion. That evening, they
engaged solely through the children. As soon as Mervyn and
Gwerfyl were in bed, Doris walked into the bedroom and shut the
door. This was Iolo's cue to make up the sofa. He lay awake all
night.

***

Pinnock and Smith met for two hours the next day to discuss what to do about Iolo. They found themselves in agreement that to make an example of him would be to draw the attention of Africans to the weaknesses and fallibility of a supposedly superior race. And making a big fuss would only heighten white anxiety. In the end, they decided to go no further than issue Iolo James with a severe reprimand.

Mr Smith walked down to the goods shed to find Iolo, who accepted his reprimand without demur. For the rest of the day, there was a spring in his step.

At the end of his shift, he dropped in at the Hartley Hotel for a couple of celebratory whiskies. He was not a big drinker, but tonight a dram or two was in order. He was in no hurry to see Doris with whom, he was sure, another difficult conversation was coming. That was the final hurdle to overcome, but it could be deferred until later.

He had miscalculated. Mr Simpson, who had heard from Mr Smith that there was to be no action taken against James, was at one end of the hotel bar with his son and a couple of other local farmers, Mr Groves and Mr Noble, along with a young man Iolo did not recognise.

Iolo realised that he had inadvertently entered the colosseum and would be lucky to get out alive. But to flee would trigger a chase. Best, he thought, to try and act normal. He went to the other end of the bar and ordered two whiskies in one go. Then he sat down at a table close to the door, as far away from Simpson and his entourage as he could manage, so that he could make a quick get-away if need be.

Iolo drank his whisky in nervous sips. He could overhear the unknown young man, well under the influence, declaring, "Honestly this is the easiest living country. All the work is done by the Africans, you don't even black your own shoes. Believe me, a white man is lord here and he rules with his tongue and his boot. When I see two Africans doing the work that they do and only getting about 8 pence a day, it makes me laugh." *Must be a newcomer*, thought Iolo.

Suddenly Noble turned his head in Iolo's direction. "Is that James?"

Simpson looked over his shoulder and nodded in the affirmative. "The cheek," said Simpson. "He brings shame on the white man and then has the arrogance to rub it in our faces by coming here for a drink."

His son, Ernest, a hot-headed young man in his twenties, upped the ante, trying to impress his elders. "As you were saying yesterday, Pa, he can't be allowed to get away with it. If Pinnock and Smith aren't willing to do anything, it's our duty. Perhaps a little roughing up might wipe the smile off his face."

Groves, an older man and less gung-ho, cautioned the younger Simpson, "We may not like it, but we are not the law and should not act as if we are. Let it go Ernest."

While these exchanges took place, Iolo was making a show of reading the copy of the *Indian Opinion* he'd brought in with him.

Half an hour passed. As they kept drinking, Simpson and his son got more and more agitated. The bartender could tell that the atmosphere was getting tense. Iolo decided against another drink and prepared to make a swift departure. Ernest Simpson saw him making his move. "Look, he is planning to run away," he shouted, "this man is a white kaffir who has consorted with Africans that want to kill us all! Stop him!"

He and his father advanced unsteadily towards Iolo. Several other men in the bar, already well-oiled and eager to join in a ruckus, got up and joined them. Iolo, startled by Ernest's call to arms, hesitated. When he did move, he was too slow. His young pursuer and a fellow drinker by the name of Jeffries got to him before he could leave.

The drinker grabbed Iolo by his arms and trapped him against the wall. "Oi, if there is going to be trouble, take it outside!" cried the bartender. The two Simpsons, Noble, Jeffries and another man dragged Iolo, who was stunned by the way things had escalated, out into the street.

It was dark. Only a few people were still out and about. Most walked on by but three other men came over to see what was happening. The older Simpson started pushing and shoving Iolo while his son and Jeffries tied his hands. "We are going to give you the punishment you deserve, you bastard," hissed Ernest.

Noble interjected, "Let's give him a good ducking in that well over there! Come on!"

It was an old well, no longer used for drinking purposes. The water was stagnant and stank. The group picked Iolo up by his feet and his shoulders and carried him towards it. He was wriggling and resisting, but to no avail. He cried desperately for help but nobody came to his assistance.

The water came up to a couple of feet beneath the lip, so it was no great challenge to submerge Iolo. He was tipped upside down, held by his feet and then plunged into the well. Iolo felt the cool wetness envelope him. He had not had time to take a breath and within moments, his lungs were bursting.

Then he was lifted out. He could hear shouting but was unable to make out what was being said. He had long enough to take in some air before being shoved back in again. When he was next raised, he heard laughter and a voice declaring, "It's a bit like ducking a witch. Come on, again!" Iolo went slack. His mind racing, he decided that his best chance of survival was to focus on taking in air and staying calm.

After five duckings, Groves forced his way through to where Iolo was still being held upside down over the mouth of the well, groaning incoherently, water pouring off him. "For God's sake, stop it!" Groves roared. "That's enough! You've made your point. You don't want to end up in jail, do you?"

The fever broke; the older Simpson, puffing with exertion, said, "OK, Groves, we'll leave it at that. Come on Ernest, turn him the right way up and untie him. Leave him here. Let's go back into the hotel for another drink." His son complied, aiming a parting kick at Iolo but missing his target. The group dispersed, subdued.

Iolo sat slumped, his back against the wall of the well, gasping for breath. As his thoughts came back into some sort of focus, he wondered whether he should go to the police, but as he struggled to his feet, he decided that he just wanted to get home and out of these clothes. He was soaked to the skin.

The journey home was painfully slow. Twice he had to stop and rest. Finally, he reached their front door. He found Doris sitting in the living room, a cup of tea on the table in front of her. Since putting the kids to bed, she had been waiting to confront Iolo.

As he entered, she said to him in a harsh tone, "At last! Where in God's name have you been? I have another bone to pick with you. We need to…" She cut her tirade short when she saw the state Iolo was in. To her surprise, a wave of sympathy for her husband came over her. "Goodness me, what has happened? No, don't say anything. I can see you are in no fit state. We can talk tomorrow. Let's get you out of these clothes and into bed."

Soon Iolo was in the unfamiliar surroundings of the marital bed, sleeping the sleep of the dead.

Chapter Ten

Bulawayo, October 1921

Michael sat down in Iolo's favourite chair in the living room. He had a glass of water in one hand and a book in the other. He liked to browse through Mr James's library when nobody was around. Mrs James was out shopping and the children were at school so he had the place to himself for a while.

He had absent-mindedly selected a slim volume in Welsh. He was about to put it back on the shelf when he saw on the dustjacket that one of the contributors had the same name as Mr James's daughter, although the spelling was slightly different. He was intrigued.

A loose sheet fell out of the book and onto the floor. Retrieving it, Michael saw that it was a poem by the same woman, translated into English. The title was, "To the vagina." As he read it, his eyes widened; then he burst into laughter. *Iolo James, you get stranger and stranger,* he thought.

131

Michael noticed there was another loose sheet in the book. He opened it. It was a handwritten letter to Mr James from a Mr Ivor Williams, dated August 1911, just before the James family left Belmont.

At first glance, the letter was also entirely in Welsh. However, when he looked again, he could see that the letter ended with a sentence in English. It read, "Please vouch for my character – my future depends on it." Then, at the bottom of the page, there was another, agitated, hand. Michael recognised it as belonging to Mr James. In capitals he'd written, "*NO! PYDRU YN UFFERN!*"

Michael had no idea what that last phrase meant. Perturbed, he put both the poem and the letter back into the book and carefully returned it to the shelf. He resumed his domestic tasks.

Michael had returned to service with the James family just before the Christmas of 1921, a decade after he'd failed to return from his Kimberley errand for Mr James. He had been in the job for over six months now. It was not going well.

Working as a domestic servant again had not been his preference. When he'd done the job in Belmont, there had been too much time to think about his lost son, Molemane. He had accidentally stumbled back into it.

Since coming to Southern Rhodesia, Michael had mainly worked on the mines. From 1917 to 1920 he'd been at Wankie Colliery, in the northwest of the colony. Michael was horrified by the filthy, overcrowded conditions in the Colliery's compound, which contributed enormously to hundreds of deaths there from the Spanish influenza in 1918. He was one of over two thousand Africans who caught the disease. At one point, he had been so sick that his friends, in their desperation, contemplated taking him to the Colliery's native hospital, from which few emerged alive. But he'd turned the corner just in time.

During the post-war years there were several strikes at the Colliery. Michael, who worked as a lasher or a trammer, loading and pushing trucks full of coal out of the mine shafts, was involved in one of them that took place in early 1920. One of the compound policemen had challenged the right of miners to sell beer. Michael was among the many workers who brewed their own beer, using sorghum and maize grains. Without the income that came from selling it, he would not have enough money to live on. The police violently broke up the strike after two days and Michael was summarily dismissed.

Unsure what to do or where to go next, he took the train down to Bulawayo where he planned to move in with a cousin living in Makokoba, as Africans called the main location, and look for work. However, not long after his arrival, he changed his mind. Michael decided to go home. He took a train south, getting off at Pilane, the station nearest to Mochudi.

**

Michael had heard from his cousin that King Linchwe was gravely ill; his powers had passed temporarily to his second son, Isang, until the child of his deceased eldest son was old enough to take over. Isang was proving to be independent-minded. Michael decided he would beg him for forgiveness and ask for his banishment to be overturned.

On arriving in Mochudi, he took a room in a hostel run by the Dutch Reformed Church. At first, he stayed indoors until it was dark, when it was safer to venture out. He bought helpings of *bogobe* and *seswaa* from women hawkers on the street outside, carrying them back to the hostel; they kept him going.

The town was dusty and unprepossessing, with ramshackle buildings scattered about, but it felt good to be back among his own people. The sights and sounds from his room were so familiar. From his hostel bed, he could overhear the chatter outside. Through the window he could see that many more Kgatla men were now wearing European clothes.

After a week, he felt confident enough to come out of hiding and go to his parents. He walked to Morwa overnight. They were overwhelmed with joy to see him.

When he turned the conversation to the subject of how to overturn his banishment, his parents urged Michael to make representations to the King's advisors. His father told Michael that they had not been allowed any contact with Molemane over the years since he'd fled.

But before he could do anything, word somehow got around that Michael was back. His former wife's family alerted the authorities and he was arrested. They told him he would now face the *Lekgotla* in person. There might even be additional punishment for absconding before the original trial, Michael was warned.

Michael, addressed by his birth name, Gopane Matala, finally found himself before the King's Court in November 1921. After hearing extensive arguments from all sides, Isang gave his judgement. It came as a pleasant surprise.

The decision to banish Gopane Matala had been excessively harsh, Isang ruled. But his sentence could only be lifted on one condition: he should make no attempt in future to contact his son, who by now was on the cusp of adulthood. He did not know Gopane Matala, having been rechristened with another Kgatla name long ago, Isang said.

Michael was conflicted. He had hoped that, if his banishment was lifted, he would be able to re-establish some sort of relationship with his son. His old stubbornness flaring back into life, his first instinct was to reject Isang's verdict, but he stopped himself, instead asking for time to consult with his family.

The King consented but warned him not to take long – he had many other cases to consider that day. His parents pleaded with him to accept. His uncle argued that Molemane now had a different family. It was too late to change that; but his parents were old and it would be an enormous comfort if they could see Michael regularly again.

Battling back tears, Michael reluctantly accepted the King's terms. Perhaps one day Molemane would seek him out, but he doubted it. He had a duty to his parents. While welcoming Michael's decision, Isang warned him that if he broke the terms of the agreement, his banishment would be reimposed.

Over the next two weeks, Michael remained at his parents' homestead, helping with the cattle and crops. They could still not quite believe that their beloved son had returned to them. It gave him pleasure to see how happy they were, but as the days passed, he just could not shake off his grief at the prospect of never seeing his son again. His ordeal since coming back to the Kgatla Reserve had rubbed salt into deep emotional wounds. If anything, with all hope now gone, the wounds were rawer than ever.

He realised that, if he was not to go mad, he would have to leave again. He assured his parents that he would return often, but explained that it was just too painful to be so close to Molemane and yet be unable to see and know him. He could not make his life here.

When he told his parents, they were distraught but knew that he could not be stopped. Exhausted, Michael could not think beyond resurrecting his earlier plans. So, in early December 1920, he took the train back to Bulawayo.

***

135

Michael was walking through the Natives only exit gate at Bulawayo railway station. In the corner of his eye, he saw a white man who he vaguely recognised. He was staring at him from the other side of the street.

"Michael? Is that you?" the man called out. It was Iolo James.

Both were astonished by this unexpected turn of events. After Michael had given a brief account of himself, Iolo insisted that he should come with him and stay in the *kia* at the back of the James' family home while he worked out his next move. Mrs James had just sacked their latest domestic servant for theft, Iolo said in passing.

On their way, Iolo asked Michael whether he had seen Samuel and delivered that package all those years ago. He assured him that he had indeed seen Samuel, and, anticipating the next question, went on to add that he had not returned to Belmont because he did not feel it was safe there anymore. He told Iolo that, given his involvement in fighting the Boers during the 1899-1902 war, he'd been worried that after Samuel was apprehended, he might be next. Iolo did not interrogate him further about it.

When they arrived, Iolo presented Michael to Doris with a mock flourish, saying that he'd invited Michael to stay in the *kia* for a bit. She was not keen. "This man deserted his post without explanation in Belmont and now you want to welcome him as our guest?" Michael was struck by her grey pallor and the way in which she slurred some of her words.

Not wanting to cause any trouble, he was ready to say that he would go, but before he could, Iolo intervened, "Michael had his reasons. I am putting my foot down."

Doris stamped out of the room, cursing Iolo under her breath.

"Let me show you your quarters. It's very good to see you again Michael!" Iolo said with a smile. "Let's talk more after dinner. You must join us." Michael thought he had misheard. He had just been invited to sit at the same table with a white family and eat with them.

Dinner was the strangest experience of his life. When Doris saw Michael sitting opposite her at the table, she looked horrified, but said nothing. She had prepared a stew. She served the children and herself but not Iolo or Michael. Iolo, with exaggerated brightness, said, "I will serve food for us, Michael." She stared down at her food, her appetite vanished.

Mervyn looked disconcerted and confused throughout the meal but kept his thoughts to himself, saying only "Good evening." Gwerfyl was much less bothered, chatting away to all and sundry.

Michael spoke only when spoken to and asked to retire as soon as he had finished eating. "No, please Michael, stay up a little longer. I'd like to talk more with you," remonstrated Iolo.

They sat on the *stoep* after dinner. Iolo talked much more than Michael, telling him about most, but not all, of the things that had happened in his life since Belmont. Michael, suppressing his feelings of unease, gave Iolo a fuller account of his visit to Samuel, but omitted the knife. When James asked about what had befallen Samuel, Michael admitted that he did not know.

Michael also mentioned that he had been involved in a strike at Wankie Colliery and then sacked, which was why he had come to Bulawayo. This excited Iolo. "Ah, Michael, it's good to see that you are still fighting the good fight! You and I have much in common. You're welcome to stay here as long as you like. I'll help you find work on the railways."

Michael wondered whether it might have been better not to tell him so much. He didn't dislike James, but there had always been something strange about him. Mrs James oozed hostility from every pore and seemed unwell. But his options were limited. Maybe Mr James could get him a job.

It wouldn't do any harm to stay for a few days, he thought. "You are very kind, Mr James, thank you. But I hope you won't mind if I don't join you for any other family meals. I think that was too much for your wife. I will eat in the *kia* for the rest of my stay."

"Call me Iolo."

Michael kept to himself over the days that followed. Doris cast malevolent glances in his direction whenever their paths crossed. Gwerfyl often sought him out. She was a charming little girl. Mervyn also relaxed and started to talk with him. As promised, Iolo had asked around the railway headquarters, but confessed to Michael that he'd had no joy.

"I sang your praises left, right and centre, but at one point I let slip that you'd been involved in a strike at Wankie," Iolo told him artlessly. "Once word got around, everybody had cold feet." Michael's spirits sank.

The next evening, Iolo approached Michael again. "I've had a great idea. I don't know why it took me so long! We need a new domestic servant. Doris gets through them at an alarming rate, but she cannot manage on her own much longer. As you may have worked out, her health is not good these days. Would you accept? We could pay you well over the going rate."

Thanks to you, it might be the only offer I'll get, thought Michael. But it would buy him some time. So, he said, "That is good of you, Mr James, I accept your offer. I will start immediately by washing up tonight's dishes after dinner."

"Wonderful news! I will tell Doris." Iolo marched into the kitchen.

The sound of a plate smashing on the kitchen floor told Michael all he needed to know about her reaction.

***

Bulawayo, October 1921

Doris felt she was losing her mind. At first, the Luminal had helped to calm her nerves and improve her sleep. She had even stopped taking it for a while in Hartley. After Iolo's Watchtower fiasco and their move back to Bulawayo, she had gone downhill again. Her anxiety returned, more acute than before. She began to take bigger and bigger doses, running out of her supplies well ahead of schedule.

When her doctor refused to increase her pills, she'd found another who was more compliant. But the more she took, the more she seemed to need. She knew she could not expect any sympathy or support from her husband. The weekly allowance she got from him was never enough. She was working her way through her mother's bequest at an alarming rate but felt helpless to stop herself. Her symptoms grew worse. She started to experience tremors.

Her state of mind deteriorated rapidly during the second half of 1921. She became obsessed with the terrifying riots in Tulsa, Oklahoma, in the United States. A black man had reportedly attacked a white woman. Armed black men had then sought to spring the culprit out of jail, leading the police and white militias to take steps to pacify the black ghetto of Greenwood. Despite resistance, the police and the militias were able to bring matters back under control, albeit at the cost of dozens of lives.

Events in Tulsa confirmed for Doris that white civilisation hung by the thinnest of threads. Whites were under siege here in Southern Rhodesia too, women like her above all. She thought back to Ignatius in Hartley. For the first year or so, she'd felt relaxed around him. But by the time they'd left, she was sure he was planning something. It was a good job they'd moved to Bulawayo before he could carry it out.

Simon, the domestic servant they had employed soon after moving back to Bulawayo, had been the same. Over the year he was in their employ, he had given her inappropriate looks. Then she had found him in her bedroom, apparently rifling through her drawers. He claimed that he was only putting away the washing, as she'd asked him to. Doris had no recollection of that. Some of her mother's jewellery was in those drawers; he must have been planning to steal it. Iolo did not believe Doris. He never did. He'd persuaded her not to press charges. In the end, they'd agreed that it would be best just to let Simon go.

And now Michael was in her house. She had to supervise him, have him close by all day. He'd betrayed them in the past and yet Iolo was treating him like a member of the family. She would never forget that evening dinner, when Iolo invited him to join them at the table. He had sat there, looking very satisfied with himself, eating more than his fair share, staring at her.

**

Bulawayo, October 1921

Iolo's luck seemed to have turned. They had decided to flee Hartley, unable to tolerate the contempt and disapproval they'd endured after that unspeakable incident with the Simpsons. They had been lucky. Frank Tindler, a longstanding friend, was working in the Bulawayo goods sheds and alerted Iolo to a job vacancy there.

The only candidate, Iolo was successful. Whatever reservations they may have had about him, the railway management was struggling at the time to cope with an acute white labour shortage. They could not afford to reject Iolo. Soon afterwards, the Rhodesia Railway Workers' Union went on strike. The stoppage was remarkably successful, and he found himself the beneficiary of a twenty five percent pay rise as a result.

Once they were back in Bulawayo, Iolo kept his head down. He was very happy in their new house on Lobengula Street, which had been hard to find. There was an enormous shortage of housing suitable for Europeans in the town.

The house was a brick and iron construction. It had everything they needed. There was a *stoep* at the front, a living room, two small bedrooms, a kitchen with a Dover stove and a bathroom with a zinc bath in it. It had running water and electricity. The servant's quarters were at the back.

Iolo liked Bulawayo. On their first posting, just up from Belmont, they hadn't stayed long enough to get to know it properly. But this time it was different. Bulawayo was attractively laid out, far nicer, to his mind, than Salisbury. The broad avenues and streets, some of them lined with exotic trees, were organised in an American-inspired grid. To the west of Borrow Street, the town had a pleasant park, through which the Amatsheumhlope river gently meandered.

Unlike Salisbury, Bulawayo also had a proper history. Meaning 'place of slaughter' in Ndebele, it had been a town during the pre-colonial era under Lobengula, the Ndebele King.

The British had captured it in 1893 during the First Ndebele War, but not before Lobengula had burnt his town to the ground. Iolo was sure that the spirit of Lobengula's Old Bulawayo had not been erased by the colonial settlement built on its ashes.

Iolo took to cycling everywhere. Bulawayo was flat, making it easy to ride around. Most days he rode the full length of Lobengula Street to Raylton and back for work. When he could, he would also cycle out of town into the hillier countryside, but the demands of family life meant he was usually too busy to go far.

Mervyn and Gwerfyl were happy too. They soon found friends, "lots and lots of them!" shouted Gwerfyl one day, doing a handstand. The only cloud on the horizon, as far as Iolo was concerned, was Doris.

She made no effort to hide her disappointment about the house, which she complained was much smaller than the one in Hartley. It had no garden at all, she said. And, from her perspective, it was also at the wrong end of Lobengula Street, the north end, opposite the entrance to the location.

The horror, thought Iolo. The north end of Lobengula Street was a border zone. He loved the fact that the different races were less segregated than usual. There were Indian stores near their house. African market stalls lined the street. Doris refused to use either, instead preferring to shop in the heart of the European town, around Market Square.

Her health was going from bad to worse. The pills she was taking were not good for her. Iolo had asked a doctor acquaintance about them who had warned that taking too many could be damaging. She looked haggard and exhausted. Although she'd kept up with the household tasks following Simon's departure, she was often abrupt with him and the children. He said nothing. She'd never listen to him anyway.

Then, out of the blue, Michael appeared in Bulawayo. Iolo was not superstitious, but he felt that this was another sign that life was on the up.

He had never been able to shrug off the pangs of guilt about Samuel, he wasn't sure why. But Michael had assuaged them somewhat by confirming that Iolo's package had reached Samuel. Now he was rewarding Michael for his good service by finding him a job within the household. The circle had been closed.

***

Bulawayo, December 1921

Iolo told his friend Frank Tindler about Samuel and Michael over a pre-Christmas drink at the Empire Bar. Frank had arrived in Southern Rhodesia from Kent, where he'd worked for the railways while pursuing his real passion, cricket. He had been good enough to make the county's second eleven. When he got to Bulawayo in 1912, he wasted no time getting involved in the local cricket scene, both as a player and a coach.

Iolo arrived in Bulawayo from South Africa a few months before Frank. He was working as a goods clerk when Frank took charge of the goods sheds. Frank shared a non-conformist background with Iolo and the two got on well from the start. He was an easy-going boss.

Frank was no apologist for the Empire and agreed with Iolo that Africans often got a very raw deal in Southern Rhodesia. He was a solid trade unionist, a stalwart of the white workers' railway union.

He knew Jack Keller, the union's leader, from back home. They'd worked together on the South Eastern and Chatham Railway, sailing from Britain on the same ship. Both had taken an active part in the great railway strike of August 1911. Keller, however, never warmed to Iolo. "I can't work him out at all," he once said to Frank.

Frank married a local girl, Harriet, in 1913. She liked Iolo, who often came round to their house in Raylton, a child or two in tow. However, she couldn't stand Doris. The feeling was mutual. Harriet found her prickly and paranoid, one of those Europeans who were unnecessarily fearful of African people. Most of the white community acknowledged that Black Peril cases were vanishingly rare, yet Doris never stopped going on about them. Their antipathy meant that the families socialised less often than they might have done.

Frank was the only person in white society in whom Iolo felt comfortable confiding. When in 1914 he'd announced that he was opposed to the war, Frank did not rush to judgement, but he did not share Iolo's maverick tendencies. He was quick to sign up. He batted the full innings, serving first in East Africa, where he won a medal for bravery in the battle of Tanga, and then going to Europe to fight.

Iolo wrote him the occasional letter, so when Frank returned to Bulawayo, he knew that Iolo had been posted away as punishment for his pacifist activities. When Iolo got in touch in early 1920 to say he and the family had decided to leave Hartley, Frank was able to pull some strings – the goods sheds needed a couple of extra European clerks – and get him back to Bulawayo.

Frank had never got to the bottom of what had happened in Hartley, although there were rumours; Iolo was said to have hidden down a well for some reason. Harriet once told him that she had overheard a group of children in Raylton singing a ditty which ran, "Ding dong dell, Monkey Nut James is down the well."

Iolo was circumspect, saying only that he had fallen out with some local officials for standing up for Africans.

"Why don't you tone things down a bit, Iolo? You're always getting in trouble. One day things could get really serious. Your kids won't thank you when they're older," Frank said as he finished off his pint of Castle beer.

"I know, Frank, but there are moments when it's wrong to bite your tongue, to opt for the quiet life. What kind of example would that set for Mervyn and Gwerfyl?"

"Well, maybe. But one day your luck might run out. And what about Doris? She's not easy to get along with, but I can't help thinking that your heroic stands are part of the reason why she lives on her nerves so much."

"I'm glad you have some insight into Doris's mind, Frank. I certainly don't!"

Frank went on, "Harriet tells me that Doris makes almost daily visits to that dodgy doctor just round the corner from yours and that some people are calling her an opium addict."

"Nonsense," replied Iolo. "I've seen no evidence of that. She does take pills, but nothing major."

There was an awkward silence. Iolo broke it. "Frank, I know you mean well, but you've got the wrong end of the stick."

"Fair enough, Iolo," Frank replied, wearing a placatory smile. "Let's drop the subject. Another round?"

Iolo accepted the peace offering. When Frank came back, drinks on a tray, the conversation moved on to less sensitive subjects.

Chapter Eleven

Bulawayo, October 1922

Iolo took Frank's advice. He made a concerted effort to avoid controversy. He stayed a member of the white railway workers' union but was not active in it. He never quite felt as if he fitted in. He was disappointed when the railway management reversed many of the gains made in 1920, leading to £3 being docked from his monthly wage; Doris complained bitterly about it.

Iolo's interest in Gandhi's activities resumed. Gandhi had taken over the leadership of the Indian National Congress at the end of 1921 and things were hotting up again. Iolo started reading Theosophical texts by Annie Besant, who was a longstanding supporter of Congress. She'd been publishing a blizzard of articles in favour of Indian independence. Iolo got to know a couple of Indian shopkeepers on Lobengula Street and often sat with them after work, discussing events on the subcontinent.

He also followed – initially with enthusiasm but ultimately with horror and disappointment – the revolt by white mine workers on the Rand in early 1922. There were violent clashes between the strikers and the police and the army. But there was also a vicious pogrom against innocent Africans. He considered the slogan of the revolt, *"workers of the world unite for a white South Africa"* an utter travesty.

***

Michael was often left to pick up the pieces at home. He was increasingly in sole charge of the children. Their father was often not there and they had grown a little scared of their mother. When she wasn't unconscious on her bed, she was shuffling around the house, muttering under her breath about the Rand Revolt, which had further fuelled her paranoia. "There will be an epidemic of miscegenation, you mark my words," she had recently declared to a bewildered Gwerfyl, pointing menacingly at her.

One morning in April, on entering the home to perform his duties after lunch, Mrs James had suddenly screamed at Michael. "Leave, or I will call the police! I can't bear to be in the same room as you!" She had a wild look in her eyes and her whole body was shaking. She had then walked out of the house at speed. He reported the incident to Iolo, but her husband only shrugged, apologising on her behalf.

Michael felt in an impossible position. He shared his dilemma with friends in Makokoba. They all thought he was in grave danger and urged him to leave. Yet Michael felt protective of the children; they could never fill the gap in his heart left by the loss of his son, but Mervyn and Gwerfyl allowed him to experience a simulacrum of parental love. He hesitated.

Winter came and went but still he did not go. By the time summer arrived, Mrs James's behaviour was nigh-on intolerable. She left the room as soon as he entered and refused to speak to him at all. Iolo still did nothing.

Michael finally came to a decision. Just one more monthly pay packet. He would go at the end of October. Perhaps he would return home to the Kgatla Reserve for a visit. He had not been back for well over a year and his parents were sending messages, asking him to come.

Before Michael could make his move, disaster struck.

On the third Monday in October, Mrs James did not get up in the morning. She was nowhere to be seen at breakfast, so Michael made sure the children had something to eat and got them off to school. Iolo assisted half-heartedly but did not go to check how his wife was before leaving for work.

Michael began washing the kitchen floor. As he sloshed the mop around, he heard a crash and a groan from Mrs James's bedroom. At first, he did not react, unsure what to do. Entering a white woman's bedroom without permission was taboo, but doing nothing would be immoral and wrong.

Mervyn and Gwerfyl would never understand if something terrible happened to their mother and he had done nothing to help her, so he approached the closed door, turned the handle and looked in.

Mrs James was writhing uncontrollably on the floor by the bed, the whites of her eyes prominent. A stream of words, none of them making any sense, emanated from her mouth, alternating with occasional grunts and groans. Michael thought he could make out "God help me" at one point, but he couldn't be sure. It could also have been "get off me".

He looked at her for a moment, paralysed. Then he reached down to pick her up and put her on the bed, where she would at

148

least be more comfortable. She was still in her nightgown. He took care to ensure that her body remained covered.

As he lay her down, placing a pillow under her head, the seizure seemed to relent. Her limbs gradually twitched less, the sounds stopped and her breath calmed. Her eyes were open, staring blankly at the ceiling. Michael reversed stealthily out of the room. He caught a glimpse of her bedside table, which had several empty medicine packets on it.

He left the door ajar so he could keep an eye on her. He thought about going around to one of the local doctors but decided against it; he was wary of leaving her on her own. He went to the front of the house and called out to a young African boy who was passing by. In return for a small amount of money, the boy agreed to take a message to Iolo in the goods sheds.

Michael scribbled a note to him and gave it to the boy. It read, *Please come now. Your wife is very ill. She might die*, he added at the last minute. He needed to make sure that Iolo came.

***

A flustered Iolo ran into the house. "Michael, what's happened? Where is she?"

"In her bedroom, Mr James. She seemed to be having a fit, but she is calmer now."

Iolo went into the bedroom and sat on the edge of the bed. Doris did not respond, her eyes still fixed on the ceiling. "Michael, please get Dr Hastings," he said, glancing back at him. "I'll stay with her."

Dr Hastings arrived within twenty minutes. He was the doctor who had refused to prescribe Doris any more Luminal. He began his investigations straight away. After a few moments, Doris spoke, "I am alright," she murmured.

149

"Well, it is good to hear your voice, Mrs James, but you are not alright, are you?" replied Dr Hastings. "I can see from your bedside table that you are still taking a great deal of that barbiturate which I warned you off." There was no response from Doris.

By noon, Doris was out of bed and dressed. She sat in the living room, transfixed. Dr Hastings departed, telling her to come and see him first thing the next day. Iolo decided that it was okay for him to return to work; they had been in the middle of an important stock taking exercise when he was called away. He asked Michael to keep an eye on Mrs James and look after the children when they got back from school. Michael felt uncomfortable about it but nodded in assent.

Doris remained still and quiet all afternoon. The children, used to this behaviour, ignored her, chatting instead with Michael as he gave them bread and jam for tea. Then, at five pm, Doris abruptly came out of her room, saying to nobody in particular, "I must go out. I have something very important to do."

"No Mrs James, don't go anywhere, please," responded Michael. "Your health is not good. It can wait until tomorrow, surely?"

The children made their own entreaties, but nothing could persuade her. She staggered out of the house and was gone.

She had not returned two hours later when Iolo got back from work. "What!" he exclaimed. "She didn't say where she was going?"

Mervyn was sitting at the table, unusually subdued. Gwerfyl was crying. "Look after the children, Michael, I've got to find her." With that, Iolo too was gone.

Doris had no friends, she didn't socialise, so where would she be going? Iolo had no idea. All he could think of was to try the Tindlers. "She's not been here," said Frank. "I suggest you report her disappearance to the police, stressing that she is not in her right mind and could be a danger to herself. Then they will send out a search party." That seemed a sensible idea so, after a quick cup of tea, Iolo made his way to Bulawayo Police Station.

By the time he got there it was 6:30 pm. An impassive Constable sat behind the front desk. "My wife has gone missing and I'm worried about her," declared Iolo.

"Ah. What is her name, sir?"

"Doris James. I'm her husband, Iolo."

The Constable was jolted into life by the name. "Doris James, you say? She has just been here to report a crime. She and two Constables are on their way to your house now to make an arrest."

"I'm sorry, I don't understand. Arrest who?"

"I'm afraid I'm not at liberty to say, sir," replied the Constable. "What I can say is that it is not you," he added, laughing at his own joke. Iolo turned straight round and ran out of the door.

He did not stop running until he was home. It was as he'd feared. Michael was being led away by the Constables. His expression was neutral, as if he was going for a normal stroll. He didn't look the slightest bit surprised.

"Why is he being arrested?" Iolo cried out.

"Your wife has alleged that this African sexually assaulted her today, entering her bedroom without permission and then lasciviously touching her body," said one of the policemen. "We are taking him into custody on suspicion of rape."

"There is no truth in it," pleaded Iolo. "She had a fit and he helped her. He may even have saved her life."

He looked past the Constables and saw Doris in the doorway. "Doris, for God's sake, you know Michael did no such thing. Please, before it is too late, tell them!"

Doris mouthed something, but so quietly he could not make out what she'd said. She was far away, in another world.

Michael said calmly to Iolo. "Mr James, there is nothing to be done. Things will now take their course. The last thing I want is

151

any more of your so-called help." Then, his face softened. "Explain this as best you can to the children. Tell them that I will miss them."

Iolo took no notice. He stood in front of the two Constables. "I will not let you pass. Release this man now."

"Jesus, Mary, Joseph and the wee Donkey," exclaimed one of them in a strong Irish accent. "We'll arrest you too if we have to. Move out of the way." He pushed past Iolo, pulling Michael along with him.

Defeated, Iolo sat on the ground against the railings, watching the three men disappear around the corner. He looked at Doris, but she refused to meet his gaze, instead going into her bedroom and shutting the door behind her.

"Mervyn, Gwerfyl, come inside. This must have been very upsetting. Let me explain what is going on," he said in a tired, sad voice.

***

Iolo's explanations only confused and distressed them more. In the end, he gave up, saying, "Come on now, bedtime. I will read you both extra stories. You have been very good this evening."

Getting them to sleep took ages. Once there was silence in the house, he lay down on the sofa and closed his eyes. Within minutes, he too was asleep. The front door was wide open all night.

The next thing he knew, it was early morning. He could hear noises and shouts emanating from the location as its inhabitants stirred for the day, girding themselves for whatever challenges lay ahead.

Soon afterwards, the children woke up. Iolo roused himself reluctantly and saw to their breakfast before sending a message to Frank telling him that he would not be at work until lunchtime at the earliest. There was no sign of Doris. He walked the children to school. They were much clingier than usual. Once they had gone in, he set off for the police station.

He got nowhere. Michael was in the cells and he was not allowed to see him. "You can get him a lawyer, if you want, Mr James, but that is it," said the policeman he spoke to, regarding him quizzically.

"I will," said Iolo. "I'll be back later today."

He spent the morning visiting lawyers, but none were interested in defending Michael. "This African has wrapped you around his little finger, Mr James," said one. "I don't touch Black Peril cases with a bargepole. My reputation would be destroyed if I defended him. Besides, I am astonished that you are arguing for this African and against your own wife," the lawyer went on. "Be careful, sir, you are treading on dangerous territory." Discouraged, Iolo decided to change tack and seek out Dr Hastings. Perhaps he would agree to give evidence about Doris's addiction.

***

While Iolo rushed around Bulawayo, Doris stayed in her room. She had only the haziest recollection of yesterday's events. She had run out of pills again. The more she tried to make sense of it, the less it made. But of one thing she was certain: Michael had sexually assaulted her.

She remembered his hands on her. She remembered feeling panic and fear. She remembered him laying her down on the bed and rearranging her clothes. She remembered him whispering to her. What else could he have been doing? She had done the right thing reporting him. No white woman was safe from him. She also remembered her husband contradicting her, the ultimate betrayal.

When she did leave her room, it was to go out for more pills. Her favourite doctor was as accommodating as ever. Soon the Luminal was having its effect. She felt calmer, more herself. But she was still exhausted. She returned to bed to sleep.

***

Dr Hastings looked up from his notes when Iolo walked into the consultation room. "Mr James, how are you? I hear you have been waiting a long time, I do apologise. It is good to see you taking your wife's situation with the seriousness it warrants. She needs to go into a clinic for treatment. Withdrawal is the only option and to do that, you need to place yourself in the hands of experts for a prolonged period. I can recommend a couple of clinics in South Africa. There are none of sufficient quality here, I am afraid."

Iolo thanked him for his concern. "Yes, you may be right. But there is a more urgent problem. In a deranged state, after your visit, she went to the police and accused our domestic servant of sexual assault. He is in custody now. It is a terrible injustice. I have come to beg you to make a statement to the police about her confused state of mind."

Hastings was shocked. "This is awful. How can anybody believe her?" He paused and then looked at Iolo. "I am sorry, I just cannot do that. It would be the end of my career. Surely you understand?"

Iolo looked at him with incredulity. "What happened to the physician's oath, Dr Hastings?"

"What? You mean 'Do No Harm'? Not quite the same as doing the right thing, Mr James." Hippocrates did not have to make a living in Southern Rhodesia. "Besides, the oath relates to medical ethics alone. I am not a lawyer. I am a husband and a father, as you are, Mr James. I cannot do this to them. It seems to me that you are in the same position. Are you prepared to commit social suicide for an African? All I can help with is your wife's medical care. On that count, you can be sure I will do my best."

Iolo gave no answer. He could see that Dr Hastings was not going to come to Michael's rescue. It was all down to him.

The meeting over, Iolo went home to see to the children. He arrived just as they were walking up the street, back from school. He ushered them inside and gave them their tea.

Gwerfyl asked him, her voice wobbling a little, "Is Michael back yet?"

"I'm afraid not." He tried to sound upbeat. "Soon, hopefully." There were tears in both his children's eyes.

A short time later, Frank appeared at the front door, having come straight from work. "Hello kids!" he said chirpily. Looking at Iolo, his smile faded. "Good God man, you look terrible. So, why did you have to cry off work today?"

The two men walked into the yard, so the children would not overhear. Iolo told Frank the whole story.

***

Frank and Harriet were supportive over the weeks that followed. Mervyn and Gwerfyl spent a lot of time with them and their children, sleeping over on numerous occasions. Iolo regularly went there for his meals. Frank allowed Iolo time off work when he needed it.

Iolo went to the police station almost every day, but he was never allowed to see Michael. He was tormented by guilt but felt helpless.

At the end of October, the European electorate voted on whether Southern Rhodesia should replace rule by the British South Africa Company either by joining South Africa or a system of partial self-government. The self-government option prevailed.

But his ballot paper was not among those counted. He had other preoccupations.

Michael's trial was scheduled for January 1923 in the Bulawayo High Court. Dr Hastings came to see Doris every day. He had gone to the doctor who had supplied her with Luminal and threatened to report him to the authorities if he continued to do so.

Hastings prescribed her a limited supply of Luminal himself and monitored her condition regularly. But she was soon in semi-withdrawal. Doris coped by drinking more and more alcohol. Any spirit would do. Soon there were empty bottles all around her bed. Iolo and Hastings tried to stop her trips to bottle stores, but she was cunning; they could not monitor her movements twenty-four hours a day.

The police had taken several statements from Doris since the incident. None of them made much sense. There was no convincing evidence of an attack. In the end, they did not charge Michael with rape or attempted rape, which potentially carried the death penalty, but with the lesser crime of indecent assault. Even so, the charge came with a long prison sentence.

For a while, the police had considered completely dropping the case against Michael, but that idea had been abandoned once Doris's lawyer got to work.

The week after the October incident, Doris had been visited by a member of the Rhodesian Women's League, Mrs Ethel McBrain. The wife of one of Bulawayo's town councillors, she was outraged to see the conditions in which Doris was living. She attributed Doris's poor state to shock.

When she asked Doris whether she had had any support from a lawyer, she'd received no reply. Taking that to mean no, Mrs McBrain said that she would return the next day with somebody who could give Doris the legal advice she needed and make sure she received justice. "The whole town is behind you," she assured her.

The lawyer which the Women's League had on retainer was a Mr Allen. He came to the house the following day. When he knocked, nobody answered. He was about to leave when a dishevelled woman came up to the door, her shopping basket clinking.

Doris looked at him but said nothing.

"Mrs James, I thought I had missed you!"

Still no response. Undeterred, he followed her into the house, "Mrs McBrain has told me about your case. I am so sorry to hear about your ordeal. As you know, there have been numerous such cases over the last twenty years. It is crucial to ensure that Africans who transgress are punished," Mr Allen continued. "Otherwise, no white woman will be safe. The Women's League is covering my costs, so you have nothing to worry about on that score."

Doris's attention was on the glass of brandy she had just poured herself. "Where is your husband, Mrs James? It would be good to get his approval."

She stared at him, growling, "I have no husband, at least no one worth calling a husband."

Mr Allen blinked, confused for a moment. Righting himself, he said, "If that is how you feel, fine. Let's proceed anyway."

For the next hour or so, Mr Allen talked. Doris did not interrupt, nor did she interact. By the end of the visit, Mr Allen was none the wiser. But no matter. The details were not important. The police would provide him with her statements now that he was acting on her behalf.

There was no family Christmas at Lobengula Street. Iolo and the children spent it with the Tindlers. Doris showed no interest in the festivities. She began spending more and more time walking the streets of Bulawayo.

It was only in part because she wanted to avoid Iolo and the children. She didn't feel safe if she stayed in one place. She was hearing voices in her head, telling her that she could be attacked again at any time.

Dr Hastings despaired. Nothing he did seemed to be helping. Her condition was awful. Things could not go on much longer, but he hesitated to do anything drastic until the trial was over. An intervention now could be misunderstood.

***

Following his arrest, Michael had spent two weeks in the cells at the police station. After the first few days of questioning, he had been largely left to his own devices. Then he was moved to the town prison.

The conditions in the prison were worse than at the station. He was in a dark, six by three-foot cell with five other men, one of whom talked constantly to himself. There was no bedding, just a blanket and the bare floor. The toilet was a bucket in the corner of the cell, which was often overflowing long before it was collected for emptying.

The food was meagre and of poor quality: congealed *sadza*, usually with nothing to accompany it. He had twenty minutes a day in a congested exercise yard. No visitors were allowed. He spent hour after hour, day after day, lost in his own thoughts.

When the police told him that he would be charged with indecent assault rather than rape, he had felt no relief. He knew that a long stint in prison awaited him. Michael swore that, if by some miracle he survived this, he would never allow white people to harm him again.

***

It was a blisteringly hot day as Judge Miles walked into the Court Building. His assistant handed him the list of cases. He sat down in his office to read through it. The usual range of petty cases would start things off. Then, after lunch, another Black Peril case involving a domestic servant.

He dreaded Black Peril cases. There was nearly always a gang of outraged citizens in the visitors' gallery, commentating from above on the proceedings. Only a guilty verdict would be acceptable. He'd read through the court papers on this particular case; the evidence was weak. The single positive thing about these cases was that, unpleasant as they were, they rarely lasted long.

The morning cases passed without note. Judge Miles ate a very decent lunch at the Bulawayo Club and then returned to work. If he could get the Black Peril case done efficiently, he might get home early, perhaps in time for a late afternoon ride on his horse before sunset. He rose from his seat. The parties to the case would be in court by now. Time to go.

As he walked down the corridor, his assistant caught up to him, a concerned look on his face. "Your Honour, before you go in… something has come up. A man has come forward in today's Black Peril case. He wants to give evidence on behalf of the defendant."

Miles stopped in his tracks. This was unheard of. "Who is this person?"

"The husband of the plaintiff, Mr Iolo James," said his assistant.

The judge laughed. "This is no time for joking."

"It's no joke. Here is his request. His signature is at the bottom," replied the assistant, pointing at a sheet of paper.

Judge Miles paused. He considered adjourning and speaking with this Mr James to check on his sanity. But this could prejudice the fairness of the trial and cast a cloud over his own reputation. He was also curious; here was something interesting.

Most days, his work was dull and predictable. If nothing else, this would be fodder for conversation at the Club. Horse-riding could wait. He decided to allow the husband to give evidence.

"Everything seems in order. Tell Mr James that I will call him at the appropriate time in the proceedings." The eyes of his assistant widened in surprise, but he made off to find Iolo.

***

Michael was led into the dock. He was not permitted to sit down until the judge was seated and the court had been called to order. He did not look around, but from the corner of his eye, he could glimpse the jury sitting to his right. It was composed of nine European men – no African had ever sat on a jury in Southern Rhodesia. Michael had decided not to engage with the trial. Soon he would know his fate.

Policemen stood on either side of him. While they were waiting for the trial to start, they had been placing bets with each other on how soon it would be over. When asked, Michael had pled not guilty to the charge of indecently assaulting Mrs Doris James, but he knew it meant nothing.

A lawyer began speaking for Mrs James, describing something that had never happened. Michael heard that he was a degenerate and a threat to all white women. Severe punishment was warranted, the lawyer said. Several policemen from the station took the stand and answered questions from the lawyer. Mrs James was portrayed as a distressed victim who was suffering from major health problems as a result of the sexual assault.

After forty-five minutes, the case for the prosecution was finished. Michael had no lawyer. He had dictated a short statement of his innocence, which did not take long for a court official to read out. Next, the jury would retire to consider its verdict. It was probably only a matter of minutes before he was sentenced.

He was caught off guard when the judge said, "We have had a last-minute request to give evidence for the defendant. I am inclined to grant it but I will hear from you, Mr Allen, if you have objections."

"I do, my lord. Permit me to approach the bar."

Michael was jolted out of his trance by this exchange and for the first time looked properly round the courtroom. Some members of the jury were looking perplexed. Above him, in the visitor's gallery, he saw several white women standing up and shouting "Shame!" He saw a man scribbling something into a notebook, a reporter, probably. Then, directly behind him, there was Mr James, sitting near the back. Staring at the bar, he did not meet Michael's gaze. *What is he playing at?* thought Michael.

After five minutes of commotion, Judge Miles called the court to order again. "I dismiss Mr Allen's objections. If those people in the visitors' gallery are unwilling to quieten down, I will order their removal. The witness should take the stand."

Iolo stood up, walked to the stand and took the oath.

"Mr James," began the judge, "I invite you to make your statement, after which the plaintiff's lawyer will be permitted to question you. Do you understand?"

The white women in the gallery above gasped when they heard his name. The reporter from the *Bulawayo Chronicle* was flush with excitement. This was going to be a big scoop.

Iolo made his statement. It was short. His voice was firm at first, but as he continued it began to crack.

"I am Mr Iolo James, the husband of the plaintiff, Mrs Doris James. Mrs James is seriously unwell. Her condition has led her to imagine something that did not happen. The defendant did not assault her in any way. He helped her when she was having a crisis. I know the defendant well. He is honest and of good character. He is innocent, my Lord. The charges should be dropped and the defendant released."

As he finished, angry cries rang out from the delegation sent by the Rhodesian Women's League to observe the trial. "Lies! How could you do this to your wife?" shouted one of the women.

"Order!" exclaimed Judge Miles. "Mr Allen, your witness."

Mr Allen rose from his desk and approached Iolo. "Mr James," he began, "you have made astonishing allegations against your wife. You seem willing to believe an African rather than her. I have met your wife. Any distress she is experiencing arises from the vicious assault that she experienced. When I asked her about you, she gave a very negative appraisal of what kind of husband you have been."

"Yes!" exclaimed one of the women in the gallery, "You are a disgrace, sir!"

"Order!" Judge Miles barked. "This is your last chance, ladies. Allow Mr Allen to do his job without interruption."

"I put it to you, Mr James," Mr Allen went on, "that your actions today are motivated by malice and spite towards your wife. I also put it to you that you were not at home when the events which have brought us here took place. So how do you know that the defendant is telling the truth?"

Iolo replied, his temper rising, "Yes, our marriage is not a good one, but I would not lie about something this important. I was not there until it was all over, you are right, but there are others who can confirm that my wife has not been of sound mind for quite some time."

"Ah, that is interesting, Mr James. Nobody else has come forward to give evidence about your wife's mental state. There is no doctor's report to back you up. If there were, that might be different, but there is not. We can only conclude that, whatever your motivations, you are not a reliable witness, Mr James."

"I refute your accusation that I am an unreliable witness. And doctors are too scared to provide such a report. Believe me, I have asked," Iolo retorted.

"Ah! So now it is all the fault of doctors!" the lawyer declared, looking at the jury. "No further questions," said a pleased Allen, returning to his seat.

"Thank you, Mr Allen," said the judge. Looking at Iolo who was staring at the floor, all passion spent, he added, "You may leave the stand, Mr James. I find your evidence unconvincing. Members of the jury should ignore it when they withdraw to consider their verdict."

Iolo returned to his seat. He looked wobbly on his feet. A chorus of insults and epithets rained down from upstairs. Michael was shaking his head as Iolo passed by. He couldn't help but admire his former employer, but his overwhelming feeling was one of incomprehension. *This man is addicted to the futile gesture*, thought Michael.

Michael was taken back down to the cells while the jury deliberated. It had taken longer than he'd expected, but soon it would end as it was always going to.

Back in his office after sending the jury out to consider its verdict, Judge Miles poured himself a whisky. Mr Allen had made short work of Iolo James. Had he been right to give him the stand? Having heard his evidence, he was less sure than he had been. He drained the glass in one go.

Chapter Twelve

The jury took an hour, which was longer than usual, but returned the inevitable guilty verdict.

"This has been an unusual case," Judge Miles said, "but in my view, the jury has reached the right decision." The judge sentenced the defendant to ten years in prison with hard labour. Michael looked directly at him as he spoke. The judge felt his hackles rise.

Impudent African, he'd thought to himself after he left the courtroom, more certain than ever that the verdict was a just one. At the last minute, he'd added two years onto his intended sentence to avoid looking soft. He was glad he had. Judge Miles now put the case out of his mind, ignoring the *Bulawayo Chronicle* reporter who tried to waylay him for a comment as he headed for the Club.

Michael was taken down to a holding cell by the policemen due to escort him back to prison. They took the opportunity to rough him up once they were out of sight. "You pervert," said one of them as they punched him in the stomach. "You'll get hell from the prison warders now that you've been sent down. They fucking hate Africans who have violated white women."

"Not only that; you seem to have corrupted that husband to boot. Maybe you violated him too," said another.

Michael said nothing, protecting himself from the blows as best he could.

***

As Iolo left the Court Building, he was accosted by the women from the Rhodesian Women's League who had been providing the running commentary from the gallery. They hurled curses at him as he kept walking.

"Nothing to say," he muttered to the reporter as he approached too, "please leave me alone." He just wanted to get away, to hide from the world. Frank had told him to come round once the trial was over. The children would be there.

Iolo had decided to testify on behalf of Michael at the last minute. Now it was done. Iolo had not thought about the possible consequences when deciding to go ahead, but the reception he had received showed that the future was going to be very difficult for him and the children.

It occurred to Iolo as he drew near the Tindlers' house that they could get dragged into it too. He and the children would not stay long.

"Good luck, Iolo," said Harriet, looking pained and drawn.

"I'll see you tomorrow at work," Frank said, giving him a pat on his shoulder.

As they walked the short distance home, Iolo was conscious of many eyes upon him, but nobody said anything. News of the sensational events that afternoon in the High Court was spreading like wildfire.

Doris was in her room as usual, being attended to by Dr Hastings. "No need to say anything, Mr James, I have heard it all. Your wife, thank goodness, seems oblivious. But now the trial is over, there is no time to waste. She needs expert medical attention which can only be found in South Africa if she is to pull through. I have managed to reduce her addiction to Luminal, but she has substituted alcohol for the pills she can no longer obtain. Let us talk about it tomorrow."

Iolo's thoughts were elsewhere. He could not think as far ahead as tomorrow.

***

The Rhodesian Women's League delegates had gone their separate ways after speaking with the reporter outside the Court Building. But there was unfinished business. Mrs Gronyer, the deputy chair of the Bulawayo branch, and Mrs Tate, its welfare officer, had agreed before they parted that Mrs James should be offered urgent refuge from that disgraceful husband of hers.

She and the children could stay with one of their members – several had large houses that could comfortably accommodate the three of them for a while. It could all be organised and carried out tomorrow. Time was of the essence.

Mrs Harper, another member of the delegation, agreed with the plan, but her thoughts had turned to punishment. Her blood was running hot; Iolo had to pay for what he had done.

Violet Harper was a married woman in her twenties who worked in the bar at the Empire, Bulawayo's main cinema. She had no children yet, but she was sure it would not be long. She'd joined the Women's League because of her concerns about the Black Peril. It was a good organisation, but sometimes she found it somewhat staid, rather too preoccupied with respectability.

The case of Sam Lewis in 1911, when she was twelve, had been formative for Violet. Two of Lewis's daughters had allegedly been propositioned by an African newspaper delivery man. Although she was not friends with them, she'd known the girls.

Lewis had reacted by taking his daughters to the offices of the *Bulawayo Chronicle* and asking them to identify the man. After they did, Lewis took him out into an alleyway and shot him dead. Lewis subsequently faced two trials. The first ended in a hung jury. In the second, the jury declared him innocent.

Violet also recalled a horrible case in Umtali the year before, in 1910, when the Colonial Office in London intervened to save an African from the gallows. The authorities had even had the gall to claim that Black Peril cases were infrequent, which every right-thinking white person knew was untrue. Although, she had to admit, there had been fewer cases in recent years.

When she'd asked her father about the Sam Lewis case, he had told her proudly, "Lewis is a hero. The justice system keeps failing us. By taking the action he did, he made everybody that little bit safer."

The Lewis case showed that direct action was sometimes necessary. And what Iolo James had done was utterly unconscionable. Violet was going to make sure he wouldn't get away with it.

Violet had a work shift to go to. She hurried to the Empire straight from the Court Building. She'd agreed to cover the last few hours for a colleague who needed to leave early. There was a queue of customers buying tickets for the films on show that evening: *Every Woman's Husband*, *The Great Gamble* and *The Final Episode*.

She went through the foyer and up the stairs to the bar. It was quiet. But sitting there, nursing a beer, was her husband, Cedric Harper. He often dropped in to see his wife at work. They greeted each other with kisses on the cheek. "How did it go in court, darling?"

She brought him up to speed, revelling in her own outrage. She ended her tale by telling him, "He must be made to pay, Cedric!"

"Too right!" he replied. "And I know how, Violet. There is a well-known instrument of people's justice: tarring and feathering."

"Leave it with me," he went on. "I'm meeting friends at the Exchange bar in half-an-hour. I'll recruit some people. We'll buy the stuff we need and swing round at nine to pick you up after work." He downed the rest of his drink in one go and dashed off, a manifest destiny to fulfil.

Cedric Harper was as good as his word. He returned to the Empire at eight thirty pm with seven other men. They'd purchased a bucket of tar and a bag of wool – they hadn't been able to find feathers anywhere – from an Indian store near the location and left it behind the bins down the side of the cinema. The group stayed for several more drinks while Violet finished her shift. Their collective exuberance only grew.

One of the men, Llewellyn Graaf, declared, grinning, that they had formed a citizens' vigilance committee to do what the stuffed shirts were afraid to do. Another, Leo Arunsen, upped the ante, saying that they were more like the Committee for Public Safety, about to unleash a reign of terror against its enemies.

Violet kept them all supplied with alcohol, enjoying the bragging. *These are proper men*, she thought. *They'll not shy away.* At nine on the dot, Cedric Harper, the self-appointed group leader, brought the group to attention.

"Right men! Violet is off work now. Let's get going. We need to find a couple of taxis to take us round to James's house on Lobengula Street. None of us are sober enough to drive our own vehicles."

There were several taxis outside waiting for cinemagoers after the films finished. After some haggling, three were hired. Two of the drivers seemed eager to play their part in the drama. One of them appeared to be acting under duress. Cedric and Llewellyn lifted the bucket of tar into the back of one of the taxis. "Quick, come on," shouted Llewellyn.

The drive to the James residence did not take long. Iolo was putting the children to bed when he heard the sound of cars outside, doors opening and shutting. He could tell there were several people. Retribution was coming more quickly than he'd expected. He thought back to the dignity Michael had shown in the dock. He would try to do the same. "Stay in your rooms, I'll see who it is," said Iolo. He took a deep breath and headed towards the front door.

"Come outside Mr James," called out Violet, "there is some business that I wish to discuss with you!" Iolo edged apprehensively outside. "What do you want?" he asked.

The men cheered. "Here he is! The traitor, the renegade, the madman James!" cried one of the taxi drivers, Vincent Hammond.

From someone in the small crowd came the shout, "It's Monkey Nut!"

"You are coming with us, Mr James," pronounced Violet. "I am Violet Harper of the Empire and we are here to tar and feather you."

Iolo recognised her from outside the Court Building. He felt his courage deserting him. He could hear his children crying. They had come out to see what was happening. "Please leave now, before I call the police," he said, with as much authority as he could muster. In the corner of his eye, he saw his neighbour, Henry Livermore, looking on. "Henry, please go and alert the police," he asked.

"No, stay where you are, sir! We are here to dispense justice," said Cedric Harper.

Livermore did not move. His wife approached Iolo's children and tried to take them inside. They resisted, wriggling out of her grasp.

For a moment, nobody moved or said anything. Then everything began to happen quickly. Three men grabbed hold of Iolo and tried to pull him into one of the taxis. Iolo fought back but it was hopeless.

He found himself being dragged along the ground, face down. His false teeth were knocked out but he managed to grab them. He could feel blood flowing from cuts and grazes. Somebody picked him up and bundled him into Hammond's taxi.

Two men sat either side of him, with another on his knees to pin him down as the vehicle drew away. Mervyn ran towards the car, screaming "Let my father go!"

Doris, who had come out of her room unnoticed to see what was happening, shouted out, "No! Mervyn!" The boy got a foot onto the footboard of the car but one of the attackers kicked out at him, forcing him off.

The two other cars followed close behind. The convoy made its way to Market Square. Iolo made several attempts to yell out as they went past pedestrians, but Arunsen, the man sitting on him, put his hand over Iolo's mouth. "Maybe we should just lynch you," he spat. "You deserve it."

Violet, sitting next to him, jabbed a finger in Iolo's direction, "You are going to pay for taking a kaffir's word over your wife's."

"That African is worth a thousand of you lot," Iolo replied, forgetting his terror for a moment. Violet hit him hard in the face with a brush.

They reached Market Square; Iolo was hauled out of the taxi. "Stand straight!" Cedric ordered him. "Violet, pass sentence!"

Violet adopted a severe tone. "Iolo James, you have been found guilty of taking the word of an African against your wife. You are nothing but a white kaffir. Administer the appropriate punishment!"

Iolo felt numerous hands on his body. They were taking off his clothes. Soon he only had a shirt and his underwear on. Then came a warm, claggy sensation. Tar was being lathered on. His skin stung. "Not on his face!" he heard somebody cry out. His eyes were tightly closed. Then, wool was thrown over him.

It was all over in moments. "Quick, finish, I think I saw a policeman!" said somebody.

Another man shouted, "Let's get out of here!"

Iolo heard car engines and slamming doors. His attackers were gone.

When he opened his eyes, he saw tar and a downy layer of wool unevenly distributed over most of his body. His face was completely uncovered, his left leg too. He tried to move his limbs. He felt heavy, weighed down. Putting one foot in front of the other hurt. But he persisted, generating some forward momentum.

He walked slowly out of Market Square, towards the nearby police station. His whole body throbbed. He could hear sobs coming from somewhere. Then he realised that it was he who was crying.

***

Sergeant Sheppey heard the doors of the police station swing open. In the middle of recording the details of an Italian man who had just been thrown in the cells for drunk and disorderly behaviour, he did not look up from his book. "Come up to the desk please. I'll be with you in a moment," he declared in a deep voice.

171

Sheppey's senses were suddenly overwhelmed by the powerful, acrid odour accompanying the new arrival. He was impelled to look up before he had finished the job in hand. What he saw was a sorry specimen. A shortish white man, unclothed, covered in a substance he could not identify, moaning and crying softly.

"My God! What in God's name has happened to you?" The man's face looked familiar, but his name eluded him. The man stammered in response as he approached the desk, limping. It was impossible to make out what he was saying.

Sheppey realised that the man needed a chair and perhaps something to drink. "Here, sit down, man. I'll get you a glass of water," he said in a soothing voice. "Then, when you are ready, you can tell me what the devil has happened to you."

The station was quiet, so Sheppey was happy to give the man time and space to recover. It was a full twenty minutes before Iolo could talk. The sergeant said little as he listened. By now he'd realised that this was Iolo James, the man whose extraordinary behaviour in court earlier the same day had been the talk of the town.

Sheppey could not pretend to understand what had made the man act so foolishly, but he had no time for those who took the law into their own hands. If Mr James was telling the truth, a group of white vigilantes had assaulted him and had to be punished. He was aware that the majority of his fellow officers would probably take a different view. But he would see to it that this offence was investigated in a proper manner.

"So, what were the names of the men who did this to you, Mr James?" Sheppey asked. Let's make a full list."

"I don't know many of them by name," Iolo said, still stammering a bit but calmer now. "There was one woman too, you know. She was called Violet Harper. Her husband, Cedric I think his name is, was the ringleader."

Eventually, Iolo came up with three other names he remembered hearing in the taxi. "OK, Mr James, thank you. That'll do for now." He gestured to a colleague. "Corporal Trapido here will help get some of that tar and other stuff off you and give you some clothing to put on. Then we need to get you home to your children. They must be worried sick."

Iolo trudged off with the corporal towards a nearby bathroom. Within minutes the police station was filled with his cries and curses – the tar was so painful to remove.

Iolo was accompanied home at three o'clock in the morning. The children were not there. Mr Livermore came out when he heard the police car draw up. "They are asleep in our house," he told Corporal Trapido. "It took an age to get them to calm down and it might be better not to disturb them at this time."

"Is that OK, Mr James?" Trapido asked him. Iolo nodded in assent, saying "good night" as he entered the house.

Trapido looked on as he disappeared inside and then, remembering his duties, shouted to Iolo, "We'll be back tomorrow morning to take a proper statement, Mr James. Please make sure you are available."

Iolo waved a hand in acknowledgement but did not turn around. He lay down on the sofa. Tiredness overwhelmed him and he lost consciousness.

He was abruptly awoken three hours later by the children. Iolo still had bits of tar on his arms and looked a sorry sight. Mervyn was silent and subdued but Gwerfyl burst into tears. He somehow found the energy to comfort them.

Mrs Livermore had brought them over. "They would not wait any longer, Mr James," she said, refusing to look him in the eye. She could not wait to leave. "I am very sorry for your misfortune, but please do not ask us to do anything more for you," she added as she withdrew. "I know the Tindlers are your friends, so my

173

husband has gone to inform them about events. That is as far as we are willing to go," Mrs Livermore finished, already out of the house, her voice fading into the distance.

Frank Tindler arrived a few moments later. He told the children to go over to Auntie Harriet straight away, where breakfast was waiting, and not to worry about dad – he would take care of him. They hesitated but Iolo reassured them, "Yes, go over. I'll see you there later. Don't worry. Uncle Frank is here now." Gwerfyl planted a kiss on Iolo's cheek and then ran off after her brother.

Frank and Iolo looked at each other. "Bloody hell, Iolo," Frank said with a weary expression. "Let me make us a cup of tea. Then we can talk."

He went into the kitchen, where he bumped into Doris, standing wraith-like at the sink, a bottle in her hand. She did not acknowledge Frank. Instead, she brushed past him and back into the bedroom, closing the door behind her.

***

The next couple of days were a blur for Iolo. One or two events imprinted themselves on his mind, but no more. He remembered the police coming and taking another statement. They would be charging his attackers with assault, they told him. A trial date would be arranged.

He remembered Frank and Harriet coming and going, sometimes with the children in tow. He remembered encountering Doris a couple of times around the house. They did not speak. Then she left with Dr Hastings and a couple of what had looked like medical orderlies.

Iolo remembered signing something, but what it was about, he could not for the life of him recall. He remembered returning to work after a few days, accompanied by Frank. Nobody talked to him but he didn't care. The job did not require much thought and it was a relief to be distracted.

A week after the traumatic episode in Market Square, Iolo began to exit this fugue state. The abrasions to his body, which a brusque doctor at the Memorial Hospital had declared on inspection were "in no way injurious to human life", were also healing. Iolo could see the children relaxing a bit. They returned home to sleep overnight. Frank and Harriet continued to provide them all with meals, for which he was grateful. A precarious normality reasserted itself. However, Iolo still felt an underlying deep unease.

Then, after work one day Frank asked him, "Do you know what has happened to Doris, Iolo? You haven't uttered a word on the subject since she left and there are moments when I wonder."

Iolo looked at him and replied, "Now you mention it, I don't – not really, anyway. I signed something for Dr Hastings but in truth I wasn't really taking much of what he said in."

Frank gulped. "Ah, I feared as much. She has been sectioned, Iolo. She is in Ingutsheni Lunatic Asylum. In due course, she is going down south for treatment. You gave permission."

Ingutsheni was on the southern edge of Bulawayo, quite near Raylton.

Iolo gasped, shaken. "Did I? How could I do that and not remember? She must be so scared. The children will never understand. My god, I truly am a monster."

He broke down. For half an hour he was speechless, bent double in his chair, repeating the same phrase again and again, "I did this to her… I did this to her… I did this to her." Frank could only sit there, stricken, staring at the floor.

Eventually, Iolo cried himself out and, calmer, he raised himself up and gazed at Frank. "I will have this on my conscience to the end of my days, Frank. I've been such a poor husband. She must curse the day she met me. I don't know how, but I've got to atone for what I have done to her." His friend returned his gaze but said nothing.

***

Bulawayo, March 1923

Everywhere Violet Harper went, she was met with embraces and handshakes. She and her fellow partners in crime were local celebrities. There were drinks on the house at bars and discounts in the shops.

Rumours that James Donald MacKenzie, the outgoing Attorney-General, was considering reviewing the ten-year sentence imposed by Judge Miles on Mrs James's African domestic servant hardened sentiment in favour of the gang of vigilantes. The rumours turned out to be false.

Their plan to offer Doris and the children safe refuge curtailed by her sudden and unexplained disappearance, the Rhodesian Women's League turned its attention to Violet. It issued a public statement commending her actions and began campaigning for the charges against her to be dropped.

Her husband, Cedric, was offered a pay rise by his boss at the garage on 3rd Avenue, where he had worked for several years – for services to the white population of Southern Rhodesia, he was told.

But beneath the euphoria and triumphalism, there was some anxiety. The co-conspirators could go to prison; assault was a serious offence. The trial was due to start on the sixth of March. Their lawyer told them to plead not guilty, not because anybody would believe them, but because it would then allow him to play to the court of public opinion.

Iolo grew ever tenser as the day approached. Sleep was not easy. When he awoke, he already felt exhausted. Frank had signed him off from work until it was all over and said that he would walk with him to court on the first day. Iolo was grateful for this act of solidarity.

The day of the trial arrived. Harriet brought over some breakfast for him and the children but he couldn't eat anything. Mervyn and Gwerfyl then left for school. Mervyn, who had always been a quiet, thoughtful boy, was sullen. It broke Iolo's heart to see him so cast down.

Mervyn insisted on giving evidence in person against his father's wishes, but Iolo's lawyer, another friend of Frank's, said that Mervyn's testimony would strengthen the case against his attackers.

"Come on, Iolo," said Frank. "It's time to go."

As soon as they got to the bigger streets where there were more people, the shouts and catcalling began. When they approached the High Court building, they found a large crowd had gathered to support the defendants. They pushed through the melee, trying to ignore the abuse being hurled in Iolo's direction. A few reporters blocked their path, barking out questions, but they rushed past and into the building, where the atmosphere was calmer.

Court officials directed them to seats near the doors to the court. As they sat down, there was a loud roar outside before the doors swung open and the seven defendants came through. Several were laughing, faces flushed.

Cedric Harper saw Iolo and Frank and gestured in their direction. "It is you who is on trial today, James. Just listen to how much support we have out there!"

After five minutes, Iolo was called in. Frank tried to give him some reassurance. "It will be fine, Iolo. Good luck, Harriet and I are on your side. I'll drop by this evening to see how it went."

Iolo's smile was weak and watery. "Thanks," he replied.

As Iolo entered the court, he looked around. It was packed. The Rhodesian Women's League was in force again in the public gallery, from where there were hisses as he was shown to his place. He glanced to his right and saw the defendants in the dock, still chatting and smiling as if they were on a day trip. Then a court official declared, "All rise," and Justice Ernest Wright entered and took his seat.

The jury filed in. None of them looked in his direction. The proceedings began with a statement by the Solicitor-General, Mr George Cooper, for the Crown, dropping the charges against Violet Harper.

"It is unfitting for a young European woman to be before a British court of law in a case of this sort," said the lawyer. "There is insufficient evidence that she applied any tar or wool to the plaintiff and so should not be viewed as involved in the assault."

This announcement was met with a deafening cheer from the gallery. Violet, who could hardly believe her luck, waved at all and sundry as she left the dock, reappearing moments later in the gallery next to her friends, who applauded as she took her seat.

Once order had been restored, the Solicitor-General began questioning the remaining defendants, who now abandoned their festive air and took on serious expressions as they replied. Clearly, they had been told to show respect for the court.

While the Solicitor-General focused on establishing the facts, the defendants kept trying to inject observations about how outraged they had been in the first trial by what James had done to his wife. Iolo felt the Crown was allowing them excessive latitude but was in no way surprised. He knew, as Michael had done, that he was already the guilty party in this society.

The court adjourned in mid-afternoon. Iolo fought his way through the throng outside and hurried home. He was very tired, but managed to put on a show for the children when they got back from school. Frank, as promised, came by for a while. There wasn't much to say.

"I'll walk with you again tomorrow morning," Frank told Iolo. "Tomorrow is you and Mervyn's big day."

Iolo gave a hollow laugh.

Mervyn, who had joined them in the sitting room, said to his father, "We're going to show them tomorrow, Dad, you'll see."

"Good lad," said Frank, giving Mervyn an affectionate hug.

***

Extracts from "Tar and feather case result", published in the Bulawayo Chronicle, 8th March 1923
The final chapter of what has come to be known as the tar and feather case was heard in the High Court yesterday before Mr Justice Wright and a jury.

Three defendants who had acted as taxi drivers were found not guilty and were discharged. The jury returned a verdict of guilty against Harper, Arunsen, Doran and Graaf, but recommended that they be dealt with leniently. His Lordship fined them each £25, with the alternative of two months' imprisonment, but said that, if it had not been for the jury's recommendation, they would have gone to prison. The charge against Mrs Harper was withdrawn by the Solicitor-General [...]

[...] Mr Advocate Watson (for the defendants): The original case last January was fully reported in the Bulawayo Chronicle?
James: No.
Mr Watson: Was it reported?
James: Yes, but it was only a very meagre report.
James later made certain allegations against his wife but was told by His Lordship to confine himself to answering counsel's questions.
Mr Watson commenced to question the witness about a pet rooster.

His Lordship: Is this supposed to be comic relief, or to affect the jury?

Mr Watson: It is to show the complainant's character, my lord.

The judge commented that it did not throw much light on the case before the court and Mr Watson abandoned the cross-examination about the rooster.

James declared that Mrs Harper had said in the car she was prepared to do time for him and denied that he said anything even resembling that he would sooner take an African's word than his wife's.

Mr Watson: But you did in this case?

James: I did not take the African's word in this case. I went by other circumstances [...]

[...] James: I was told near my house that I would be lynched.

Watson: Are you being serious, Mr James?

James: I am very serious. I fully made up my mind to it and resigned myself to death. I did not hear anyone say no violence was to be used. It didn't look like it, pulling me along the ground. And the physical injury was nothing in comparison to the mental agony.

Jury Man: Did you think you had given provocation sufficient for them to lynch you?

James: I was not conscious of having given any provocation [...]

[...] Complainant's son, Mervyn, stated he saw his father seized by a number of men and put into the motor car.

Mervyn: I got on the motor car and someone pushed me off. My father was dragged about 50 yards.

The boy broke into tears in the witness box and was unable to finish his testimony [...]

[....] Addressing the jury, the Solicitor-General contrasted the control which had been shown by the public in a very serious recent

assault by an African on a European woman with the attitude alleged to have been taken up in the present case by the accused.

Mr Watson laid stress on the attitude the complainant had adopted in the High Court in January in connection with an African found guilty of sexually assaulting his wife. That case was published in the paper, and whether or not a full report was published, the main facts, which are the only facts necessary to consider, were correctly published. In view of the position of white women in this country, counsel submitted that there had been provocation for the assault on James [...]

[...] In the course of his summing up, His Lordship said that the jury's most difficult task would be to try and put out of their minds any ideas they might have had on the case, anything they might have discussed with their friends or read in the papers, and any opinions they might have formed before the came into the court. It was the jury's duty to judge the case before them on the evidence before the court. The question was really a very simple question, whether the accused were guilty or not of taking part in the assault on James.

His Lordship: There is always a danger when people take the law into their own hands that it will not end there. Where people are apt to take the law into their own hands is where the people think the courts of justice are not strong enough or fair enough to do justice.

No legal defence or legal provocation had been proved for the assault, said His Lordship later, and reviewing the evidence against the three men who drove taxis, he agreed with Mr Watson that there was very little evidence to go on [...]

[...] The jury considered their evidence for nearly half an hour, and on their return at 4.30 pm, the foreman announced they found Harper, Doran, Arunsen and Graaf guilty of assault under great *provocation. The jury strongly recommended that they be treated very leniently [...]*

[...] *His Lordship: You have been found guilty by the jury of an assault on James, and as you apparently imagine that manual violence is the way in which people should be treated, I should have, but for the recommendation of the jury, made perfectly sure that you would have gone to prison, even for a short time, that you might have tasted some of the disgrace and mental suffering you have made Mr James taste. I should very much like to have made you taste it yourselves. Owing to the recommendation of the jury, however, I will give you the opportunity of paying a fine.*

The lenient sentence prompted wild cheering in the public gallery. The trial ended at 4.45 pm.

***

Editorial, Bulawayo Chronicle, 9th March 1923

The extraordinary Tar and Feather case reached its conclusion in the High Court two days ago. Justice Wright found four of the defendants guilty but, responding somewhat reluctantly to the plea of the jury to show leniency, he saw fit to give them the option of paying a fine instead of serving time in prison.

The evening after the verdict, a packed public meeting was convened by the Rhodesian Women's League at which an appeal for funds towards the cost of the fines was launched. Within 24 hours, the full amount of £100 was raised.

We have received letters criticising our coverage of the case. We have been accused of forgetting that the real victim of this whole unedifying episode was his wife. This is unfair. The husband should not have acted the way he did. Equally, his attackers went too far. Hopefully, everybody can agree that there should be no further assaults of this nature, nor any incidents that can be construed by anyone as justification for such action.

Chapter Thirteen

Bulawayo, July 1923

Doris had barely slept. The cries and screams from the African wards had gone on all night.

Ingutsheni Lunatic Asylum was established in 1908 to warehouse individuals certified as insane and dangerous, either to themselves or others. Harmless lunatics were usually allowed to remain with their families. Prior to its creation, lunatics had been sent to South African asylums at great cost or had mouldered in prison cells, forgotten and neglected by society.

Africans called the asylum *Enhlanyeni*, the place of mad people. The asylum was initially intended for African men only and not for Europeans, particularly not European women, for whom it was deemed an entirely unsuitable place.

But African women and Europeans were soon, for lack of alternatives, being housed there too. The small number of

European women sent to it were considered temporary inmates who, wherever possible, were to be sent south for treatment.

Many of the Europeans who ended up there were poor, but racial boundaries were nonetheless rigidly maintained. Europeans and Africans were placed in different wards. They ate different food. The African inmates were required to work, but the Europeans were not. They were also subject to different therapeutic treatments, insofar as any were attempted.

When things were peaceful, the asylum's inmates could hear, in the distance, the clanging of the railway yards and the hubbub from the closed compounds which housed the African workers.

The asylum had a dairy herd and some farmland. It was also experimenting with growing cotton. Doris liked listening to the sedate lowing of the cattle. It calmed her.

Despite not being formally admitted as a patient, Ingutsheni had been Doris's home for four months now. She felt contented these days, but during her first weeks, she had been anything but.

It had been a period of enforced detoxification. No pills, no alcohol, nothing. She had only the vaguest memories of that time. Constant seizures, fever, delirium, weeping and pleading for somebody, or something – anything – to take away the pain.

The mainly male European attendants, known as keepers, kept her in a locked room, opening the door only to pass her food and water, which she barely touched. Occasionally, they had to force-feed her.

At first, she had paced around the boundaries of her tiny room obsessively, shouting insults at her captors whenever they passed by. They ignored her.

Every so often, a number of other European men would come by, spend five minutes or so observing her through the grill and then depart. Among them were the Assistant Superintendent, Mr

Smeaton, and the Head Attendant, Mr Warren. The others, she came to realise, were doctors.

After a week or so, torpor descended. She spent hours lying on the thin mattress in the corner of her room, staring at the ceiling and sleeping. The seizures were less common now, afflicting her every day or so.

She retreated into a dreamworld. There, she had all sorts of adventures. The thing she enjoyed most were the recurring conversations with her father. At some level, she knew he was dead, but he felt alive to her as they talked. His presence bathed her in love. She had always been a daddy's girl and his death during the Kimberley siege had left her bereft.

Their discussions centred around what had gone wrong with her life. He was full of good advice, as ever, although the precise details eluded her when she tried to recall them afterwards. Her favourite moments with him were when he embraced her. She could sense his warmth and he would whisper endearments in her ear which filled her soul with joy.

Sometimes in the background, as they talked, she could hear the voices of children, calling to her. They would say things like, "Mother, mother, we're hungry" or "Look, look, mother!" She had no idea who these children were. She tried to ignore them, but it wasn't always easy.

One of the European doctors began visiting and trying to talk to her. She refused to reply. He was interrupting her. Then one day, he came into her room with a couple of keepers and a chair. They put the chair down and they tried to lift her onto the seat. At first she resisted, but they overpowered her and manoeuvred her limp body onto the seat, propping her up by holding her shoulders back.

The doctor placed his hand on her chin and raised her head. Doris could hear what he was saying, but she kept her eyes firmly shut.

"Doris, can you hear me? How are you feeling, Doris? I want you to say something to me." She did not respond.

The doctor eventually gave up and she was returned to her mattress. Doris was relieved. She had won. Now, where was her father?

But they kept coming back. The same ritual. Her irritation grew. Couldn't they see she just wanted to be left alone? She ignored them, keeping her eyes closed every time. Then, after several days of stand-off, the doctor said something that forced a reaction from her. "Doris, you must come around. Your father wants you to."

Her eyes burst open. Looking directly at the doctor, she screamed, "What do you know about my father? He is none of your business."

"You talk to him all day, Doris," the doctor said, "We can hear you."

She hadn't realised that some of her conversations with her father had been out loud.

The exchange wrenched her back into the real world. From that day onwards, she started surfacing. The conversations with her father continued, but she now took care to make sure they only took place in her head. She began to eat and drink too, although not much.

Once a day, the keepers let her out of her room, walking with her to the toilets or into the exercise area. As she shuffled along, she could see other inmates, Africans, through a dirty window. She could not make out whether they were indoors or outside. The conditions looked filthy.

There was a mirror in the toilets. When she was ready to look into it, what she saw was hard to recognise. Grey, unkempt hair. Grey, lined skin. Hollow eyes. "How can that be me?" she asked herself.

Several days later, she was moved to a different room. It had a proper bed. There was a painting of the Victoria Falls on the wall. The door of the room was left unlocked. Soon after the move, the doctor, whose name she learnt was Arthur Newsome, started to hold short sessions with Doris in his consulting room.

He was friendly and pleasant enough in his manner. He explained to her why she was here. Dr Hastings and her husband had thought it was best. She had been drinking herself to death and had begun to wander the streets of Bulawayo day and night in a state of total inebriation. She needed help, so here she was.

"Where is here?" she had asked after the doctor had said the same thing several times.

"It is called Ingutsheni," he explained. "You will be here until you are well enough to go to South Africa for proper treatment."

Doris came to enjoy her daily sessions. She looked forward to her time with the nice doctor. He spoke much more than she did. He talked about his background and his family. When he asked her questions about her life, she talked about nothing other than her father. He smiled in response, but she could detect discomfort and concern on his face.

At other times he talked medical talk. He had ideas about what had caused her condition. She did not pay much attention to them. She was feeling better. Her physical strength was increasing. Her body felt more robust. Her mood was better. If she could just stop having the seizures, she thought, she'd be fine.

Then, one day, as she entered Dr Newsome's consulting room, she saw that there was another man there, with whom she was not familiar.

"You have a visitor, Doris. It's your husband, Iolo. He's been asking to see you for some time and I think that you are now well enough. Go on, say hello."

Newsome watched Doris's expression change from equanimity to puzzlement. "My husband? But I don't have a husband," she replied. "My father died in the Kimberley siege before I could find a suitable match. Nobody would have me after that."

She could see a look of shock on the face of the strange man. She was taken back to her room. Doris was unconcerned. "That was a funny episode," she said to herself. Within minutes, another seizure took hold of her. Once she had recovered, she resumed her conversations with her father.

***

Iolo regathered himself and turned to Dr Newsome, "Can she really not know who I am?"

"I am afraid so, Mr James. She hasn't spoken about you or the children at all. I thought your visit might prompt her memory. Clearly, I was wrong. But it may only be a temporary state of affairs. Let's hope so. I suggest you come back again in a week's time. Between now and then I will work on helping her to remember. But one way or another, Doris must leave soon. She doesn't belong here."

Iolo thanked the doctor for his time and efforts and was escorted out of the asylum by one of the keepers. The shouts and screams he could hear as he walked out were spine-chilling. What a god-forsaken place, he thought to himself.

The European populace in Bulawayo knew about Ingutsheni, but it never gave the place much thought. It was close by and yet a million miles away, out of sight and out of mind. Iolo had been no different in his thinking. Until now. He shuddered. The doctor was right; the sooner Doris was out of there, the better.

Iolo made several more visits to the asylum over the weeks that followed. Every time he was met with blank indifference by Doris.

***

Dr Newsome was not just one of the doctors at Ingutsheni; he was the superintendent, the man in day-to-day charge. He was a recent arrival to the colony who had trained at Cambridge under W.H.R. Rivers. When the veteran Medical Director for Southern Rhodesia, Andrew Fleming, contacted Rivers to ask for suggestions for the vacant role, Newsome's was one of the names mentioned.

Rivers described Newsome to Fleming as a modern man who had been exposed to some of the new thinking in psychology, including the Austrian, Sigmund Freud. Rivers was sceptical about some of Freud's ideas, but strongly endorsed his underlying proposition that madness could sometimes be amenable to treatment and should be treated as a health issue.

Fleming was also open to such approaches. He visited London in early 1922 and interviewed several candidates. Newsome was appointed.

Almost from the moment he'd arrived at Ingutsheni, Newsome found himself embroiled in fierce battles with the European staff over the merits of a more progressive approach to treating the clinically insane. For the rest of his colleagues, the primary purpose of Ingutsheni remained incarceration, keeping the European community safe rather than rehabilitation. "The African mind is a mystery to himself, let alone to Europeans. No point trying to make sense of it. Most of his problems come down to Syphilis, witchcraft and smoking marijuana," Assistant Superintendent Smeaton had informed him on his first day.

Newsome did not agree. He had read Freud's *Totem and Taboo*, which argued that the psychic problems of primitive peoples were no less amenable to treatment than those of civilised ones. Newsome did not like Freud's use of the term primitive, but he agreed that, in all human beings, mental anguish manifested in physical symptoms such as convulsions, epilepsy and amnesia. This was because traumatic memories were being buried, rather than confronted.

However, neither Fleming, nor his deputy, William Eaton, were able to give him much support in his battles with the staff at Ingutsheni. Newsome had come to realise that it would be next to impossible to provide any meaningful treatment for the African inmates.

He faced less internal resistance from asylum staff in trying out new therapeutic ideas on European patients. In the course of his many sessions with her, he developed several hypotheses about what was wrong with Doris, including why she did not, or at some level, refused, to recognise Iolo.

A few weeks after Doris was admitted, Newsome sent a telegram to Wulf Sachs, a fellow enthusiast for Freud who he'd got to know in London, asking him to take her on as a patient. Sachs had emigrated with his family to South Africa in 1922. He was working as a general practitioner in Johannesburg, but Newsome knew that he was keen to undertake more psychology practice, with a view to setting up his own clinic.

There was not much space for exposition in the telegram. All Newsome could say was that Doris was a "very interesting case" and would hopefully be well enough to travel soon. Sachs was quick to reply that he had confidence in Newsome's assessment that he could help and would be happy to take her on. Newsome promised Sachs that he would put a detailed assessment down in writing, to arrive with the patient.

When Newsome told Iolo that he had found somebody good to treat Doris in South Africa, he was delighted. Iolo emphasised that money was no object, he just wanted the best for her.

Nevertheless, he felt sick when he found out how much Sachs would be charging. It would be nearly a third of his monthly wage.

"I strongly recommend him, Mr James," said Dr Newsome. "I am sure you would be able to pay in instalments over an extended period if your financial situation demanded."

"That would help," replied Iolo. "I am no plutocrat," adding "Doris has longstanding friends in Johannesburg." He was referring to the Mackenzies, with whom he and Doris had stayed on their way to and from Tolstoy Farm more than a decade earlier. "I'll ask if they can offer her lodgings while she is being treated."

"That sounds perfect, Mr James," said Newsome, smiling. Reverting to a business-like tone, he asked, "The question is, how do we get Doris there? She does not see you as her husband, so persuading her to go with you could be tricky. There is also the problem of her continuing seizures. I suggest that you take one of our keepers on the journey to ensure that she is compliant. I have one in mind, he is reliable and experienced. We wouldn't charge you too much for it." Iolo assented, relieved that he would not be on his own with Doris.

Frank and Harriet agreed to look after Mervyn and Gwerfyl while Iolo was away. The day of departure arrived. It was a bitterly cold July morning when Iolo, Doris and the keeper seconded to the party, Walter Messiter, were picked up from Ingutsheni and driven to the railway station by Frank, who was keen to show off his first car, a Morris.

Doris had been anxious about travelling with the strange man who kept coming to see her, but she was reassured to hear that Walter was coming too. In his forties, Walter towered over everybody at six-foot five, but had a calm and gentle demeanour. He had been kind to her. She was pleased when Walter told her that they'd be passing through her hometown, Kimberley, on their way to Johannesburg.

When they got to the railway station, Harriet was waiting at the entrance with Mervyn and Gwerfyl. Iolo had agonised over whether the children should be allowed to see their mother before she left, before deciding that it would be unfair to deny them the opportunity.

Iolo had talked to Mervyn. Gwerfyl, now nine years old, was still too young to make much sense of it all. Mervyn said that, however difficult it might be, they should see their mother. How he had matured over the past year, Iolo thought. Besides, Mervyn added, seeing them might jog her memory. That helped to persuade Iolo.

Mervyn stepped forward tentatively, Gwerfyl under one arm, half-hiding. "Hello mother," he whispered, his voice wavering.

Doris looked around before realising it was her that the boy was addressing. "I'm very sorry," she said, a kind expression on her face, "but I think you have the wrong person. I'm not your mother."

Gwerfyl cried out and ran back into Harriet's arms. Mervyn stood his ground, trying to maintain his composure, but could not hold back from replying, "Well, it's true that you have been no mother to us for a long time. Perhaps you are right!"

Iolo put a hand on Mervyn's shoulder, ushering him away. "OK, Mervyn," he murmured. "Let's hope that she returns to us restored from Cape Town. Don't give up on her." Mervyn was too downcast to speak. "Take care of your sister, Mervyn," Iolo went on. "I'll be back in a few weeks, once your mother has settled in."

"Come on, you two, let's go," said Harriet. "Ice-cream at home."

Gwerfyl cheered up in an instant and rushed back to the car, shouting "Bye!" to no one in particular. Frank had remained in the driver's seat with the engine idling. Mervyn, disconsolate, followed his sister without looking back.

Iolo looked at Harriet, embarrassed, "Thanks again. I don't know how to repay you and Frank."

"Go on," she replied, gesturing towards the train.

Iolo, Doris and Walter boarded and sat down in their allotted compartment. Walter extracted some pills from his pocket and passed them to Doris. "Take these." She obeyed, as she had grown used to doing at Ingutsheni.

Dr Newsome had given Walter the medicines just before they left the asylum. "The most important pills for the journey are the sedatives, Mr James," Newsome explained. "It will reduce the chances of your wife having a seizure on the train, which could be hard to manage. The pills were more powerful than the ones she'd been on, and she was not to take more than two every four hours.

A few moments later, the train pulled out. They were on their way to Johannesburg. But to what, Iolo was unsure.

***

Extracts from Case Report dated 24th July 1923 by Dr Arthur Newsome – Private and Confidential. Mrs Doris James: For the attention of Dr Wulf Sachs, General Practitioner, Belleville, Johannesburg.

Mrs Doris James was brought to Ingutsheni Lunatic Asylum on 2nd February 1923 by Dr George Hastings, a General Practitioner in Bulawayo, with the consent of her husband, Mr Iolo James. Dr Hastings described a long history of addiction to the drug Luminal on the part of Mrs James, partly replaced by an alcohol addiction when he tried to reduce her intake of the pills. She was suffering from regular physical seizures and mental delusions [...]

[...] Dr Hastings described a troubled marriage between Mr and Mrs James, which had culminated in a court case in January 1923 in

which her husband had testified on behalf of his African domestic servant, disputing her claim that she had been sexually assaulted by said servant [...]

[...] Mrs James suffers from periodic seizures that can last for up to ten minutes. The symptoms resemble epilepsy. Their number has reduced since she arrived. She has one or two a day currently. While her addictions have been sufficiently severe to play a part in triggering her seizures, I am not convinced that they are the whole cause. I consider that there is a psychological dimension [...]

[...] One of Mrs James's delusions is that she is able to converse with her deceased father. These conversations boost her mood. She is unwilling to disclose the contents of those conversations with anybody. Given her fragile state, we have not challenged this delusion.

Another of her delusions is her insistence that she does not have either a husband or children. We have pushed harder in this respect to persuade her that she is wrong, so far without success. Visits by her husband have elicited no apparent recognition [...]

[...] My training does not qualify me to diagnose Mrs James's malaise with absolute confidence. I can only posit a hypothesis which might be worth exploring once she is in your care. This is that the catastrophic and shameful failure of her marriage has led her to wipe it from her conscious mind, along with the children who are its progeny. On the other hand, her conversations with her father bring her a degree of comfort, partially alleviating her mental distress. But this delusion must eventually also be challenged.

Overall, I believe that her mental distress is expressing itself through physical seizures. Reading the newspaper coverage of the two court cases involving her and her husband earlier this year, it appears that this has been a dysfunctional marriage for a long time. It cannot be ruled out that her husband has been violent towards her. Mr James's behaviour has clearly been highly unconventional in the past. He has notions which, to put it mildly, are strongly at variance with the dominant mores of European society. Mr James is not my patient. He appears genuinely concerned for the well-being of his wife. At first sight, he does not manifest any obvious neuroses. For obvious reasons, I have not shared these hypotheses with him [...]

[...] So, to sum up: Has Mrs James perhaps progressively internalised the shame that her husband should be feeling for his conduct? Has doing this now become unbearable, leading her, as far as possible, to bury this powerful part of her life-experience deep inside her unconscious, in the process eradicating her husband and children from her memory? Has her father 'reappeared' to help her make sense of her plight and sooth her distress? Does this trauma manifest in the physical world in the form of her addictive behaviour and seizures? I wish you good luck in disentangling this case. Please keep me informed of your progress.

***

"Drama at Kimberley railway station", Diamond Fields Advertiser, 27th July 1923

Kimberley railway station was the scene of an unexpected drama yesterday when a disturbed European woman travelling south to Cape Town escaped from the custody of her husband and an accompanying warder while their train temporarily stopped at the platform to allow passengers to embark and disembark. The dishevelled woman leapt out of the train shouting, "I'm coming, father!" and ran out of the station. She was pursued by her husband and the warder. Station staff joined in the chase.

After about 100 yards, she was apprehended but then fell to the ground in a fit, where she remained for some time. Our reporter encountered the incident as he was walking to the newspaper office and assisted in returning the lady to the train once her seizure had passed.

A large crowd had gathered by this time. Fortunately for the party, the train had been held on the platform and they were able to resume their journey without delay. When our reporter sought the names of the woman and her husband, the husband declined to give them. All he said was, "Thank you for your assistance. As you can see, my wife is very unwell." Nobody in the crowd recognised them.

Part 4   **Bulawayo, Southern Rhodesia, 1924-45**

Chapter Fourteen

RESTRICTED AND CONFIDENTIAL: The 1945 African railway workers' strike: Private briefing for the Prime Minister (E.G. Howman, 7ᵗʰ November 1945)

You asked for an urgent briefing ahead of tomorrow's Cabinet meeting on the significance of the African railway workers' strike. I hope that it assists you in your preparations for the meeting.

I assess the recent strike by African railway workers to be highly significant. Unless prompt action is taken, it could have a demonstration effect on African workers across the whole country. While external factors may have played some limited part in triggering the industrial action (the election in Britain of a Labour Government/the growing attractiveness of Communist ideas), I consider the strike to be predominantly 'home grown' and non-political in nature.

The strike is the symptom of a wider failure by employers and political authorities to meet the economic, social and health needs of a rapidly growing urban African population.

The view still prevails amongst most Europeans that African men in towns are temporary visitors who should return to their 'homes' in the rural areas once their work contracts are complete; African women and children should not be in towns under any circumstances. This philosophy is dangerously outdated. A substantial number of Africans already consider the towns to be their permanent place of residence. The trend will only accelerate over the years ahead.

In our official report, published last year, on the conditions of Africans in the urban areas, we set out a wide range of welfare measures that should urgently be implemented. They echoed the excellent report, published in 1943, on the survey carried out by the Reverend Percy Ibbotson from the Native Welfare Society.

I urge the Cabinet to revisit *all* the proposals set out in these two reports. I very much hope that Sir Robert Tredgold's current Commission of Inquiry into the causes of the railway strike will also endorse their recommendations. I warmly welcome the decision taken during the strike to establish Native Labour Boards in the main industrial sectors. That is a good start, but much more action is needed.

We have had plenty of advance warning of the coming storm. If some in the Cabinet are not persuaded by humanitarian considerations, perhaps they might be motivated by the possibility that implementing such measures will encourage African trade unionism, which must now be accepted as a reality, to develop in a moderate direction.

There will continue to be strong opposition to the more progressive approach being advocated here from conservative elements within European society, despite the fact that it is very much in their long-term interests too.

In Bulawayo, where the Native problem, as traditionalists misguidedly call it, is perhaps most acute, the railway management and the Municipal Council are particularly backward in their thinking. But these conservative elements must be overridden if the railway strike is not to be the harbinger of existential threats to colonial rule in the future.

I will end by repeating the final paragraph from our report (paragraph 97). I believe that it is more germane than ever:

"The sudden transmutation of a simple tribal people into a modernised industrial community is full of complexity and ugly currents of change; it cannot take place without an abnormal degree of social and personal demoralisation; the disruption of the old is a necessary preliminary to the emergence of the new, but if we see in it the opportunity to stimulate, mould and discipline the slow processes of reorganisation and renewal which are already in action, there is no reason whatsoever that sound, healthy, efficient and prosperous urban African communities should not be built up."

***

Bulawayo, November 1945

The three members of the Commission of Inquiry re-entered the hot and airless room which had been their home for over two weeks. At their head was the chair of the Commission, Sir Robert Tredgold who, until 1943, had served as the colony's Minister of Defence and Justice. When his old boss, the Prime Minister, Sir Godfrey Huggins, asked him to take on the role, he was duty bound to accept.

The Commission was established at the beginning of November, by which time the strike, which had caused widespread consternation within white society, was largely over. It was easily the biggest strike by African workers in the history of Southern

Rhodesia and had caused significant economic disruption. The Commission was expected to complete its business within three weeks. It had taken evidence from many quarters, including from some of the strikers. The strike had spread to Northern Rhodesia and the same panel was also separately investigating the strike there.

Sir Robert was known as a liberal on African matters. In 1934, instructed by Masotsha Ndlovu, the General Secretary of the Industrial and Commercial Workers Union, he had got the municipal by-law forbidding Africans from walking on Bulawayo's pavements struck down by the courts.

Tredgold had been shocked by what he had heard so far about the conditions in which African railway workers were living. By all accounts, their housing was so abominable that he could only wonder at their moderation in calling a strike rather than a rebellion.

The commissioners were under considerable time pressure and were keen to move on to drafting their report. But first there was a last witness to hear from. He had been added to the list late in proceedings. His name was Iolo James. They had never heard of him. They'd been informed that he knew the African workers in the Bulawayo goods sheds, who many thought had been behind the strike.

By this stage of the Commission of Inquiry, the sessions were sparsely attended. There were at most one or two members of the public and a few journalists. But for Iolo James, the audience had filled out again. A large number of Africans had turned up. The members of the Commission could see some of the strikers who had already given evidence sitting at the back of the room.

The door through which the public entered swung open. Through it walked a short man in late middle-age, unremarkable in every respect. He made his way to the desk at the front and sat down opposite the members of the Commission, who were on a raised platform. Some of the Africans at the back shouted out in encouragement.

Sir Robert Tredgold called the session to order. He welcomed Iolo and invited him to make an opening statement after which there would be questions. Iolo looked at the chairman and said, "Thank you, Sir Robert. Yes, I have some remarks prepared, if you and your colleagues will bear with me."

"Proceed, Mr James," replied Sir Robert. "We are keen to finish as soon as possible," he added, his impatience bubbling up. Nervous, Iolo began his statement.

"I was employed in the Bulawayo goods sheds until my retirement in August 1932. From twenty-five years ago, Africans in the goods department have been sending in complaints of their living conditions and applications for better wages. But always the reply came that nothing could be done." There were murmurs of assent from the audience which distracted Iolo for a moment. He lost his place in his notes but soon found it again.

"A lot of times, the Africans would suddenly drop their work and go over to the station and demonstrate in front of the traffic manager's office, making a loud clamour for redress. During the 30 years I was in the goods sheds, until my retirement in 1932, this happened almost every year."

Iolo's mouth was dry but no water had been provided for him. He disliked speaking in public and began to speed up in order to get it over with.

"The traffic manager would send his well-paid African clerk to interview them and convey his reply. It was wrong for the *Bulawayo Chronicle* to suggest that the Africans have not resorted to the usual course in putting forward representations. While it has since corrected that impression, it still owes them an apology. Of course, it has not yet been received. I suppose that kaffirs cannot expect one. I use that word advisedly."

The hum of approval from the audience behind him grew louder. Somebody cried "shame!". Sir Robert intervened, "Mr James, we do not use such words here. Please desist. I presume you are being ironical, but it serves no purpose. You are also digressing. Please stick to the point and bring your statement to a close."

"I apologise, Mr Chairman," Iolo replied. "I have nearly finished. To conclude, contrary to what many of my fellow Europeans before this Commission of Inquiry have said, the African workers on the railways have long had legitimate grievances which have been largely ignored. They are no less entitled to form a Union than we Europeans in search of redress. This strike was justified, and there will be more strikes in future unless the attitude of the railway management changes dramatically. Thank you, Mr Chairman. I am now ready to answer any questions you or your colleagues may have."

Several Africans in the audience stood and applauded loudly. Sir Robert looked on irritably and, after a few moments, exclaimed, "Silence please! Let us move on to questions for Mr James."

As was his prerogative, the first came from Sir Robert. In the course of his answer, Iolo told the chairman about a brief but successful strike by African railway workers in the goods sheds in 1915.

"Is there something different about the African workers in the goods sheds that they should be particularly firm in their demands?" asked Percy Ibbotson, another of the commissioners.

"It has been mentioned that there has always been a kind of wasps' nest among the African workers in the goods sheds," replied Iolo. "It was said, I am led to believe, in the form of a complaint. But these are the best educated Africans on the railways. They have to be or else they will be of little use. Is it not the function of education to create a desire for improved conditions for both body and mind? They are the best workers in Bulawayo."

"In your opinion, what is the biggest complaint of the African strikers, Mr James?" The question was asked by the third member of the Commission, Mr Low.

"I hesitate to speak on their behalf, but I can say that one of their greatest complaints is that they have no kitchens, and the kitchens that are there at the present time have been built mostly by the Africans themselves or by their women folk. To my mind, the cause of this trouble on the railways has been, since I have known it, the failure at all times by the company, or the various general managers and heads of departments, to take any fatherly, let alone motherly, interest in the welfare of the people. Things were much better on the Cape Railways when I worked for it all those years ago."

Sir Robert then asked Iolo, "Do you feel from your experience that they are able to run an Association such as they have commended and that this Association should be recognised?"

Iolo smiled. "Well, it will be after this. They have capable men amongst themselves, and they have taken a lead from the others. I should say, yes."

"Would you say that you have been a champion of the Association?" Mr Low interjected.

"Do you suggest I instigated it?"

"No."

"Until the other Sunday after the strike when they consulted me on what they had done, I had not seen any of them for ten years," said Iolo.

"Have you seen the constitution of the Rhodesia Railways African Employees' Association?" asked Sir Robert.

"No," replied Iolo.

Sir Robert Tredgold frowned at him for a moment before composing a smile and thanking him for his evidence. "This is the last of our public sessions. We will now adjourn to consider the evidence."

There was another round of applause from sections of the audience as the members of the Commission filed out of the room.

Chapter Fifteen

Iolo got up to leave. The journalist from the *Bulawayo Chronicle* approached him, his hand outstretched, to ask some questions, but he waved the man away. He had not spoken to that rag since 1923 and had no intention of ever doing so again.

As he emerged onto the street, blinking as his eyes adjusted to the brilliant midday light, he was surrounded by some of the Africans who had been in the audience. There were pats on the back and cries of "thank you", "well done", "you showed them".

Iolo felt satisfied with his efforts. With just a few exceptions, his evidence had been entirely truthful. He had, in fact, seen the new Association's constitution in early 1944, at the time it was formed. Indeed, he had commented on the draft they had shown him beforehand.

He had met some of his former African workmates from time to time since retiring in 1932, giving advice when asked. But he had not been closely involved. He'd had no hand whatsoever in the decision to strike.

Initially, he had been reluctant to appear before the Commission, but they had urged him to do so. He'd been visited by Willie Sigeca, the secretary of the Association, who'd arrived to work in the goods sheds a year or so before Iolo left. Educated to Standard Seven, Willie was now the most senior African employee in the goods sheds' records office. Iolo had been impressed by Willie's intelligence and industry from the start. He was not surprised to find out that he was one of the leaders of the strike.

Willie had said to him, "Mr James, we need somebody to convince them that this strike and our Association did not come out of thin air. African workers on the railways have had longstanding grievances and have tried everything to be heard. As somebody who has supported us, you know this well. Dozens of our members have given evidence, but at the moment, the commission is not taking us seriously. Perhaps you could help persuade them to change their mind."

"I doubt it, Willie," Iolo had replied. "I am a person of no significance in European society. I may no longer be considered a menace, but most people still see me as an eccentric, a bit of an anomaly. Which I suppose I am. Are you sure you want me to do this?"

In truth, Willie had not been sure. But the strikers were not spoiled for choice. He had put out feelers to some of the more sympathetic leaders of the white Rhodesia Railway Workers' Union, but nobody was willing to take the risk.

Then Sipambaniso Manyoba Khumalo, a community leader based in the location, and one of the founders of the newly formed Bulawayo African Workers Trade Union, had suggested Iolo as a possibility.

Iolo did not have much to lose by way of status or reputation, Willie thought to himself. That was the upside. He could speak forthrightly. But there was a downside; he was indeed a nobody.

His treatment by the members of the Commission confirmed that Iolo's evidence would not make much of a difference. He'd also found some of Iolo's comments, while well-intended, patronising and demeaning, but he kept this to himself.

So, while Willie joined in the approbation of his comrades, his mind was already elsewhere. The Association had lost some members since the strike had ended – a substantial minority had been opposed to going back to work without anything really concrete on offer.

He anticipated that some rank-and-filers would be disappointed by the recommendations of the Tredgold Commission of Inquiry. There was a risk that the Association might collapse. There was urgent work to do to prevent this happening.

***

After a while, Iolo made his excuses, unlocked his bike and headed for home, which was still on Lobengula Street.

He was living alone. Mervyn, now in his mid-thirties, was in the army. He had survived the war unscathed, to his father's great relief, fighting first in North Africa and then in Europe. Mervyn shared his father's pacifist convictions but had decided to put them to one side in response to the threat of fascism, a stance which his father understood.

Mervyn was stuck in Greece, waiting to be demobbed. A history teacher by training, he had been working at a European school near Durban when war broke out. He hoped to return there. He'd been promised that his job would be kept for him.

Gwerfyl had gone to Britain in 1937 and never returned. She was married and living in Swansea with two children of her own. She now called herself Gwen; only her family still used her original name. Iolo would have loved to go back to Britain and see her, but money was always tight; paying for her berth had left him short for quite a while. All they could do was exchange letters and photos.

Iolo had been a single parent since 1923. He remembered the years after Doris left the stage as tiring and tough, but they had survived. Being the son and daughter of somebody who, at least for a while, was a social pariah had not been easy for Mervyn and Gwerfyl. They had suffered bullying at school and neither had found it easy to make friends. When Gwerfyl had told him that she was leaving, she said she couldn't bear to live in such a sick country any longer. He'd understood.

Frank and Harriet had continued to support the family as best they could. They ignored the flack they got for associating with Iolo. It helped that Frank was one of those people who others found impossible to dislike. He appeared to navigate his way through life without breaking into a sweat.

From time to time, Harriet dropped hints that she thought Iolo had been a poor husband, but she was strongly committed to his children. And her own had cheerfully adopted Mervyn and Gwerfyl as supernumerary siblings.

As for Doris, Iolo's view was the less said, the better. Between 1923 and 1925 she had been in Johannesburg, living with the Mackenzies while under the care of Dr Sachs, seeing him twice a week for therapy sessions. Sachs sent brief monthly reports back to Dr Newsome and Iolo. For the first six months there wasn't much progress. Her seizures had continued.

During the second six months there was a marked improvement, although this was not an unalloyed blessing for Iolo. She edged out of her own private world, recognising that the conversations with her father were the product of her illness. At some point, they stopped. She came to accept that Iolo was her husband and that they had two children, Mervyn and Gwerfyl. The seizures became rare.

But there was a great swell of bitterness and anger in her. Doris could never forgive Iolo. And when she thought of her children, she could not see beyond him. She knew that this was unfair, but it was how she felt.

She baulked at the idea of returning to normal family life. No amount of cajoling could persuade her. After a year of therapy, Dr Sachs discharged her from his care. The Mackenzies assumed at this point that she would return to Bulawayo, but she refused to leave. Doris had begun drinking again.

After another ten months, following an ugly confrontation, the Mackenzies expelled her from their home. For a time, she fell out of sight. Then she reappeared in Bulawayo, finding a room in a poor white area of town. For a month, Iolo had no idea she was back.

One day Gwerfyl returned from school, breathless and exclaiming, "I saw mother on 4th Avenue today! I said hello but she did not say hello back."

It took Iolo some time to find out where she was living. There was no joyful reunion. In fact, little was said. She smelled strongly of alcohol. When he gave her some money, she did not reject it, but there was no expression of gratitude.

This perfunctory encounter set the tone for their relationship over the following decade. Iolo would often visit her and give her a little money – sometimes, to make himself feel better, he would call it an allowance. There would be no conversation. Doris never asked how he or the children were. He knew that most of what he gave her would go on alcohol. She had also started to smoke heavily.

From time to time, he would lose track of her as she moved from one temporary lodging house to another. Landlords soon tired of her failure to keep up her rent payments. But then he would find where she was and things resumed much as before.

He heard reports that Doris was having more seizures again, but he had not seen her have one himself. She had several more stays in Ingutsheni in the late 1920s and early 1930s.

Iolo did not visit her when she was in there. She'd improve enough to be released but, after a while, relapsed into her old, destructive ways. Dr Newsome was long gone from Ingutsheni. He'd moved on to a job in Northern Rhodesia, working for one of the mining companies there, Iolo was told. He was not replaced for some time.

Whenever he saw her, Iolo could tell that Doris was in a terrible state. He had a feeling that things were coming to a head, but he was unwilling and unable to help her.

Chapter Sixteen

Bulawayo, November 1935

Wulf Sachs parked his car near the house on Lobengula Street. As he levered himself out of the driver's seat, he said to John, the man sitting next to him, "Stay here and keep an eye on the car. I am not planning to be long."

John smiled and nodded. John's son, Daniel, who was travelling with them, was lying on the back seat, fast asleep.

Sachs and his fellow passengers were on their way back to Johannesburg after spending a few weeks at John Chawafambira's village in Manicaland. John was the son of a famous traditional healer there. Sachs had known John since 1933, first as a patient but now, he hoped, as a friend.

Sachs had left John and Daniel at the village, but before he'd got far, the car had broken down.

To his surprise, while he was waiting for the repair to be completed, he encountered John and Daniel again, back on the road. Apparently, John had been compelled to flee the village after various things – Sachs was unclear what had happened – went wrong. He resolved that as soon as they were in Joburg, they would sit down together and get to the bottom of what had happened.

Stopping in Bulawayo on the way home had not been a definite part of Sachs's plan. He'd kept it in reserve, on the off chance that circumstances would permit it. He'd always wondered what had happened to Doris James and, on deciding to make the journey to Manicaland, had retrieved the family address from his records, just in case. Sachs needed to be home in three days, but that gave him enough time for an overnight stay.

He'd booked a room at the Bulawayo Club on arrival and then driven round to the James family home. It was early in the evening. He saw a light being switched on as he approached the front door. He was in luck. Sachs knocked twice. A male voice responded, intonation rising, "Coming! Give me a second."

Moments later, a man whom Sachs presumed was Iolo James opened the door. They'd never actually met when Doris came down to Johannesburg. Mr James had dropped her off at the Mackenzies and then hot-footed it back to Southern Rhodesia. Their only contact subsequently was by letter. The man looked at Sachs, saying, "We don't know each other. Can I help you?"

Sachs introduced himself and explained the purpose of his visit. As he spoke, Sachs watched the colour bleeding out of Mr James's face. "This is a surprise, Mr Sachs," he stammered. "It would have been much better had you given me some advance notice."

"I wasn't sure I would have the time to seek you or Mrs James out," Sachs replied by way of explanation. "I am on my way home to Johannesburg and don't have long. So let me get straight to the point; how is my former patient?"

"Not at all well, I'm afraid," Iolo James replied, unwilling to meet Sachs' gaze. "But I have very little contact with her these days."

Sachs tried to elicit more information about Doris's condition from her husband, but he was unforthcoming. It was clear to Sachs that she and Mr James were estranged. The man just wanted him to go away.

After several more fruitless exchanges, Sachs tried to force the issue, "Perhaps you could take me round to where she lives? I would very much like to meet her. As you will recall, I was concerned, all those years ago, that her treatment had been brought to a premature end."

Iolo James blushed, "As you know, she was her own worst enemy. Besides, I don't know her exact address at the moment. She moves around a great deal. All I can suggest is that you ask around the lodging houses on 4th Avenue." He began to close the door on Sachs, "Now, Mr Sachs, I think this conversation is over. Goodbye."

And with that the door slammed shut. Iolo James immediately closed all the curtains to the front windows overlooking the *stoep*. Sachs retreated back to his car.

His initial reaction to this lack of cooperation from Mr James was one of surprise but, on second thoughts, he should have anticipated it. While Sachs was treating Doris, he'd come to some conclusions about her husband too. From what she'd told him, Sachs thought it highly likely that Mr James had experienced some sort of trauma during his childhood.

It was too late now to do a search of the lodging houses for Doris. He would do that first thing tomorrow and then resume the drive south after lunch. He might even take Mrs James back with him to Johannesburg if she agreed.

Early the next morning, Wulf Sachs went to 4th Avenue. John and Daniel said they had some business to attend to in the main location.

Sachs had been told by somebody he'd met over breakfast at the Bulawayo Club that 4th Avenue had once been decent and respectable. But after its residents began moving to the suburbs, the housing there was taken over by landlords, mainly Afrikaners and Greeks, and converted into cheap accommodation for poor whites. This had been Doris's milieu for the last decade.

Sachs had no idea where to start, so he simply approached the first person he met, an elderly Afrikaner woman sitting on a stool in front of a run-down bungalow at the junction with Abercorn Street. He struck it lucky at the first attempt.

"Doris James? Yes, I know her," she told him. "She is one of my tenants. She was asleep in her room when I passed it half an hour ago. Sozzled as usual, no doubt. She's three months behind on her rent. By rights I should throw her out, but she's a sad case. Abandoned by her husband, I'm told."

"Can you take me to her room, Madam?" Sachs asked the landlady.

She ushered him into the bungalow. There were five rooms, each occupied by different tenants. Some of the doors had been left open. He could see white women of various ages, two of them with young children. Everybody was wearing dirty and tattered clothing.

This is absolute squalor, thought Sachs. Doris had sunk as low as it was possible for a European to sink. Finally, the landlady pointed to the closed door of a small room at the rear of the bungalow, which likely had once been servants' quarters. "She's in there," she said, adding, "You'll not get much out of her, I'm afraid."

Sachs pushed the door open. The stench was overpowering. An emaciated, grey-haired woman was lying motionless on a filthy bed, eyes closed. Only her mouth was moving, but it was impossible to make out what she was saying. The floor could not be seen. Empty bottles and cigarette butts were strewn everywhere.

Sachs knelt down and whispered, "Mrs James... Doris... it's Wulf Sachs, your doctor in Joburg... can you hear me?" There was no immediate response from Doris. Then her legs began to tremble and kick. Sachs noticed that her left foot was missing its big toe.

Her voice, hoarse and rasping, suddenly rang out, "Father? Is that you? I've not heard from you for so long." She took hold of Sachs's right wrist and gripped it tightly. Sachs was unable to pull it free.

Doris leapt up and started to hit Sachs, her arms whirling, "You abandoned me. I thought that, of all men, I could trust you. But no!" she wailed. She pinned Sachs against the wall. She would not relent. Then she lunged at him again, falling off the bed. Suddenly, Doris lost all energy; she collapsed on the floor.

As she lay there, she looked up at Sachs, her expression calmer now. "I used to be white, you know," she said quietly.

Sachs retreated into the corridor while he had the chance, but he had lost all composure. *Come on, man, you are a professional! Pull yourself together*, he reproached himself. The shock began to wear off. She was so much worse than he had imagined. It could be irreversible alcohol-related brain damage, advanced dementia, or both. As for her missing toe, it was probably peripheral artery disease. There was nothing to be done for her. It would be a mercy if one day she didn't wake up.

He walked back through the bungalow. As he did so, a well-dressed woman carrying what looked like a bag of clothing appeared out of nowhere and gestured that she wanted to get past him. He made to give way, but then she stopped abruptly.

She gave him an appraising glance and asked, "Who are you?"

Before Sachs could say anything, she went on, "If you are from the Council, about time. It is disgraceful that you leave it to volunteers like us to provide support to the wretched people living here."

Finally able to get a word in edgeways, Sachs shook his head. "No, I am not from the Council. I am an acquaintance of one of the tenants. I came to check on her well-being."

"Well-being? Well, la di da!" the woman mocked. "There is no well-being to be found here, sir, only poverty and misery, the white race laid low while Africans roam the town freely, walking down the pavements as if they own them. If you want to do some good," the woman went on, "tell the Council to pull its finger out. Tell them that Violet Harper of the Vigilantes Association sent you. That so-called socialist, Mayor MacIntyre, will be quaking in his boots." She laughed and then continued on her way, good works to perform.

Back on the street, Sachs saw the landlady. She was back on her stool again. He made to walk away but then had second thoughts. "Thank you for your help, madam," he said. Reaching into his jacket pocket, he pulled out his wallet and gave her all the notes he had, "Here, please take this. Does that cover her rent arrears?"

"*Verdomde hel*, more than enough!" she exclaimed. "It covers the next six months too."

"Good. Thank you for your help."

Sachs went back to the Bulawayo Club, where he, John and Daniel had agreed to meet. They would depart straight away, he decided. There was no need for lunch – he'd lost his appetite.

***

220

A month after Mr Sachs's unwelcome visit, a police officer visited Iolo at home to tell him that Doris had died.

"Choked on her own vomit yesterday," the officer mused. She was found in her room in a dive on 4th Avenue, he told Iolo. She was now in the morgue at Memorial Hospital. Her family needed to identify her.

Iolo went immediately. Afterwards, he went home to Lobengula Street to tell Gwerfyl, who was still living at home then, working in Meikles, Bulawayo's biggest department store. Mervyn was in Johannesburg, training to be a teacher. He sent him a telegram.

Doris's funeral was held at the Anglican church five days later. The congregation was tiny. Iolo and Gwerfyl, Frank and Harriet, and two women at the back of the church that Iolo did not know. One of them, youngish and well-dressed, glared at him throughout the service. The other, much older and wearing old clothing, had a bored look, as if she did this regularly.

At the end of the service, Iolo approached the women to thank them for coming. As he drew close, the old woman withdrew, muttering under her breath, clearly not keen to speak with him. The younger woman stood her ground, however. Only when it was too late to retreat did he recognise her. It was Violet Harper.

Violet strode towards Iolo and, before he could react, slapped him hard on the right cheek. "You are still a disgrace, James. Nothing has changed since you got your just desserts in 1923. Doris's death will always be on your conscience. I hope she haunts you in your dreams." Then, she turned on her heels and strode out of the church.

Iolo, not for the first time in his life, was dumbstruck. Gwerfyl rushed up to her father to make sure he was alright. "Sit down for a moment," she said. "That woman is insane. Who was she?"

"I have no idea," he lied. After five minutes, he had recovered enough to begin the walk back to Lobengula Street. Iolo was lost in thought. Violet Harper was right. His selfishness and lack of love had played a big part in blighting Doris's happiness. Mervyn and Gwerfyl had been very loyal to him, but they did not know the full truth. Nothing good would come of telling them. And he could not bear the thought of losing their affections. That would destroy him.

There never was a great family reckoning about what had happened to Doris. Instead, they barely spoke of her again.

Chapter Seventeen

By the time of Doris's death at the end of 1935, Iolo had been retired for three years. He hadn't wanted to stop work, but the Great Depression had led to big retrenchments on the railways. Frank did his best to fight Iolo's corner with the management, but ultimately couldn't keep him in his job. Capable Africans like Willie Sigeca were available and came a lot cheaper. Iolo accepted it without much of a fuss. He accepted that the world was changing; indeed, it needed to.

At first, his retirement had been quiet and uneventful. His confidence had been knocked for six by the tarring and feathering imbroglio and he was also short of money. Doris and the children, in their different ways, continued to be a financial burden.

But Iolo did not need that much to live on and he had little difficulty finding things to occupy his time. For a start, he reconnected with his Welshness by helping to establish the Bulawayo Cambrian Society.

He'd got to know Manibhai Vasanji Naik, one of the Indian shopkeepers at his end of Lobengula Street, particularly well, and often spent time talking about life and politics with him. M.V. Naik's store was famous. Known by Africans as 'Kumalo bazaar', it sold clothing, pots and pans and other miscellaneous items to its customers, many of whom lived in neighbouring Makokoba.

Iolo also became obsessed with the world of physical culture, a life reform movement which promoted things such as vegetarianism, fasting, high-fibre dieting, breathing exercises, meditation and bodybuilding.

He keenly followed the exploits of one of best-known figures in the movement, the veteran South African strongman Tromp Van Diggelen. He had a large private collection of magazines full of pictures of muscle-bound men performing physical poses, often browsing through them in the evening before bed. His favourite was an American magazine called *Strength and Health*. He'd not had any desire for physical intimacy with another person for over a decade by then, but that did not mean he could not appreciate the beauty of the human body.

For several years, that was about the sum total of his life. However, Iolo had not forgotten his conversation with Arthur Shearly Cripps of two decades ago. At the end of the 1930s, he resumed his search for meaningful ways to discharge his moral obligation to the African majority.

Iolo decided that a good first step would be to support African sporting activities in Bulawayo. He was soon drawn towards the growing boxing scene. He had witnessed his first bout in 1938 while taking a walk around the strip of land encircling the town known as the Commonage.

There had been an animated crowd of thousands on that day. As far as Iolo could make out, a Manyika boxer was taking on a

Ndebele opponent. The Manyika's supporters were dressed in blue. Those in the Ndebele corner wore red and black.

It was not boxing as Europeans understood it. Few blows were traded. There was no raised ring. Iolo struggled to work out what was going on. After about an hour, the Council authorities arrived to break up the unauthorised throng.

At the time, there was a big debate in official circles about what attitude to take on African boxing. Some government officials viewed the contests as little more than an excuse for drunken hooliganism, asserting that they should be banned. Others argued that boxing, if properly channelled, could inculcate discipline and act as an emotional safety-value for Africans far from their rural homes. Iolo took the latter view. What was needed, he thought, was for African boxing to be brought in line with the Queensberry Rules.

African sporting and cultural activities in Bulawayo were overseen by the Native Welfare Society. Its leading light was a liberal, if paternalistic, European called Reverend Percy Ibbotson. Iolo made contact with Ibbotson in 1939 and became a foot soldier in the Welfare Society. Iolo did not know it then, but he was to cross paths with Ibbotson again in 1945, before the Tredgold Commission.

For several years, Iolo was an inconspicuous figure at Welfare Society events, always in the background, helping out. As time passed, he got to know another important figure in the Society, a charismatic young Ndebele man called Sipambaniso Manyoba Khumalo. It was to be a significant relationship for them both.

Sipambaniso was an excellent footballer and all-round man about town. He was a powerful figure in Makokoba. Sipambaniso became intrigued by Iolo. "You are an unusual man, Mr James," he said, after hearing Iolo recount how he had defended Michael against the false allegations made by his wife back in 1923, "What you did must have had many consequences for you."

"It did. In many ways I am still living with them now," Iolo replied, going on to tell Sipambaniso how he'd been tarred and feathered as a result. "But those days are over. A quiet life for me now."

***

In early 1942, Sipambaniso approached Iolo with an unexpected proposal. He wanted Iolo to attend Council meetings and submit brief weekly reports about what had happened there to Sipambaniso. He would circulate them. He did not specify to whom and Iolo did not ask.

Sipambaniso explained that while important decisions were being made there which affected all Africans in Bulawayo, he did not have time to go himself. "I do not trust the reports in the *Bulawayo Chronicle*," complained Sipambaniso. Iolo knew what he meant.

So it was that Iolo became a fixture at Council meetings. Once he had found his bearings, he began to ask questions. Not used to being subjected to scrutiny, his probing interventions were resented by some of the councillors on the receiving end; others applauded his civic commitment. Of course, he never revealed that he was writing up reports for Sipambaniso.

Sipambaniso was grateful. One day in 1943, at one of their regular get-togethers in the back of M.V. Naik's store, he told Iolo, "You don't know how useful your reports are, Mr James. We are never taken by surprise by the actions of the Council now."

By that time, Sipambaniso was one of the leaders of a campaign against the overcrowded and unsanitary conditions prevailing in Makokoba, whose population had more than doubled since 1939.

Iolo's European friends were amused by his new hobby of going to Council meetings. At one point, Frank said to him, "Why the hell have you started attending them so diligently? They are as dull as ditch water. You must have better things to do?"

Iolo said only, "Less boring than you think. And I'm keen to have a better understanding of what the Council is up to. It affects all of us."

"Maybe," replied Frank. "But you'd make more of a difference if you stood as a councillor."

"How many votes would I get, Frank?" laughed Iolo. "I am still *persona non grata* in this town."

"Less than you used to be," countered Frank. "Things have improved a lot since that Violet Harper moved down south a couple of years ago. I don't hear you being called Monkey Nut much these days. At this rate, people will soon be calling you Citizen No. 1 instead."

"That would be a step in the right direction," said Iolo, laughing.

Iolo felt that he was at last beginning to make a difference.

Then came his moment of fame in front of the Tredgold Commission. In the weeks following his testimony, he experienced an upswing in abuse from Europeans as he moved around town on his bike. But it soon petered out.

Meanwhile, inspired by the example of the railway workers, Africans in Bulawayo began organising and mobilising on an unprecedented scale. Three days before Iolo appeared before the Commission, Sipambaniso, along with several others, had established a Bulawayo African Workers Trade Union. Jasper Savanhu, who was also a leading figure in the Southern Rhodesia Bantu Congress, became its president, and Sipambaniso its secretary.

Thousands attended its first meeting in Makokoba. There were plans for coordinated strikes. Sipambaniso sent a message to Iolo saying that his reports would be shared amongst the members of the new umbrella Union.

A few days before Christmas 1945, Sipambaniso sent him a typed copy of a speech given by Jasper Savanhu at the inaugural meeting of the Union. A young activist called Joseph Msika acted as the courier. Iolo had heard that the speech caused uproar but had been unable to find a copy – typically, the *Chronicle* had refused to publish it.

Savanhu said, *The Railway strike has proved that Africans have been born. The old Africa of tribalism and selfishness has died away [...] We have found ourselves faced by a ruthless foe – exploitation and legalised oppression by the white man for his and his children's luxury. The days when a white man could exploit us at will are gone and gone forever. The employer who ill-treats one of the least of African workers does it to all of us. We must not fail in our duty to suffer with him.*

When Joseph Msika passed Iolo the copy of the speech, he'd told him, "Sipambaniso has said that you can be trusted."

That simple sentence made Iolo feel happier than he had done for many years. Africans were on the move across the country. Change was in the air. And Citizen No. 1, Iolo James, was, in his own small way, part of it.

Part 5   Epitaph/Epilogue, 1958

Chapter Eighteen

The mourners, about sixty-strong, began filing out of the Presbyterian Church into the rain. Among their ranks were the Mayor of Bulawayo and the General Manager of the Rhodesia Railways, signifying the esteem in which Iolo James had come to be held.

It had been a low-key service, in accordance with the wishes of the deceased. People murmured to each other as they left, "A good service."

"What he would have wanted."

"Frank's tribute was a fitting one."

These were among the well-meaning tropes Mervyn overheard as he stood by the door, waiting to greet attendees and thank them for coming.

Mervyn had spent much of the previous three months looking after his father. It was lucky he had moved back to Bulawayo in 1956. After nearly twenty years in Durban, where he had ended up as deputy headmaster, an opportunity to return home and take up the role of headmaster at Willoughby School had come up.

With his father becoming more fragile, Mervyn had leapt at the opening. He had never married or had children, so there were no family complications to hold him back. His father had told him there was no need to move on his account – he was fine. But Mervyn could see that, beneath the surface, Iolo had been relieved and pleased.

Gwerfyl was unable to travel back from Swansea to Southern Rhodesia for her father's funeral. Although her children were now grown up and had moved out, she and her husband still had little spare money. He was a foreman on building sites and she was working in a toy factory.

Mervyn had seen her between being demobbed and sailing to South Africa in 1946. Neither spoke much about their father. Nothing was said about their mother. She remained a taboo subject.

Mervyn mainly saw his father at the weekends. They shared a love of cycling. In his later years, his father had fallen in love with the untamed granite hills of the Matopos, so it was often their destination. "I have no idea why it took me so long to explore it properly," Iolo had said. "This is a magical, sacred place."

He was not interested in Rhodes's grave at World's View or in the wildlife. What excited him were the Ndebele political and religious sites there. "I had a good friend in the Welfare Society, Sipambaniso Manyoba Khumalo. Sadly, he died in 1952, far too young. He had an enormous funeral, and I attended," he reminisced. "He taught me a lot about the Matopos. Europeans just treat it as a tourist playground, but it is so much more than that. The recent wave of forced removals there is sickening."

His father had a favourite story about the Matopos which he told to anybody willing to listen. He had once bumped into two

African trade unionists and nationalists of his acquaintance there, Grey Bango and Joshua Nkomo. Both had grown up in the area.

The two men were downcast. Grey Bango informed Iolo that they'd just visited the High God Shrine at Dula, where the Voice had prophesied that freedom from white rule would not be achieved for another thirty years. "I said that he shouldn't worry. It would happen far quicker than that. Grey Bango told me not to tell a soul about the prediction, which I never have."

Iolo was pretty fit for his age. He was robust enough to travel on his own to attend Arthur Shearly Cripps's funeral at Maronda Mashanu in August 1952. His short-term memory could let him down and he was rather deaf – he refused to get a hearing aid – but his mental faculties were still good. "Regular attendance at Council meetings helps me stay sharp," Iolo told his son, who could not tell if he was joking or not.

Father and son did not talk much about politics. They argued about the joining together, in 1953, of the two Rhodesias and Nyasaland, known officially as the Central African Federation. Iolo opposed it, fearing that Southern Rhodesia would try to extend its colour bar to other territories. He was convinced that the Federation could not last.

Mervyn supported the Federation because he hoped that the new constitutional arrangements which accompanied it might erode the colour bar in Southern Rhodesia, rather than extend it.

Iolo was jubilant when Ghana gained its freedom in March 1957. "I've met quite a few of the up-and-coming Southern Rhodesian African leaders here, Mervyn," he said one day. "They pass through M.V. Naik's home and store. They are capable and, what's more, willing to work with other races."

Mervyn shared his father's enthusiasm for the cause of African independence, but he was less optimistic about Southern Rhodesia's prospects. Until recently, he had been living in South

Africa; he feared that Southern Rhodesia might be heading for something closer to *Apartheid* than freedom.

"No, no, Mervyn," his father would say, smiling. "It is only a matter of time. I am sure I will see majority rule here before I die."

His father was wrong. He did not have long left to live. As Frank said during Iolo's funeral service, his end was simultaneously tragic and ironic.

In early July 1958, Iolo was returning on his bike from a Council meeting. Along the way, he performed a few errands, which required him to cross some railway tracks that were not part of his usual route.

An observer reported that he saw Iolo having trouble with his bike. It looked like one of the wheels had somehow got stuck in the tracks. Preoccupied with releasing the wheel, he seemed not to hear a fast-approaching goods train, or the cries of warning from those nearby.

The driver hooted the horn and put on the brakes, but it was too late. It was a direct hit. Iolo was dragged along for fifty yards before the train came to a halt. His right foot and left arm were severed in the accident.

The doctors in Memorial Hospital did not expect Iolo to survive, but for a while, in a coma, he clung on. Mervyn handed over all school duties to his deputy and moved into his father's place so that he could visit him in Hospital every day. He and Frank took it in turns to sit by his bed.

Iolo's vital signs seemed to be picking up, giving Mervyn cause for hope. But then a respiratory infection took hold. Within three days it overwhelmed him. He finally died, just short of his 81st birthday, on the 22nd of July 1958.

During his hospital vigil, Mervyn had not bothered to look through his father's magazines and documents, which were piled up, higgledy-piggledy, all over the house in Lobengula Street. But he had found a piece of paper sitting on top of the writing desk entitled 'Last Will and Testament'. It stipulated that he did not want a fuss made when he died, just a small service and burial in the European cemetery. No headstone please.

Frank was to be asked if he'd be willing to say a few words. It should not be anything approaching a tribute, his father directed. The final sentence directed that all his possessions were to pass to Mervyn and Gwerfyl, but that there was little of value apart from the house itself, which was to be sold. The rest of his possessions, except perhaps some of his book collection, could go direct to the rubbish tip.

***

Frank spoke well at the service, which was held three days after Iolo's death.

"Iolo always did his own thing," he said. "He thought for himself and did not follow the herd. That got him into trouble sometimes. Most of you will be aware of what happened back in 1923. Those were tough times for him. His marriage was ruined. I won't lie, I sometimes thought his actions were unwise. In later life, he became somewhat secretive about what he was up to, which was sometimes irritating. But I always respected him as a genuine seeker of truth."

At that point, the Minister presiding over the service, John Manod-Quinnell, raised a hand unexpectedly, "Sorry, Mr Tindler, permit me to interject. You talk about his propensity to get into trouble. As a man of faith, Iolo James would have been well familiar with the Gospel of Luke which calls on us all to fight injustice, to not be bystanders. This is what we sometimes call making 'good trouble'. That, I think, is a fitting epitaph for the man."

"He was a good worker and always treated Africans with respect," went on Frank. "I enjoyed working with him in the goods sheds very much for all those years. The hand the railways had in his death was one of the strangest episodes of an unusual life. Above everything else, he was a loving father to Mervyn and Gwerfyl. He was very proud of them and was so happy to have Mervyn close by again in recent years. I am sure we will all miss Iolo James."

Tears welled up in Mervyn's eyes. As had occasionally happened over the intervening years, images and impressions from 1923 suddenly flashed up. He'd always struggled to make much sense of it all. He knew that the emotions of abandonment and betrayal he'd felt towards his mother had made it difficult to form relationships with women. He'd never been able to let down his guard and he regretted that.

When he thought about his mother, all he could see was her standing outside the house, detached and uncaring, staring ahead, as his father was dragged out of the house by that vigilante gang. It was so unnatural. What could have made her behave like that?

Was there another side to the story? Father was no saint, he knew that. But no, she was to blame. Over twenty years after her death, he still felt angry and confused.

***

Mervyn was due back at school in a few days' time, so the next morning he got down to the job of sorting through his father's voluminous papers, which were scattered all over the house. He'd become a hoarder in his later years. Mervyn was determined to be ruthless. He would not succumb to the temptation of reading everything.

Vast quantities went straight into rubbish bags. After a day of hard graft, he had made good progress. There was not much more to do. Mervyn turned to clearing out the drawers of his father's writing desk. Some of the stuff in those drawers might be worth keeping, he thought to himself.

The first drawer was full of letters from Mervyn and Gwerfyl, going back over three decades. He put them in a cardboard box to go through at leisure. The second drawer contained a short manuscript called 'Origins'. His father had mentioned that he'd written an account of his early years but had never showed it to him. Mervyn had heard all his father's stories. He did not expect to read anything he did not already know. He decided he would look at it later.

There was one last drawer. When he opened it, he found three envelopes inside. The first one, on which his father had written 'Doris, 1923-25' on the cover, contained several reports from a doctor in Johannesburg. Mervyn hesitated. Did he really want to read any of these? It would only bring back painful memories.

The second envelope was slim. Iolo had marked it 'Michael'. The third envelope was the thickest and was unmarked. He opened it to find dozens of single-page reports of Council meetings going back about twenty years. He took them out and flicked through. They appeared unexceptional, not interesting enough to read through. None of them were addressed to anybody. Maybe they could be offered to the municipal librarian?

At the bottom of the pile of reports was a letter from the Federation of Bulawayo African Trade Unions. Mervyn pulled it out and began reading.

Letter of thanks from Grey Bango, President of the Federation of Bulawayo African Trade Unions, 5th May 1948

On behalf of the Federation, I am writing to convey our gratitude for your valuable service to the cause. Your accounts of Bulawayo Council meetings have helped us to anticipate how it would respond to our activities. They assisted us in identifying the Council's weak points! This was particularly useful for our comrades in the Municipal African Employees' Association, who were in the vanguard of the recent general strike.

As you know, the general strike started here in Bulawayo before spreading to the rest of the country. Our white rulers must by now realise that African workers are an unstoppable force in this country. The only thing that can hold us back is if we allow ourselves to be divided. Don't believe everything supporters of Benjamin Burombo say about how the African Workers Voice Association was the real power behind the strike. You have backed the right horse in the Federation!

It is rare to find a European who does not think he knows better than we do how to conduct our affairs. Please continue with your work, which will be more important than ever over the period ahead. Joseph will remain your contact point. Secretary Sipambaniso Manyoba Khumalo asks me to convey his greetings.

Grey Bango's signature followed.

None of it meant much to Mervyn. He had been in Durban in 1948, but he had noticed that his fellow Europeans still talked with apprehension about the African general strike.

His father had been up to more than he let on, thought Mervyn.

That evening, a whisky poured and sitting in his father's favourite chair, Mervyn opened the envelope marked 'Michael'. There were two documents inside. The first was in his father's hand. It was dated January 1923 and entitled 'The confession of Iolo James'.

It was two-pages long. A glance through suggested that a middle page was missing. It was full of crossings out, done with wild strokes of the pen. At a couple of points, the strokes had penetrated right through the paper, suggesting to Mervyn that his father had been in a state of agitation when he wrote it.

Extracts from 'The confession of Iolo James', 12th January 1923

Doris is lying, I know it! There is no way Michael would do such a thing. She is seeking revenge on me through him, which is despicable. All my attempts to see him in prison have been unsuccessful. If I don't do something, I am complicit in this injustice. I [indecipherable]

I must do something. I must do something. I MUST do something! But WHAT?

Why did I ever come to this terrible country? Racial prejudice corrupts everything it touches, including me. I have never believed in it, yet I came here. The biggest mistake of my life [...]

[...] normal relationships between Europeans and Africans are just not possible. I blunder around [indecipherable]

I owe Doris nothing. She has never understood me. I must do what has to be done even if it destroys us both [...]

I'm scared of the consequences if I go ahead and testify. Will it make any difference? Probably not. But if I don't try, I will never forgive myself [indecipherable]

[...] but what about Mervyn and Gwerfyl?

Mervyn was stunned. As a child, he had sensed his father's distress, but he'd not appreciated until now just how great it had been.

He stared ahead in the half-darkness for a long time before hesitantly opening the second document. It was a short letter written in June 1925 from Michael, in Bulawayo prison, to his father.

Letter from Michael to Iolo James, 9th June 1925

Dear Mr James,

I have not opened your recent letters. Please stop writing to me. I want no more contact with you.

I am very sorry to hear that you suffered a painful punishment for defending me in court. The prison warders took great pleasure in telling me about it. You did not deserve that. But every time a letter comes from you, they single me out for persecution and harassment.

You tried to do your best, but you could not. You have often been a danger to those you want to help. Do you still understand nothing about how things work here? If you want to do something useful, you should leave Africa and take all of your fellow Europeans with you.

Goodbye, Mr James.
Michael

Iolo had written something at the bottom. "*This is nothing more than I deserve. I'm a fool.*"

The contents of the letter shook Mervyn to the core. He downed the rest of his whisky in one go and poured another one. He had always thought well of Michael. But this letter revealed him to be ungrateful and rude. *To hell with him!*

He turned to the envelope with Doris's medical reports in it. He hadn't intended to open it but, angry and distracted, he did so without thinking. The top document was marked 'Discharge Report'. *Too late*, he thought, *I'm going to have to read it now.*

Extracts from 'Discharge Report by Dr Wulf Sachs: Mrs Doris James', 20th July 1924

In our sessions we have made good progress in addressing her delusions. But this has not brought tranquillity. Indeed, her anger and sense of injustice have increased. The focus of her anger is her husband, who she accuses of having been unloving and callous. According to her, he has always put his principles ahead of her and the family's best interests. He did not take her feelings and opinions seriously. He did little practical care of the children, leaving it all to her. She is insistent that she will never return to him or the family home [...]

[...] *her physical symptoms have improved. Her seizures have reduced but not disappeared. But her prolonged alcoholic self-abuse means that they may never stop completely. Given her previous addiction to Luminal, I would not recommend that she resumes taking it. She could be tried on potassium bromide, but there are risks that this could destabilise her mental state again. I have observed that she can be obstinate in refusing to take medication. Although the evidence base is patchy, perhaps the least risky recourse in her case might be a Ketogenic diet (rich in fat and low in carbohydrate). But again, this would require discipline which she may not have without proper supervision* [...]

[...] *I believe with continued treatment Mrs James's recovery would further advance. But I am not optimistic that she will be able to sustain the improvements described in the absence of a supportive environment. Despite our best efforts, she has obtained alcohol and drunk to extreme excess on several occasions over the last year. She remains an alcoholic and still lacks clear insight into her condition* [...]

[...] *It is a great shame that, despite my offer to be extremely flexible in the matter, her husband has said that he is no longer willing to pay for her treatment. Even at this late stage, I plead with him to reconsider his decision.*

For a while, Mervyn sat paralysed. Then, all of a sudden, he leapt up and threw his mother's medical reports into the fire. Everything in the envelope marked 'Michael' followed them in, as did the reports of Council meetings. He kept only Grey Bango's letter, putting that into his briefcase.

The next day, Mervyn sorted through his father's book collection. He filled a box with the ones he'd decided to keep; he put aside most of the Welsh language books to give to the Bulawayo Cambrian Society. Some of the others could be donated to a second-hand bookshop near Market Square. The rest would be disposed of.

He also put the house on the market with Knight Bros, which placed an advert in the *Chronicle*. They were sure it would sell quickly. It did, to an Indian family. *Father would be pleased about that*, thought Mervyn.

In the weeks that followed, Mervyn tried to go back to his normal life. But was any kind of normal life possible here in Southern Rhodesia? He was not sure anymore. He could not get that letter from Michael, with its stark injunction, "leave Africa", out of his head. He developed acute insomnia. A doctor advised him to take sedatives, but he refused.

Finally, after another long, sleepless night, came an epiphany. Michael had shown him the right thing to do; yes, he'd been angry at first, it was hard to accept, but he could see it now. A month after returning to the school, he handed in his notice. In October 1958, fifty-two years after Iolo had sailed into Cape Town, Mervyn headed the other way, boarding the Athlone Castle for Southampton in search of a new beginning.

Chapter Nineteen

Michael eased himself into the Metsimotlhabe River. The water was bracingly cold, as was to be expected in July; he found it invigorating. Michael was a good swimmer. It helped to keep him strong and flexible, well, as much as a man in his mid-seventies had any right to expect. He came as often as he could.

He had not left the Kgatla Reserve since returning from Bulawayo in 1932. He was released from prison a year early, and as soon as he was out, he'd got as far away from the white man as possible.

As he swam, his arms and legs moving in tandem through the water, he thought back to the day of his release. He'd got on the train south. His cousin, the only person who visited him during his incarceration, gave him the money for the one-way fare. Michael had been utterly penniless.

When he'd first travelled on it, the railway had felt like liberation, a great adventure. But, by 1932, it seemed more like an artery through which poison entered his bloodstream. "Hopefully this is my last journey on it," he said to himself as he boarded.

The train had pulled into Pilane Station in the middle of the night. A few dozen people stepped sleepily onto the platform and dispersed in silence. Mochudi was eerily quiet, but there were sounds of revelry in the far distance. He had walked out of the village, towards his family home in Morwa.

Michael should have felt joy at being back, but two events cast a big shadow. One of them was the death of his father in 1927, which he had heard about from his cousin. His younger brother had been looking after his mother since then.

"Your father never recovered from what the white people did to you," his mother told him, adding, "It broke his heart."

But even worse was the fate of his son, Molemane. While in prison, Michael had tried not to think too much about him, but it had not been easy.

Awaiting his trial at the start of 1923, his cousin had informed him that Molemane had joined the thousands of Kgatla who went every year to work underground on the Rand mines.

Every time his cousin visited him after his conviction, Michael would ask for news. The story never changed much: he was living and working in Johannesburg. Michael grew frustrated with his cousin. "Can't you tell me anything else?" he would ask.

Michael suspected his cousin knew more than he was letting on – his eyes were often averted when he insisted that he had no more news to share. But he could not prise it out of him. Now he was home, he was determined to find out more.

The day after returning to Morwa village, he told his younger brother that he was thinking of approaching his former wife's family for news about Molemane. This would have violated the undertaking he had given to King Isang in 1921.

His brother urged him not to do anything rash.

"We cannot lose you again," he said. "Let me talk to our mother."

"Be quick," Michael had said. "I can't wait much longer. It's killing me, this sense that there is something I don't know."

Two days after this exchange, his mother had called him in from the fields.

"My dear son, sit down," she told him as he approached the bench on which she was sitting. "I will tell you everything about Molemane. We did not think it would be fair to say anything while you were in prison, so far from the family that might comfort you."

Michael felt sick. Now he was finally about to find out, he wasn't sure that he wanted to. His mother went on, her voice choking at points, her hands trembling, to tell him that Molemane was dead, and had been since 1926.

There was not much detail. It appeared that Molemane had recently been promoted to a semi-skilled job by the mine management but had been violently attacked on his way back to the compound by a group of white miners, outraged that the position had not been given to a European.

The group had beaten Molemane with metal bars until he was unconscious and then thrown him in a nearby pond of industrial slurry. The compound police saw what was happening but did not intervene until the assault was over. They eventually pulled him out and took him to the mine hospital. He died from his head injuries a day later. His body had been returned home and laid to rest with proper ceremony.

"It was not just what had happened to you which so hurt your father," his mother said. "Molemane's death was another heavy blow. He didn't last long after we got the awful news. He couldn't help wondering if Molemane's life would have gone differently if he'd returned to our family, as he was entitled to do when he'd grown up. But he never contacted us."

Michael and his mother hugged each other tightly in their shared anguish. He could not feel angry with her or his cousin for hiding the truth from him. He now understood why.

Michael flipped himself onto his back in the river, tears welling up. He stared into the clear, late-afternoon sky. Even today, nearly a quarter of a century since being told the truth, thinking about Molemane's sad end triggered a surge of grief.

After learning the truth, Michael began his own private mourning for the son he had never known. Several months later, he approached Molemane's second family through his younger brother, to ask for permission to visit his grave. They relented and, one afternoon, he stood before it, saying goodbye.

Gradually Michael began to contribute to family and community life again. As the eldest son, he was now the head of the family; his increasingly frail mother lived with him.

He waved away any suggestions that he might marry again. One or two neighbours, friends of his former wife's family, periodically tried to spread negative rumours about him, but they washed over most people, who were well aware that any African who ventured into white society ran a high risk, one way or another, of being criminalised or worse.

In 1940, Michael's mother died. She had been ailing for a while, so it was not a major surprise when she did not wake up one morning. It was a peaceful death. Michael presided over the funeral and mourning arrangements.

He enjoyed discharging his family responsibilities but was unable to prevent the young men under his guidance from following previous generations to South Africa, or, in a smaller number of cases, Rhodesia, for work. There just weren't enough opportunities for them to make a life in the Kgatla Reserve.

All he said to them before they departed was, "Never trust a white man. Take great care. Remember what happened to me and my son, Molemane. Get back home here as soon as you can."

Michael swam towards the river's edge, his usual twenty minutes up. It was shallow. He walked out of the water to where he had left his towel. He did not really need one. The warmth of the late afternoon would dry his body in no time.

***

Survival, thought Michael as he ran the towel over his arms and legs. He'd never forgotten that conversation with Samuel in Kimberley prison, when they'd agreed that it was the most they could expect in this life.

Michael never thought he'd see Samuel again. Then, in 1957, Michael bumped into him in the crowded main market in Mochudi.

Samuel was visiting relatives. Although he was now an old man too, he hadn't changed at all, apart from his limp becoming more pronounced. They embraced, overjoyed to see each other. For the rest of the day, they drank and talked in a nearby beer hall until they were asked to leave, catching up on everything that had happened to them since their last meeting nearly half-a-century earlier.

"That knife you smuggled in came in useful more than once," said Samuel, laughing. "I was in there for the full seven years. No reductions for me. But it did mean that I got out too late to fight in the white man's next war."

Michael grinned. "They needed me on the mines, rather than on the front. So what did you do after you were released?"

"In the 1920s, I worked on the gold mines. Through God's grace, I came to no harm. I ended up as a foreman, earning decent

249

wages. My family and I moved to Saulspoort in 1931. I'd saved some money, so I was able to open a general store. From that date onwards, I have been my own man. I've been lucky, my friend," he reflected.

"You were due some luck," Michael said.

"Probably," chuckled Samuel.

Michael shared his own story with Samuel, who shook his head as he listened. "I am so sorry," he exclaimed, "you have experienced things no man should experience. But you have conducted yourself honourably. You have nothing to reproach yourself for."

"Maybe not," replied Michael. "But I do reproach myself for allowing Iolo James back into my life. That was a terrible mistake."

"Yes, it is a lesson we all learn the hard way. Nothing good can come from allowing white people to get too close," said Samuel.

As Michael reminisced about Samuel, he reached for his trousers and shirt and slipped them on. For a moment he could not locate his sandals, but after a brief search he found them, half-obscured by the riverside reeds. It was time to go home and eat something. He walked along the path back to the village. It was quiet. Everybody had finished their tasks for the day.

He and Samuel had also talked about politics. He had told Michael that he was a supporter of the African National Congress, but did not support the Freedom Charter. He felt that it showed that the ANC was moving too far towards multiracialism. He was also uneasy about the alliance it had formed with the Communist Party.

One thing Samuel said had particularly impressed Michael, "The Afrikaner government in Pretoria is trying to deceive us into believing that the Tswana in South Africa can have some sort of self-government under their so-called *Apartheid* system. A few of us may fall for this ruse, but most won't, thank God. Either all of South Africa is free, or none of it is."

"The British are having an easy time of it here. Many people are looking to Seretse Khama, but I worry that he might be a bit over keen to please the colonisers," responded Michael. "And he has married a white woman!" he went on to say, shrugging his shoulders.

Samuel threw his hands up in the air. "Hmm, not wise. You are right, Michael. The Tswana here do need to wake up. Look out for a promising young activist from the Okavango who is currently working with the ANC in Western Transvaal. His name is Motsamai Keyecwe Mpho. He was one of those acquitted in the treason trial last year. Another good man is Ismail Matlhaku. He runs a taxi service in Johannesburg but is also heavily involved with the ANC. He passes through Saulspoort regularly."

"I am glad to hear that there are people you have confidence in, Samuel," Michael had replied. "The Kgatla royal family have always had strong links with the ANC and I hear that Linchwe, King Molefi's son and heir, is very committed to the cause. That bodes well for the future."

When they parted, both agreed that, now they had found each other once more, they should meet whenever Samuel was in Mochudi.

***

They were never to see each other again. In January 1958, Michael heard that Samuel had passed away.

Samuel's eldest son, Albert, had sought Michael out when visiting Mochudi to inform him. "He often spoke about you," he told Michael. "And in his final days, as he was putting his affairs in order, he gave me this document to pass on to you, saying that, of all his friends, you would be most likely to appreciate it. I confess

251

that I haven't read it, so I can't tell you anything about it, but here it is."

Albert had pushed an envelope in his direction. Inside was a tatty typescript and a note. The spidery, nearly indecipherable, writing said, "*Michael, I am so glad we found each other again! You may enjoy this piece by a black American, Ethiop, written a hundred years ago, just before the American civil war. Mpho gave it to me as a gift.*"

Michael got home. He'd felt cool and refreshed after the swim, but as usual, in the course of the walk back, he had become warm and sweaty again. He would have a drink of water, then eat. Nobody else was there, but his eldest niece had left some food on the table for him, covered by a cloth. He picked up the plate of food – *seswaa*, his favourite – and sat down on a bench outside his house to eat.

It was on this same bench not long ago, at around this time of the day, that Michael had sat down to read Samuel's parting gift. Michael smiled in recollection. "Farewell, my good friend," he'd said aloud after he finished it. He put the typescript in his desk drawer.

Michael polished off the delicious *seswaa*. Night had fallen. The cicadas were in full-throated chorus. He reached into the drawer and pulled out the piece by Ethiop. *The article may come from a different time and place,* he reflected, *but it still resonates today.* He read it again in Samuel's honour.

That night, as he had often done over the years, Iolo James turned up in Michael's dreams. His presence was always unwelcome. James usually hung around in the background, muttering incomprehensibly, sometimes waving his arms around, giving Michael no peace. Whenever he had such dreams, Michael would wake up anxious and tired, feeling harassed.

That night, however, the dream was different. After a while, James, with a surprised expression on his face, receded into the distance before vanishing completely. This had never happened before.

"Good," said dream Michael, "Go away and don't come back!"

The next morning, Michael felt rested and refreshed. Iolo James never appeared in his dreams again.

Extracts from "What Shall We Do With The White People?", Ethiop, The Anglo-African Magazine (New York, 1860)

It may seem strange that a people so crushed and trodden upon, so insignificant as the Anglo-Africans, should even ask the question 'what shall we do with the whites?' [...] but the truth is that these white people themselves, through their press and Legislative Halls, in their pulpits and on their Rostrums, so constantly talk of nothing but us black people, and have apparently got so far beyond everything else that it would seem their very instincts regard us as in a measure, able to settle and make quiet their restlessness, and hence they have actually forced upon us the question which is the title of the article. [...]

What is the cause of all this discontent, this unquiet state, this distress? This answer we think may be found in this, viz: a long, continued, extensive, and almost complete system of wrongdoing. [...]

And verily they have triumphed, and in that triumph and what else we have instanced, who does not see that this people are on the direct road to barbarism. [...]

Seriously do we hope, that if the peace of the country is to be so continuously disturbed, that that they would withdraw. We have arrived at a period when they could easily be spared.

Acknowledgments

In 1997, I wrote to Doris Lessing to ask if she knew anything about Iorwerth Jones, the man on whom my lead character, Iolo James, is loosely based. I was pretty desperate by this time, having tried intermittently for over a decade, without much success, to find out more about Jones and the two trials that are at the heart of this novel.

The great writer had not heard of him, but said in her reply that she felt "much fellow-feeling for Iorwerth Jones, who must have had a hard time of it then, with those opinions."

In my letter, I'd also confessed that I was tempted to write the story up as a work of fiction, given my difficulties filling in the historical gaps. She asked, "Does it have to be fiction?" Perhaps she was worried that a crime against literature might be committed. Her question drove me to redouble my efforts to fill in those pesky gaps. However, despite several moments when it looked like there might be a breakthrough, I remained stymied. Finally, in 2021 I gave myself permission to try writing a novel. Here it is, duly published. After nearly forty years, the circle is finally closed.

I'm not sure whether I now qualify as a *bona fide* novelist. I certainly haven't completely shed my old identity as a historian. Indeed, I haven't wanted to. I've enjoyed inserting extracts – some of them extensive and near verbatim – from genuine historical documents into the story, not to mention incorporating a range of real people and events as well.

At the same time, I have played around with some of the facts. Where I have done so, hopefully it was with good cause. For example, I turned the first trial of 1923, an assault case, into one involving sexual assault. Why? Because, although they were rare, numerous historians have persuasively argued that Black Peril cases offer powerful insights into the social pathologies of European settler-colonialism.

In a 2017 article published by the *Guardian* another great writer, Hilary Mantel, sums up perfectly what I have tried to combine in this novel:

To retrieve history we need rigour, integrity, unsparing devotion and an impulse to scepticism. To retrieve the past, we require all those virtues, and something more. If we want added value – to imagine not just how the past was, but what it felt like, from the inside – we pick up a novel. The historian and the biographer follow a trail of evidence, usually a paper trail. The novelist does that too, and then performs another act, puts the past back into process, into action, frees the people from the archive and lets them run about, ignorant of their fates, with all their mistakes unmade.

Readers must decide how well I've succeeded.

For those who are interested, following this acknowledgement there is a note on sources; it gives an indication of how and where this novel draws on the archive.

But before we get to that, let me offer thanks and praise.

My thanks go first to those who are long dead but without whom this novel could not exist. Above all, they go to Iorwerth Jones and his wife, Alice. While several of the episodes described in this book are factually based and drawn from their lives, many are complete fabulation.

Thanks also go to the other main character, Michael, or Gopane Matala. The archive reveals next to nothing about Michael, not even his name. As a consequence, virtually everything about Michael is made up.

Thanks go too to the secondary characters who feature in the novel as themselves, despite sometimes being placed in situations that never actually occurred. The list is long. A few names, such as Mohandas K. Gandhi and Joshua Nkomo, may be familiar to readers, but others – for example, Arthur Shearly Cripps, Sipambaniso Manyoba Khumalo, Wulf Sachs and Willie Sigeca – very likely will not be.

I can only apologise if readers, or relatives, feel that I have taken unacceptable liberties with the lives of any of these people.

My gratitude also extends to those characters who are purely the product of my imagination. They feel no less real to me. I'm not expecting any recriminations from them.

Turning now to family and friends who have contributed in all sorts of important ways to making the novel possible, much love goes to my wife, Suzan Quilliam, and to our daughter, Nancy Quilliam. I dedicate this novel to them both.

Thanks go as well to those friends who gave me invaluable support, whether as readers, or in terms of research and ideas. There are too many to thank all by name, but Vaughne Miller, Ben

Smith, Dale Lewis, Patricia Hayes, Josi Frater, Jeremy Krikler, Nancy Wood and Brian Wood all deserve special mentions. Nancy and her son Brian granted me the character of Frank Tindler, who is based on their relative, Frank Candler.

I must also acknowledge the many writers and scholars whose work I have drawn upon in writing the book. Any inaccuracies – I am sure there are plenty – are purely my responsibility. The most useful works consulted are acknowledged in the note on sources.

Finally, Samantha Rumbidzai Vazhure, the award-winning poet and founder of Carnelian Heart Publishing, has been a fantastic supporter of this project. From start to finish she has been a pleasure to work with. Gratitude goes too to my editor, Lazarus Panashe Nyagwambo. And last but not least, thank you Emma Minkley for doing such a great job on the artwork for the book cover.

Note on Sources

This guide should be taken as indicative, rather than comprehensive.

Archival Sources

The following archival sources were invaluable: "Magistrate gets a surprise", *Bulawayo Chronicle*, 20th January 1923 (First trial)

"What happened to Jones. The 'Tar and Feather' Case", *Bulawayo Chronicle*, 27th January 1923 (Second trial. I also drew on coverage of this trial in the 3rd February, 10th March and 17th March editions of the newspaper.)

National Archives of Zimbabwe (NAZ), S404, Case Number 2460, High Court of Southern Rhodesia, Criminal Cases, Bulawayo, 7th March 1923 (Second trial)

NAZ, D3/6/116, District Courts, Criminal Cases, Case No. 325, 1923 (Second trial)

NAZ, ZBQ 2/1/1, African Railway Strike Commission, 1945, Oral Evidence of Iorwerth Jones

"'Citizen No. 1 dies in hospital", *Bulawayo Chronicle*, 23rd July 1958. I also drew on coverage of his accident and funeral in the 7th July and 26th July 1958 editions.)

Doris Lessing Archive, DL/2/10/2/1/63a and 63b (My letter to Doris Lessing, dated 12th January 1997, and her reply, dated 19th January 1997. Both letters are in the 2013 embargoed deposit in the University of East Anglia Library.)

I also took some shorter quotes or extracts from the archives:

Paul Kamwana's preaching at a Watchtower service in Hartley and the Watchtower leaflet are both based on primary sources in Sholto Cross's unpublished doctorate on Watchtower (pages 136-140; see below). Native Commissioner Smith's statement about Watchtower is also taken from Cross. Kamwana and Smith are invented characters.

The statement by the newcomer in the bar in Hartley beginning, "Honestly, this is the easiest living country" was discovered by me in Manchester Central Reference Library. (Letters from Rhodesia Collection, 24th May 1937)

The quotation from a 1944 report on Africans in the urban areas, which features at the end of a fabricated briefing written for the Prime Minister, Sir Godfrey Huggins by E.G. Howman in November 1945 is genuine. (See *Report on Urban Conditions in*

Southern Rhodesia, paragraph 96) Both Huggins and Howman are real characters.

Jasper Savanhu's speech beginning "The railway strike has proved" is genuine and much cited by historians; see, for example, Richard Gray's *The Two Nations* (Oxford, 1960, page 137).

The prediction made by the Dula shrine in the Matopos to Grey Bango and Joshua Nkomo, telling them that Southern Rhodesia's freedom would not be achieved for thirty years, is referred to by Nkomo in his autobiography (pages 13-14; see below). However, the chance meeting between Iolo James and the two men in this novel is fabricated.

Important secondary sources

Anderson, Daphne, *The Toe-Rags. A Memoir* (London, 1989)

Becker, Howard S., *Outsiders. Studies in the Sociology of Deviance* (New York, 1963)

The Book of Luke (8:11)

Césaire, Aimé, *Discours sur le colonialisme* (Paris, 1955)

Cripps, Arthur Shearly, "The Black Christ", in Nicholson D. and Lee A. (Eds), *The Oxford Book of English Mystical Verse* (Oxford, 1917)

Cross, Sholto, "The Watchtower Movement in South Central Africa, 1908-1945", unpublished doctorate, University of Oxford, 1973

Dhlamini, Jacob, *Askari. A Story of Collaboration and Betrayal in the Anti-Apartheid Struggle* (Oxford, 2015)

Douglas, Mary, *Purity and Danger. An Analysis of the Concepts of Pollution and Taboo* (London and Oxford, 1966)

Dubow, Saul, "Wulf Sachs's Black Hamlet: A Case of 'Psychic Vivisection'?", *African Affairs*, Vol. 92, No. 369, October 1993

Ethiop, "What Shall We Do with The White People?", *The Anglo-African Magazine* (New York, 1860, pages 41-45)

Gandhi, Mohandas K., *Satyagraha in South Africa* (Ahmedabad, 1968)

Ginsburgh, Nicola, *Class, Work and Whiteness: Race and Settler Colonialism in Southern Rhodesia, 1919-79* (Manchester, 2020)

Hartman, Saidiya, *Wayward Lives, Beautiful Experiments. Intimate Histories of Riotous Black Girls, Troublesome Women, and Queer Radicals* (New York, 2019)

Jackson, Lynette, *Surfacing Up. Psychiatry and Social Order in Colonial Zimbabwe, 1908-1968* (Ithaca, 2005)

Krikler, Jeremy, *Revolution from Above, Rebellion from Below. The Agrarian Transvaal at the Turn of the Century* (Oxford, 2011)

Kufakurinani, Ushehwedu, *Elasticity in Domesticity: White Women in Rhodesian Zimbabwe, 1890-1980* (Leiden, 2019)

Lessing, Doris, *Under My Skin. Volume One of My Autobiography, to 1949* (London, 1995)

Lunn, Jon, *Capital and Labour on the Rhodesian Railway System, 1889-1947* (London, 1997)

Macdonald, Sheila, *Sally in Rhodesia* (London, 1926)

Hilary Mantel, "Why I became a historical novelist", *The Guardian* (UK), 3rd June 2017

McCulloch, Jock, *Black Peril, White Virtue. Sexual Crime in Southern Rhodesia, 1902-35* (Bloomington, 2000)

Mechain, Gwerful, "To the Vagina" (circa 1480; original in Welsh). Available in Gramich, Katie, *Orality and Morality: Early Welsh Women's Poetry* (Cardiff, 2005, pages 8-9)

Morton, Fred, "Linchwe I and the Kgatla Campaign in the South African War, 1899-1902", *Journal of African History*, Vol. 26, Issue 2-3, March 1985

Mushonga, Munyaradzi, "White Power, White Desire: Miscegenation in Southern Rhodesia, Zimbabwe", *African Journal of History and Culture,* Vol 5(1), January 2013

Nkomo, Joshua, *Nkomo: The Story of my Life* (Harare, 2001)

Patel, Trishula Rashna, "Becoming Zimbabwean. A History of Indians in Rhodesia, 1890-1980, unpublished doctorate, Georgetown University, 2021

Phimister, Ian, *Wangi Kolia: Coal, Capital and Labour in Colonial Zimbabwe 1894-1954* (Harare, 1994)

Phimister, Ian and Raftopoulos, Brian, "Kana Sora Ratswa Ngaritswe: African Nationalists and Black Workers: The 1948 General Strike in Colonial Zimbabwe", *Journal of Historical Sociology*, September 2002

Ranger, Terence, "Pugilism and Pathology", in Baker, W.J. and Mangan, J.A, *Sport in Africa* (New York, 1987)

Ranger, Terence, *Voice from the Rocks: Nature, Culture and History in the Matobo Hills of Zimbabwe* (Oxford, 1999)

Ranger, Terence, *Bulawayo Burning. The Social History of a Southern African City, 1893-1960* (Woodbridge and Harare, 2010)

Sachs, Wulf, *Black Hamlet: The Mind of an African Negro revealed by Psychoanalysis* (Manchester, 1937)

Schapera, Isaac, *A Handbook of Tswana Law and Customs* (Oxford, 1938)

Schapera, Isaac, *A Short History of the BaKgatla-BagaKgafela of the Bechuanaland Protectorate* (Cape Town, 1942)

Sheers, Owen, *The Dust Diaries. Seeking the African Legacy of Arthur Cripps* (London, 2004) [I have borrowed a quote about Cripps on page 89 of this book, beginning "I know in my heart he is right"]

Steere, Douglas, *God's Irregular: Arthur Shearly Cripps. A Rhodesian Epic* (London, 1973)

Stuart, Ossie, "Good Boys, Footballers and Strikers: African Social Change in Bulawayo, 1933-53", unpublished doctorate, University of London, 1989

Swan, Maureen, *Gandhi: The South African Experience* (Johannesburg, 1985)

Vera, Yvonne, *Butterfly Burning* (New York, 2000)

Vickery, Kenneth, "The Rhodesia Railways African Strike of 1945, Part I: A Narrative Account", *Journal of Southern African Studies*, Vol. 24, No. 3, September 1998

Vickery, Kenneth, "The Rhodesia Railways African Strike of 1945, Part II: Cause, Consequence, Significance", *Journal of Southern African Studies,* Vol. 25, No. 1, March 1999 [The evidence given by Iorwerth Jones, described here as a "white pensioner", to the Tredgold Commission of Inquiry features briefly on page 64 and is cited in footnote 105]

Van Diggelen, Tromp, *Worthwhile Journey* (London, 1955)

Milton Keynes UK
Ingram Content Group UK Ltd.
UKHW041829100823
426686UK00004B/115